GEORGE MICHAEL IS ALIVE

By
Chris Harris

MAPLE
PUBLISHERS

GEORGE MICHAEL IS ALIVE

Author: Chris Harris

Copyright © 2024 Chris Harris

The right of Chris Harris to be identified as author of this work has been asserted by the author in accordance with section 77 and 78 of the Copyright, Designs and Patents Act 1988.

ISBN 978-1-83538-225-7 (Paperback)
978-1-83538-226-4 (E-Book)

Cover Design and Book Layout by:
White Magic Studios
www.whitemagicstudios.co.uk

Published by:
Maple Publishers
Fairbourne Drive, Atterbury,
Milton Keynes,
MK10 9RG, UK
www.maplepublishers.com

A CIP catalogue record for this title is available from the British Library.

This book is a memoir. It reflects the author's recollections of experiences over time. Some names and characteristics have been changed, some events have been compressed, and some dialogues have been recreated, and the Publisher hereby disclaims any responsibility for them.

CONTENTS

Disclaimer

George Michael is Alive is of course, the figment of my imagination and is based purely on a wish that George was still around, living a fit and healthy life to the fullest.

Everything in my story based in the present day, is of course fictional, but wouldn't it be amazing if some of, if not all of these events were to be true, what a beautiful world we would live in.

The other characters in my story, although well known, in this scenario are fictional and none of the scenes described, actually took place. The events that took place on my journey with George are also fictional and didn't actually happen.

I can confirm that all of the flashbacks that Chris takes you to, are true and happened almost exactly as described in the story. It is important to include these in the story as I feel it gives you an understanding of where the story came from and the bond that Chris had with George, even though they never became the close friends. They could have been friends, if their paths were slightly different and they had of met, maybe if they had turned a different corner, things could have been so different.

Whilst writing my book, I often wondered what George would have made of the world today and whether he would be furious with how things were going. George could see way back in the 90's, the path we were being taken down when he wrote Praying for Time, and 20 years later during his Symphonica tour he reminded us that we had ignored his warnings. We should have listened to him, but I fear it's too late now and it will take another ten or twenty years before we can mend the damage we have done.

George Michael Is Alive, is fictional but every inch of me, wishes he hadn't left when he did, and that he was still with us today.

Acknowledgement

I would like to start by thanking the inspiration for my book and the biggest influence in my life, and the one constant in my life for the last 40 years. As you will discover whilst reading the story, George has help make my life a whole lot more enjoyable, and thanks to his incredible talent, I have no doubt that many of you reading the book, will agree, he has the ability to help us all in so many ways. I would like to thank the team at my publishers for their help in bringing my creation to life, and guiding me through the process of not just writing a book, but all of the other technical issues that needed to be covered to make the book look good and read well, as well as the legal issues. My editor really got into the vibe of the book, and any small alterations only added to the story, finding the words, I wish I had thought of.

To anyone who reads my book, who may well recognise their role in the story, thank you for adding something to my life that has stuck with me all of this time. Let's face there are only so many events in our lives that we remember whether good or bad.

⊷⊶◆⊷⊶

Dedication

It would be nice to dedicate the book to George Michael even though he will never get to see it, but hopefully his family will. He played a massive part in my life and was probably the most constant part of my life for over 35 years.

Prologue

On Christmas Day 2016 the world lost one of its favourite sons, a talent possibly, or should I say probably, definitely, never to be replaced?

George was one of those people who endeared himself to so many of us from his simple beginnings in Wham to the mega star he was to become with all the trappings of being a mega star holds.

He lived his life in full view of us all, warts and all and we loved him for it. In fact, the bigger the story the more we seemed to love him. George himself said he had a self-destructive personality, but somehow for some reason the big red button he kept pushing, never seemed to work in fact it seemed to have the opposite effect.

Numerous stories of George were to hit the headlines during George's long and distinguished career, because the media were determined to ruin his career. The trouble was for the media, they didn't factor in the loyalty of George's fans? No matter how much mud they threw, the fans just shrugged it off and continued to play George Michael even louder.

George will be very sadly missed, but fortunately he blessed us with the everlasting legacy of his music, and we will always be able to see him in his amazing videos. For those of us who fell in love with George in the early days of Wham to the new generation who are discovering his music today. He had the ability to create timeless music that holds up to time and fashion like few others have been able to achieve, and watching the reaction of Generation Z listening to his music and viewing his videos for the very first time, reminds me of the effect he had on me the first time I heard his music. He is (I refuse to say was) a genius.

How many of you have wondered if, in 100 years or possibly even more, people will still be listening to the music of George Michael? I hate to be a pessimist, but I would be more surprised if the world was still inhabitable in 100 years' time, and if that is the case, if the human race hasn't already blown ourselves out of existence, George's music could possibly out live everybody?

Whilst reading my story, please remember, when Chris takes you back to his past, the stories he tells you, are all true, they actually did happen. I found writing the story incredibly cathartic and was able to finally answer a lot of questions of why I am the man I am today.

I was also left with a lot of questions, so if you get to the end of my story and you have questions too, don't worry, if I can't work out the answers, how can anyone else be expected to? I hope you enjoy the journey that you are about to embark on.

George Michael is alive, is of course mostly fictional, or is it?

Chapter One

It was December 23rd 2016 George was at home at Mill Cottage in Goring-on -Thames, Oxfordshire. Mill Cottage is a 16th century house that George had completely refurbished with his partner at the time, Kenny. It had beautiful low ceilings, that George regularly banged his head on because of his height, people were much shorter when the cottage was built. Mill Cottage had beautiful views out onto the river Thames, and whatever the season, to look out of the window was a complete pleasure. George was sitting in his favourite chair in his favourite room. The room had those low ceilings with original beams and an open fire burning away. George had also situated his piano in the room, the piano previously owned by John Lennon no less, and the very same piano that George had drafted so many of his own songs. One of George's additions to the house was the library, which of course had been filled with old looking books bought in bulk to make the library look old and regal. George had never actually read any of the books, he just admired them from a distance. There was a large picture on the wall by a, not so particularly well-known Russian artist, but George liked it. He always said, *"Once you start putting really expensive art up, you'll have to start locking the doors".* George was very proud of his home, and one of the stories he loved to tell people was about his next-door neighbour. Baroness Buscombe, was a member of the House of Lords and when she heard that the rock star George Michael was moving in next door, she had a line of trees planted to block out all the parties she envisaged George to be having. George thought this was highly amusing and no doubt Baroness Buscombe was deeply disappointed when George didn't shatter her windows with all night raves.

He was sat in his chair pondering what the hell he was going through, hoping the doctors were wrong, hoping he could ride it out and come out the other side, stronger than ever. The trouble was, like a cat with nine lives, George knew he had used up eight of his nine lives and that the prognosis this time was one that he couldn't fight. He knew this time unless a miracle occurred, this was his last life.

George had become something of a recluse over the last few weeks, even months, he was almost unrecognisable to himself, let alone anybody else, he had put on loads of weight and his face looked all bloated. He was missing going to his favourite pub in the village and getting into the Christmas spirit with the locals. He loved helping out behind the bar and having a laugh with people, it was his piece of normality, away from the mega star persona, that is George Michael.

No, this year was to be very different, this year George was keeping himself very aloof, this year George would not be involved in the village festivities and the candle light parade through the village that he had loved so much in previous years. Mill Cottage was George's favourite home because the locals didn't make a fuss of him and to them, he was just another regular person, living a regular life, doing a regular job, although everybody knew George wasn't just a regular guy. They gave him this taste of normality as a thank you for all the pleasure he had given them over the years and George loved every one of them for giving him that taste of freedom.

George was thinking about all of the songs he had written and all the ones that he hadn't. He had been just as successful with other people's songs as he had from his own. Be it Elton John, Stevie Wonder, Queen, Marvin Gaye, the list went on and on. He thought about all the amazing people he had sang with over the years, other mega stars such as Whitney Houston, Beyonce and of Course Aretha Franklin. He had been one hell of a lucky guy when it came down to his music and the people he got to meet. Not many people could say they had as many famous friends as George, and they were friends. He thought about his videos and all the amazing people he worked with on those like, Linda Evangelista, Naomi Cambell, Christy Turlington, Cindy Crawford and Tatjana Patitz. Not many other artists good claim bragging rights to having that many supermodels in one video. And the fun he had with them behind the scenes, well, he'll keep those secret, but wow was he a lucky boy.

Yeah, when he thought about it, he could lay claim to some pretty amazing things, far more than the average guy in the street.

From his chair George could hear people walking past, laughing and giggling singing Christmas carols as if nothing was wrong, oblivious to what was just around the corner. On the radio, he could hear the familiar festive bells chiming to the bestselling Christmas song, destined never to reach number one. It was the most loved Christmas song of them all, with everybody knowing every word. The very same song that would ring out at every Christmas party, and numerous secretaries would pinch a sneaky snog off their Managing Director under the mistletoe. The very same song that would fill the air in every shop, pub, restaurant and club around the world. If only I got a penny for every time that song was played somewhere in the world, I would be a very rich man! George thought.

George is a very rich man, but right now all the money in the world couldn't change what was about happen. All he could do was sit thinking to himself how grateful he was for the talents he was blessed with and all the magical moments he had experienced. Yes, he had his fair share of crap dished out to him, and behind the smiles quite often the truth was very different from what the public was allowed to see, but George was a professional and knew how to wear his mask for his adoring public. For George Michael, is of course a fictional character made up purely for the public and Georgios Kyriacos Panayiotou or Yog to his friends was the real man behind the mask. Yog was the one who had to deal with real life and all the shit that came with it. George Michael got to have all the glory.

So, there he sat thinking about all the amazing things that he had achieved, all those amazing concerts he had held over the years. Yeah, they knackered the hell out of him, but once on that stage, George gave his adoring fans the time of their lives. They didn't know what was really going on in his life, and as sad as it sounds, many of them probably didn't care. Like the Freddie Mercury tribute concert, when George gave one of his best performances ever, knowing the love of his life was fighting for his life, a fight that he lost. They just knew they were going to have a totally awesome night and that they would go home buzzing, wishing the show had never come to an end. For they could have stayed there all night and watched the show over and over again, because when you go to a

George Michael concert you know you are going to be taken to a whole new place. Just like George, any worries you have? Any shit going on your life at that time is forgotten, wiped away, for two hours plus those worries, that shit doesn't exist, for those two hours you are transported into euphoria. For those two hours George Michael and the thousands of fans singing along with George, knowing every word of every song, creating a sense of unity. Neither George nor any of his fans had any shit in their life for those two hours and it was a bliss.

Some extra loud steps outside and a particular loud laugh snapped George out of his trance like state. A young couple started to sing Last Christmas, then shouted "Happy Christmas George!" as they disappeared down the lane that ran past George's front door. George smiled to himself, and a tear appeared in his eye as he thought how happy that young couple sounded, how excited they were about spending their first Christmas together. Not that he knew it was their first Christmas, but it was, and it would be one they would never forget.

George thanked the lord the curtains were closed, because quite frankly he didn't want to see his reflection in the glass and most definitely didn't want anybody else to see him. George had put on a lot of weight, he no longer looked like that mega star people associated him with on the cover of his faith album or the sex god from the Fast Love video, or the cheeky policeman from Outside, which of course was in response to his Beverly Hills experience. The very same experience that all of the media thought would finally kill off George Michael, but to their surprise, and even more to George's surprise, his fans loved him even more than ever. No George had put on weight because he wasn't well, he wasn't well at all.

George and his father Jack, had recently flown out to Austria to see George's Osteopath regarding his ongoing condition that he had had for some time. After his visit, his physician recalled a conversation they had while George was with him. He thought what George was saying was strange and that he was actually planning dying. He had put all of his affairs in order and was thinking really short term which was unlike George who normally had such elaborated plans for the future. In many ways it was as if he had woken up and was seeing things vividly, but maybe he had just removed all worries because somehow, he knew his days were limited. Despite an intense session they still managed to laugh and joke around, George even joked that his weight gain made him look like a bloated Elvis Presley. George had planned a follow up session, but that was never to happen. For George knew his days were numbered, for Jack, who had lost his wife so cruelly, now had to prepare himself to lose his one and only son. Jack who wasn't as confident that his son was going to be a worldwide mega star, Jack had wanted his son to get a proper job as an accountant. But George had a dream, and nobody was going to stop him, not even his father.

The flight home was a very quiet one between George and his dad. Although they both had so much, they wanted to say to each other, neither of them could muster the strength to speak. It was hard enough to breath whilst trying to hold back the tears, you know the pain you get between your eyes when holding back the tears? Multiply that by a thousand. They were both giving themselves agonising headaches just trying to hold themselves together, to talk would have been impossible.

Chapter Two

Chris was in his new house, he had bought it with money he won on the lottery, a lot of money, it was the Euro Millions draw and it was a whopper. Chris would tell himself he is as rich as George Michael, because he is a huge George Michael fan, he has been ever since the early days of wham and is now 49 years old, but Chris would never forget when he first met George.

It was August 1983 and Chris had invited a few of his friends round for a bit of a party while his mum and dad were away on holiday. Nothing too big, just the usual bunch that he could trust, or who he thought he could trust, one of them did decide to fill one of the toilet cistern with beer cans? Chris was all in black, as usual, that was his usual look because he was into the Stranglers and they always wore black, that's right, Chris was a punk. Not a hardcore punk, just a quiet mind his own business type of punk. But something was about to change and change beyond anybody's expectation, especially Chris's?

The girl Chris fancied madly, was at the party. Karen was gorgeous, funny, incredibly sexy, and she had big hair along with a huge smile and was always happy, always bouncing around happy to see everyone. She was totally out of Chris's league, not because Chris was homely, but Karen went for bad boys, and Chris was a good guy. Yes, you guessed it right, Chris was friend zoned. (The worst place to be when you fancy the pants off someone). Unrequited love is the most painful and of course, it comes with a huge dose of eternal hope. If I keep trying, eventually, she will fall in love with me, the same way that I love her. The trouble is though, if the other person is perfectly happy in the friend zone, then they are getting what they need from the relationship, why muddy the waters with love when you have a great friend? Chris didn't know if Karen even knew how he felt. If he hadn't told her, why and how would she know? He knew Karen felt safe around him and that he would do anything for her, but did she know why he was so eager to please? Or did she just think "oh that's Chris doing his normal nice guy thing"?

Karen however, was about to change his life forever, not by taking him upstairs and banging his brains out, although that was what he was hoping for. God what would he have done to sleep with Karen? Of course, Chris wanted Karen to be his girlfriend, but if he couldn't have that, one night between the sheets, naked with her would have been enough. One night kissing every inch of her gorgeous body would have been incredible. Instead, Karen was going to have an even bigger impact on Chris. She was not going to become the biggest love of his life, but she was going to introduce him to the biggest love of his life, for under her arm was an album. Karen knew Chris was into the Stranglers and she didn't really fancy listening to Golden Brown and Peaches and Nice n Sleazy all night, so she had brought her copy of Wham Fantastic to balance things out a bit. Wham was a new band, that Chris hadn't taken much notice of. Wham were soul boys and Chris was punk.

Karen thrust the album into Chris's hands, gave him a kiss and said,

"Here you go moi lover, stick this on."

Chris dumbstruck by the kiss and being called Karen's lover had nothing to argue so headed over to the hi-fi and set up the record. The first few beats rang out

"WHOOW! WHOOW! BAD BOYS! STICK TOGETHER"!

and it sounded okay, in fact it sounded better than okay, it was brilliant. Young Guns, Club Tropicana, Wham Rap and of course Bad Boys, Karen liked bad boys, didn't she? The first time Chris played the album it resonated with him, something connected like he had been hit by lightning. When one side finished, Chris flipped it over and played the other side. The B side was a bit more chilled, Club Tropicana and Ray of Sunshine, and when that had finished, he flipped it over and started all over again. Nobody seemed to care that the same album seemed to be playing on a loop, they were all too pissed to notice, trying to throw sausages through the smaller upstairs windows. Chris could hear Woody in hysterics in the garden but didn't pay too much attention as Woody was a very excitable chap and normally didn't get up to anything that would have caused any long-term damage, just a bit of mischief. On one occasion, whilst intending on going to the local nightclub, The Orchard, or the "The Chad" as it was known locally, Woody had been upstairs, landing, laughing his head off, and slapping his thighs in excitement, shouting for Chris but struggling to get his words out because of his intense laughter.

"Chris! Chris! look! Look!"

Chris turned around to see that Woody had a pair of his sisters' pants on his head, which Woody thought was highly amusing? Chris didn't pay too much attention to this, after all, Woody was easily amused, and Chris's other mate, Andy (also known as Jim) was in Chris's bedroom shouting,

"They don't fit! They don't fucking fit!"

Andy was trying to get a pair of Chris's trousers, past his knees, the "Chad" didn't let you through the door in jeans. It was at that point Chris's dad had called out from the bedroom,

"Chris is everything okay? What's going on?"

Chris's dad, who they thought was out because his car wasn't in the drive. The car wasn't in the drive because Chris's sister had borrowed it. In fact, mum and dad were in bed and heard every word of Woody's pant wearing antics, and Andy's desperation at not being able to get Chris's trousers on. Oh, did Chris's dad relish the moment Woody would knock on the door, so that he could let him know that he knew what exactly young Woody was doing with his daughter's underwear, and when the moment came a couple of days later, he milked every second of it. The doorbell rang and as usual it was left to Chris's dad to answer it.

"Hello Mark" he said.

"Hello Pete, I mean Peter, I mean Mr Harris" Woody replied sheepishly.

"Have you come to try my daughter's pants on again?" he enquired, trying desperately not to laugh. With a nervous giggle Woody replied,

"Ummm no, I don't think I'll be doing that again, Pete, I mean Peter".

"I'm glad to hear it. Would you like me to get Chris, you weirdo"?

"Ummm yes please Pete, uh uh Peter".

"You had better come in, CHRIS!!! Mark's here! Make sure he stays out of your sister's pant drawer!!! You might as well go up Mark."

"Thanks Pete, I mean, sorry, Peter".

Chris could never work out if Woody called his dad Pete just to wind him up. Or because he was just a little bit stupid. Chris's dad on the other hand, thought he was just, stupid?

Back at the party, Chris was completely overwhelmed by the album and not just by the music but the cocky duo on the cover sleeve and in particular, George Michael. What was it about this guy? Okay so he had a great voice, but there was something else. What was that?

The party came to its natural conclusion, a few sausages had made it through the windows much to Woody's delight, but apart from that and the larger cans, Graham had put in the toilet cistern, the house was pretty much unscathed. When Karen came to leave, Chris asked if he could hold onto her album until he was able to get to HMV and get his own copy, and of course to give him an excuse to go around to her house, to give her album back. Any excuse to see the girl of his dreams.

"Of course, you can gorgeous, I'm glad you liked it, I thought you would. Give me a kiss".

Karen leaned forward, puckered up her lips and let Chris gently give her a goodnight kiss. Well that just blew his mind, Karen called him gorgeous, for one? And she asked him for a kiss. Did she really think he was gorgeous? How did she know Chris would like Wham! She knew him better than he thought? But she didn't stay the night, he didn't see her naked, he didn't get to kiss every inch of her beautiful body that he had so hoped, and dreamed he would. Maybe another night? But she did change his life that night. What if the girl of his dreams hadn't come to the party? What if the girl of Chris's dreams hadn't bought

'Wham Fantastic' with her that night, how would his life have been different? He didn't see her naked, he didn't kiss every inch of her beautiful body, but Karen did change his life.

Back in the real world, Chris was sat in his massive new living room, he was sat at his grand piano that he had brought with his lottery win. It was essential, the room demanded it. He had positioned the piano in the corner by the patio doors, looking out onto the patio and the pool outside, not that he would be going in that in December, but he didn't have to; the house had an indoor pool too, heated to 30 degrees, perfect for the winter.

Chris was playing his compilation of George Michael's songs on his piano, he took great pleasure in mixing them up, skipping from one to another, trying to blend them seamlessly, from Fast Love to Outside, to Freedom to I'm your man, to Careless Whisper to Amazing to A Different Corner, Chris knew all the tracks' lyrics word by word and had played them so many times where his piano got their pitch perfect. Many years ago, he had a go at writing some of his own songs, a few of them were quite good, but he had lost the book with them in, if only he could find them, he thought he might be able to put some music to them, now that he had his new toy. Chris was looking forward to spending Christmas in his new home albeit alone, he was looking forward to just chill out and enveloping himself in the luxurious home he now owned. Chris had planned what he was going to get to eat over Christmas to the finest detail, it was going to be absolutely, awesome! Chris was used to spending time alone, he had made a habit of it. Even at school he wasn't really what you would call a follower? He was happy to go along with what the rest of his mates were doing, but only if it suited him, if he had his own ideas, then that's what he did.

George meanwhile in Goring, was feeling knackered, and although the heart was willing, the body had no energy, or was it the other way around? Everything took so much energy these days, George himself knew his condition but he was far too scared to admit it, he was in serious trouble, he was frightened and who could blame him.

Leaning back in his chair, he closed his eyes and drifted off into happier times, letting his memory replay images of all the fun he had had with Andrew, David, Kenny, Anselmo and of course, his beloved mum. It was like a video player in his head as clear as if they were in the room with him. George relied on these times now, they gave him a feeling of hope, even though in his own words, "hanging onto hope, when there is no hope to speak of" reverberated in the back of his mind.

George stayed in his chair for another hour, people could be heard outside and at least three or four more "Happy Christmas George" could be heard. George loved the fact that people cared about him, who doesn't enjoy being loved, it is all George ever wanted, even more than being famous or rich, being loved was everything. He made his way upstairs to bed only two more sleeps till Christmas.

Chapter Three

December 24th, Christmas Eve 2016. George woke up in a symphony of misery, each bone in his wretched frame throbbing in protest. His exhausted body, a battleground of agony, begged for respite as if every organ conspired to showcase its presence in an unruly parade of discomfort. George lay there for a while getting his bearings, what day is it? What plans did he have? Who was in today? Did he have to pretend that everything was okay? But the overriding thought going over and over in the back of his mind was, why me? For god's sake, what have I done to deserve this? I'm a good man I really don't deserve this!

George dragged himself out of bed and slowly made his way downstairs. There was some rustling in the kitchen and he could smell coffee, Noom, the housekeeper, was in and busy tidying up.

"Morning darling" George said to Noom as he entered the kitchen.

"Good morning my lovely George, how are you feeling this morning"? Noom replied

"I've felt better my lovely," said George.

"Ohhhh George, you look soooo tired!"

Noom was one of the few people in George's inner circle, that he truly trusted and of course, he had sat her down and narrated to her about his condition. It was a difficult conversation with plenty of hugs and tears. George loved Noom and appreciated everything she did for him, and of course Noom loved George to bits, he was a lovely, funny, generous man and she loved working for him. When George poured out the raw truth about his ailment, her heart shattered for him. She adored her boss and dreaded the thought of losing him to the cruel grip of sickness. He was such a graceful man that she would have worked for him for free if it meant she could keep working for him.

"Yeah, feeling a little bit crap today," said George.

"Can I get you a coffee and something to eat dear? You must keep your strength up" Noom replied.

"A coffee would be perfect, and some toast would be great" asked George.

"It will be my pleasure. We have some eggs, why don't I make you poached egg on toast darling"?

"You know what? That sounds lovely Noom, thank you"

Noom whipped up a quick coffee for George, the rich smell giving a cosy vibe. George leaning by the window with his first smoke of the day, —his mini-break, a simple pleasure dance with the morning hustle.

"Have you got any plans for today"? asked Noom.

"No not really. Fadi is coming over later, not sure what time though" George replied.

"Ohhhh, alright, that'll be nice I guess"?

Noom didn't like Fadi, he was messy and expected her to follow him around, cleaning up after him. She worked for George, not Fadi. She loved George; she couldn't stand Fadi. She also knew George well enough to know that he wasn't that bothered about him either. She had been there when George and Kenny were together and she could tell

George didn't feel anything like as involved with Fadi as he did with Kenny, it was a very different atmosphere in the house when he was around.

"Yeah. I suppose it will" replied George.

George was aware that Noom harbored no love for Fadi; it was more of a tolerated truce. Deep down, George found himself agreeing with her sentiments.

"I'll make sure he doesn't trash the place" added George.

"Don't worry my darling, you have enough on your mind to be worrying over how much mess he is making. I'll deal with it". Said Noom.

"You are an absolute diamond, I don't know what I would do if I didn't have you, give me a hug".

Noom giggled shyly as George wrapped his arms around her and gave her a huge hug and a kiss on her forehead.

"You know how to flatter a girl George, but if I wasn't here, somebody else would be".

George laughed; he had been rumbled.

"But nobody would be as good as you, Noom".

"Yeah, yeah yeah" she replied

"Your poached eggs are done, come and eat something" she said holding back her tears.

"Coming, I'll just finish my cigi" George called across the room.

"Put that damn thing out, you know you've been told to cut down on those things"!!

"Yes mum" George laughed, putting off his cigi to go for breakfast .

"That looks delicious, thank you Noom".

"You are very welcome" replied Noom.

Noom glided past George, her fingers grazing his shoulders, a gesture of affection for the man who wasn't just George but also Michael. Beyond his fame, it was George Michael's inherent kindness that she adored. The looming loss of him in the not-too-distant future weighed on her heart, yet she masked her sorrow, not wanting George Michael to perceive her emotional turmoil.

"I'm going to do some hoovering" Noom said, holding back her tears.

"Okay, but don't worry too much, it's Christmas and it'll only get trashed by your mate" George replied tucking back into his breakfast.

"Okay" Noom really struggling to hold the tears back now, she had to get out of the room, and really fast.

Chapter Four

Chris woke up from a great night's sleep. The new bed he had bought, was so comfy, he slept so well. Chris was in a good place, he couldn't be happier, even though he was single at the moment, that didn't bother him in the slightest. Chris had convinced himself that he was actually better off single. When you're single you can do everything, you want, whenever you want, however you want. He could get up and go to bed when he wanted. He could watch whatever he wanted, whenever he wanted. He had the freedom to do what he wanted, whenever he wanted. He could eat anything he desires, whenever he feels like it. Being in a relationship involves compromise, adjusting into other person's preferences. It means making joint decisions on what to do, where to go, when to go, what to watch on TV, when to watch it, what to eat, when to eat, and whether to go for spicy, meat, veg, or even, God forbid, vegan. But not Chris; he preferred making all the decisions himself, at least for now.

The truth was, the only people who knew about his lottery win were, Camelot, him and the bank. He did have a surprise plan for some close friends. He knew when he was going to tell them, just not quite yet. Money can do funny things to people, and as soon as people know you've won the lottery, they start laying claim to their share of it. As far as Chris was concerned, he had been playing the lottery for years and nobody had offered to contribute to the thousands of pounds he had spent, so why do they suddenly feel like they are entitled to a percentage of his winnings? They weren't interested in a percentage of all of the £2.80 wins he had or even when he won a few hundred pounds, nobody said they were entitled to a percentage, but he knew if he let them know that he had won over £100 million, everybody would want their share.

Chris rolled out of bed and his feet sank into the new carpet on his bedroom floor, He had insisted on the finest underlay, and oh, the transformation was profound. The carpet cradled his feet, embracing each step with a luxurious tenderness. Walking became a tactile symphony, a melody of comfort that resonated deep within him. He was still getting used to how far it was from his bed to the kitchen. Chris would laugh to himself, "Do I need to go to the loo before I start the journey"? That always made him chuckle and he planned to use it when eventually he did have someone stay over.

The house was in the style of a Spanish villa and the hall and landing were central to the house. It was like a tall tower from floor to ceiling with a massive pendant light in the stairwell. At the bottom of the stairs, you could turn right down a corridor to the indoor pool and a door on the right, took you into the cinema room. Behind you was the door to the living room and his pride-and-joy, grand piano. Straight ahead was the front door, to the left was the door to the dining room and next to that, was another corridor that took you to the kitchen, which was a masterpiece. Chris loved his home and because of the lottery win, he didn't have a worry in the world.

The kitchen was massive, everything in this house was huge. In his previous house, before the big win, he would struggle to do 10,000 steps a day. In this house, it felt like 10,000 steps from the bedroom to the kitchen. When he was watching television in the living room, if he wanted a drink he would have to plan when it was best to get it, so he didn't miss too much of his programme. Thank God he didn't watch the BBC anymore, he would have either died of thirst or missed most of the programmes he was watching. That's what he told himself anyway, it probably wouldn't have taken that long in reality to go get a drink.

Despite being a multimillionaire, Chris didn't feel the urge to splurge. His weekly shopping routine remained unchanged, for he believed in using resources wisely. Wasting food didn't sit well with him; he disliked the idea of discarding what others could cherish. To Chris, minimizing waste was a straightforward concept—plan your meals and buy accordingly. Proudly, he rarely disposed food, practiced recycling diligently, steered clear of unnecessary plastics, and maintained a commendably low carbon footprint. He did not need the likes of Extinction Rebellion pointing him how to behave, in Chris's mind Extinction Rebellion were some of the biggest hypocrites on the planet and, should practise what they preach.

Chris took a cereal bowl from the cupboard and put two Banana Weetabix in it and poured enough semi-skimmed milk to cover both biscuits. He had a certain way of eating them, scooping up the milk first then eating the softened Weetabix. He took his breakfast over to the comfiest area of the kitchen. It probably sized like a huge living room, it housed three sofas, a coffee table, a couple of other tables with lamps, all centred around a 55" flat screen TV on the wall. Chris didn't really watch the telly in the morning he just put it on for background noise. He looked out onto the patio and as per every morning there was his friendly pigeon staring back at him. The pigeon was in fact there, every morning, waiting for Chris to feed him. The patient, poor pigeon awaited Chris, assured of a meal after he finished his Weetabix. Chris, feeling a connection, pondered the possibility of coaxing the pigeon to eat from his hand, a thought that warmed his heart.

After Chris had pottered around a bit, it was time for his daily workout, an hour on the treadmill then 30 minutes in the pool and then a relax, in his 'Mammon' (Turkish style steamed room) He wasn't really into pushing weights, just keeping trim. At the ripe old age of 49, it was probably too late to aim for Mr Universe. Chris used this time to do a lot of his visualisation, affirmations and manifesting. He was convinced this was how he had manifested his lottery win. About a year earlier, he decided he needed more money in his life. Not keen on changing jobs, he delved into researching the law of attraction, seeking ways to harness its power. Shortly after he started practising visualisation and affirmations, he started to see regular wins. He hadn't changed anything, he was still using the same numbers he always had and, is still using those same numbers today. The only thing he was doing different, was his daily visualisation and affirmations and he started winning every week. Most weeks it was just small amounts, but Chris was grateful for every win, it was important to be grateful, no matter how small. Chris believed that it was like playing a one-armed bandit, the more times you pull the lever, the more likely you are to win. And every time he won, he was another pull closer to the big win, and he was absolutely, right.

How or why do you need to manifest or visualise when you have so much money? Well, the truth is our whole life is a series of manifestations. Take a look around you, everything you see was once somebody's thought, an idea. That thought or idea then becomes a creation, but it has to be designed via visualisation first. So, whether we believe in visualisation or not, the fact is, we bring into our lives what we think about, whatever that might be, good or bad. That is manifestation and we all do it, every single one of us.

Chris wielded his power of manifestation wisely and was now living his dream, and nobody could pursue him that what he had was pure fluke. He had worked hard to manifest his new lifestyle and continued to add to his wish list, the only thing was, that his wish list was now bigger and more expensive. He would debate with himself how many cars he, actually, really needed? His favourite of the moment was his Mercedes AMG C63, a 6.2 litre V8 2 door coupe. It was a good everyday car but also an absolute beast. He was considering buying a Ferrari, but he knew he would be too afraid to park it anywhere. One of his pets peeves was car park dings. Why can't people open their doors without letting them swing into the adjacent car, causing hundreds of pounds of damage? If you can't park next to another car without denting it, don't park near other people's cars. Chris would always park in the empty section of the car park, even if it was furthest point away from the shop. Even before he left the shop, he would start to think about someone parking next him? Why? When they have a choice of hundreds of spaces, why do they have to park their piece of shit next to my car? They better not have dented my door? It wasn't dented when I left the car so if it's dented now, it must have been them? God help anyone who Chris actually caught letting their car door hit his car, and it had happened, and the red mist did arrive, and they did get a new arsehole ripped into them. Nope the next step could only be to have his weekly shop delivered, then he would have one less reason to brave the minefield that is the supermarket car park.

Fortunately, Chris had done his Christmas shopping early to avoid the worst of the crowds, and the risk of a car park ding. To be fair, his Christmas shopping wasn't that much different to his regular weekly shop. He was still only cooking for himself, and he could only eat so much. He didn't stock up on tins of chocolates as tempting as they may be, they are the devil's work, and he knew a tin of celebrations would probably take a month on the treadmill to get back to the weight, he was before he had devoured the chocos. Chris never understood why people felt the need to stock up with quite so much crap at Christmas, they must spend the whole time stuffing something in their mouths, there just wasn't enough time in a day to eat that much food? And he knew fully that those very same people would be back, if not Boxing Day, the day after, stocking up again because the greedy sods had eaten the lot. They would then be back again to stock up for New Years Eve. For Christ's sake, He was a multi, multi millionaire, but couldn't work out where they all got their money from, but more importantly, where they had put all that bloody food? Having said that, it was very obvious where the food had gone, these were walking heart attacks. Any minute now at least one of them was going to go crashing to the floor holding their chest and screaming in agony as their poor heart declared "enough is enough, I can't cope anymore"!

Surely this is pre-meditated murder, what they are doing to their kids? Surely, they know how much damage they are doing to themselves and their offspring. But obviously they don't care? How can they care? It's obvious for everybody to see? This was yet another thing that irked

Chris during his trips to the supermarket, making the idea of opting for delivery increasingly tempting.

Chapter Five

George was feeling a bit better after his breakfast and had disappeared to his living room and switched the telly on. He was busy scrolling through the TV guide to see what rubbish was aired this Christmas, hoping he would find something funny that would divert his mind off things. It turned out it was the same old rubbish. George started to think about how many films there are out there and yet the TV stations give us the same few every year. Toy Story 1 – 3, Despicable Me, Chitty Chitty Bang Bang, Mary Poppins, and so on. I mean how old are those, can't they find anything newer.

"If I was in charge of programming, I would find better films than this rubbish". Muttered George to himself.

"Who you talking too George"? asked Noom. She had been dusting quietly behind him.

"Ooooops, talking to yourself is the first sign of madness isn't it"? George retorted

"So, I hear". Noom replied

"The second is hairs on the palm of your hands" George suggested with a bit of a giggle in his voice and keeping a close eye on Noom.

Noom immediately turned her hands over to check her palms, and George fell about laughing.

"The third sign is looking for them"?

"Oh, very funny George, I see you haven't lost your sense of humour"? Snorted Noom, although obviously happy to see George kidding around.

"The old ones are always the best" he giggled, feeling pretty pleased with himself.

"Ohhhhh Noom, why is there nothing on the bloody telly? Don't they know everyone is at home desperate to watch something different"?

"I know darling, I was looking last night and couldn't find anything to watch. Why don't you put some music on? That George Michael guy is supposed to be okay"?

"Okay?" chuckled George

"I heard he's bloody brilliant"? He quickly followed up with.

Noom winked at him, *"Yeah I heard that too"!*

"Stuff it, I'm going for a cigi" George said as he disappeared into the kitchen.

"You're supposed to be cutting back"!!!!! Noom called after him.

"I know"!! came a distant reply.

"He's never going to give up" Noom whispered to herself.

"I heard that"! George shouted. He hadn't but he guessed Noom would probably say something like that out of ear shot.

"How does he do that"? Noom asked herself

"I heard that too"!!!

"Whaaaaat"????

George hadn't heard either of them, but he was feeling bored and in one of his funny moods. God knows he needed something to entertain himself and Noom was the only one available, easy target really.

Noom had followed George into the kitchen with a view to nag him about his smoking, but when she got there, George was just staring blankly out of the window. Maybe this wasn't the time?

"You okay darling"? Noom asked

"I'm good my lovely, I was just wondering if I needed to do anything for tomorrow"?

"I think everything is done; you just need to turn on the stuff at the right times" Noom replied.

"I'm sure it will all be just fine". Replied George

The front door slammed shut, which meant only one thing. Fadi was here.

"Sounds like you have someone else to tease now"? said Noom

"Nahh, he's had a complete sense of humour by-pass, never gets any of my jokes" replied George

Noom sensed an abrupt shift in the atmosphere; George's playful demeanour suddenly turned subdued within seconds. It was apparent that George wasn't particularly thrilled about his presence. She didn't say anything it wasn't her place, but she couldn't help feeling that George really needed as much happiness in his life right now.

"Where is everybody"? Came the voice from the hallway.

"Kitchen" replied George.

"What are you doing?" asked Fadi

"Just having a cigi" replied George

"Cool light one up for me"

"Light your own". Said George passing him a pack of Marlborough Lights.

"Lights? You know I don't like lights"?

"No, well, buy your own then you won't have to smoke mine".

"Touchy"? replied Fadi

"Whatever". Retorted George

An uneasy silence settled in the room as they smoked their cigarettes. Noom quietly excused herself, seeking solace in the library. George, igniting a fresh cigarette, appeared to seek comfort in the routine, using it as a distraction from interacting with Fadi.

"I'm just going to take the Abby to the garden" mumbled George, Abby being George's pet Labrador, which he loved like a child. Fadi didn't respond.

The sun was out and it felt quite warm considering it was Christmas eve, and George followed Abby around the garden, taking in everything, thinking to himself, how beautiful everything looked. How much longer would he get to enjoy his garden. There was a huge sundial in the centre of the garden that Kenny had got George for his 40th birthday, George loved that sundial, Fadi would never think of something as cool as that. As he strolled around, he knew the likelihood of seeing another Christmas was never going to happen.

Abby had been incredibly affectionate ever since George and his dad brought her home from Austria, as if she could sense something was amiss. Animals, they say, have a keen intuition, and Abby had unmistakably detected that her dad wasn't well. George would often be spotted strolling with Abby around the village, reluctant to part with her when he had to go on tour. She was undeniably

George's closest friend. They played with a ball for a while until it accidentally bounced into the swimming pool and Abby knew the water was going to be really cold to bother chasing the ball in, much to George's relief.

Meanwhile, the voice of Fadi interrupted this attention,

"Hey George, what are we doing later"?

"I haven't really thought about it" replied George

"Do I have to think of everything"? shouted Fadi

"His life is so tough, isn't it?" muttered George to Abby.

"What do you want to do"? Fadi tried again

"Like I said, I haven't really thought about it"! Replied George.

"Jesus, leave it up to me, I'll think of something"! retorted Fadi

"Whatever" sighed George. Fortunately, he had found another tennis ball, so he could play with Abby a few more rounds. Anything to put off going back into the house.

Abby got tired of playing and went to sit by the door. George figured she wanted to go back inside. Before, she was sleeping by the warm fire, and it took some convincing to get her to join George in the garden. Fadi didn't open the door for her; she had to wait for George. Once he opened it, Abby quickly went back to her comfy spot by the fire.

"I'll get the door for Abby then"! George snapped

"What"? replied Fadi

"Never mind" George sighed

"It's only a bloody dog" Fadi returned, clearly, he had heard what George had said.

"She's my dog and she is a 'she' not an 'it' " hissed George

"Maybe "she" should learn how to open the door then"? Fadi quipped

Bad move.

"What did you say"? snarled George

"Maybe she should learn to open her own doors" Fadi repeated

"Fuck off you wanker." Ripped George

"WHOOOAH! I was only joking man"! returned Fadi

"Really? You wouldn't know a joke if it slapped you round the face"

"Hey chill out man". Fadi clearly sensed he had crossed a line.

"Don't tell me to chill out in my own house." Ripped George.

"Okay okay"

"No, it's not okay! You come in here, treat it like it's your fucking house! You trash the place and expect Noom to clean up after you, you're a joke"! Ranted George

"That's Noom's job isn't it"? Came back Fadi

Another bad move

"Fuck off is it her job to clean up after you? Have some respect"!

"So, what is her job then"?

"I'll tell you what it isn't, and that's to follow you around picking up your shit"!

"Oh, right so, she's only here to pick up your shit"?

"What the fuck? Whose house, is it? Who pays her wages? Who treats her with respect? NOT YOURS! AND NOT YOU!

"So, I don't have a say? I don't count around here? That bloody dog gets more respect than me"!

"You have to earn respect"!

"HEY! I DON'T NEED THIS FUCKING BULLSHIT"!

"NO"? Replied George

"FUCK YOU" Replied Fadi

"Really"? Retorted George

"Seriously! I'm outta here"! returned Fadi

"Good" shouted George, *"Do us all a favour and fuck off"!*

"FUCK YOU!" Replied Fadi

"No FUCK YOU"! Returned George

"I don't need this shit!" mumbled Fadi as he made his way to the front door.

"Enjoy Christmas on your own loser" Fadi shouted as he opened the door.

"I definitely will! Shut the door behind you" screamed George.

BANG!!! The door slammed shut and Fadi was gone.

George sparked another cigi, his hands trembling with adrenaline from the clash with Fadi. Pissed off and surprised it escalated over something so minor, he mused about his typical Cancerian temperament. Massive fuses, but when they burn out, steer clear of an about-to-blow Cancerian. George had a long fuse, mastered frustration with others, and in no shape for stressful arguments. Noom had been upstairs, but she had heard the argument kick off and it was only now that she felt it was safe to come downstairs. She had attempted to join in, a couple of times, making it to the stairs then going back into the bedroom, sitting on the bed, then getting up, going to the stairs then wimping out and going back into the bedroom for a couple of minutes.

Noom hesitated, scared to face George after their argument. She knew he wouldn't be mad and would act like nothing happened, but going downstairs felt daunting. George needed her, needed a friendly smile, not more stress. Noom took a deep breath, counted to ten, then mustered the courage to get up. She quickly tidied the bed, took another moment, and tiptoed downstairs. Glancing into the kitchen, she didn't spot George, so she headed to the piano room and she found George on the floor, cuddling Abby, blowing raspberries into her belly. Abby was all over the place, legs up, tongue out, and tail wagging. It was a joyful scene, and Noom couldn't help but smile at the heart warming sight.

"Look at you two" smiled Noom

"Hiya lovely, sorry if you heard any of that" replied George.

"Are you okay my George?" she replied not wanting to let on that she had heard everything.

"Yeah" sighed George.

"Can I get you a drink"? she asked.

"You know what Noom" Announced George.

"It's Christmas Eve and we haven't had a drink yet. Will you join me for a Christmas bevvy"? George continued.

"Of course, I will, what shall we have"? Noom inquired.

"You know what? I fancy some bubbly; shall I crack open a bottle of the bubbly stuff?" Asked George.

"Well, it is Christmas, isn't it?" Noom knew George only kept the good stuff in the house, so it was going to be a lovely glass or two of the fizzy stuff.

They polished off, not one, but two bottles of the bubbly stuff and it could have been called medicine. After they had polished off the first bottle the pair of them had become quite giggly and everything they looked at or said was funny, so it made perfect sense to open the second bottle.

They flipped through the TV guide, hoping to find something decent to watch, but even when you're upset, Christmas TV is pretty shit. There was nothing worth watching. You'd think with better technology and so many movies out there, there'd be plenty to choose from. But no, it felt like every year the options just got worse. It seemed like the BBC wasn't putting the license fee to good use in getting us a good Christmas movie selection.

"Polar Express"? suggested George

"Have seen it" slurred Noom *"A milwian terms"*

"The Grinch" giggled George

"Seen it, two milwian terms" came the answer

"It's a wonderful life"?

"Geeeoooorrrge, that one makes me cwy"

George was enjoying Noom getting more and more pissed, he had never seen her drunk before.

"Geeeoooorge, I dinnnnn't finishhh the hoooovwering toooodayyy"

"That's terrible Noom, you should be ashamed"

"I ammmm vewy assshhhammmmmed George"

"I don't think you should try finishing now, do you"?

"Ummmmm, nooo. I will finishhhh it tomowwow"

"It's Christmas day tomorrow Noom you're not coming in tomorrow"

"Yes, that's right, it's cwistmas day tomowwow, I won't be in tomoowwwow"

"Are you drunk Noom"?

"No……. I am………. Absolutely………fine…….youuuu lovely……lovely …….man"

And with that final attempt to deny her drunkenness, Noom fell asleep. George found a blanket and covered her up. She looked so sweet and cosy, and she snored.

An hour or so had passed. George had gone out to the kitchen several times for a cigi. The giggles had worn off and he was thrust back into reality. From the corner of his eye he sensed that someone had joined him in the kitchen. George turned around and it was Noom, looking a little bit sheepish.

"Hello you," said George

"Hi" replied Noom

"How do you feel?" he asked

"I'm fine…… I didn't embarrass myself did I?" Noom asked nervously.

"No, you were a very well-behaved piss head"

"Oh, don't George………I can't believe how quickly it went to my head, I'm so embarrassed"

"don't be daft darling, you behaved impeccably"

"hmmmmmm"……… Would you mind if I head home"?

"Of course not, but you're not driving, I'm getting you a cab, there is no way you're driving"

"How will I get back"?

"Let me know when you're coming over and I'll book a cab to pick you up".

"That would be fantastic, you're the best George".

George laughed, *"You're worth it"*

Once Noom had left, George grabbed some nibbles and plonked himself down in front of the telly. Shortly after George had made himself comfortable on the sofa, Abby raised an eyebrow and spotting a new comfy zone, did an 'SAS' style crawl along the floor, then bounced up onto the sofa. This totally caught George unaware.

"Aaaaghhhhh Abby"!

Abby started doing her impression of a seal and managed to position herself between the back of the sofa and George nuzzling herself in his armpit, on her back, legs in the air, tail waggling furiously so that her whole body wobbled. George, amused by her antics started to tickle her tummy causing her not only to wiggle more but make some weird mixture of moaning, growling, mumbling sound, the sort of sounds that only dogs do so well when they're enjoying themselves. Eventually she settled down and the weird moany, growly, mumble turned to a snore. George rubbed her exposed tummy while he tried to get back into the film, then out of the blue'

"Woooahhhhhhhhhhhh!!!!!!!!"

"Abby! That's gross!!!!!!!"

Yep, Abby had dropped an air bomb of gigantic proportions.

"Oh my god Abby, that's got some hang time?" holding his breath

"Jesus, what you been eating? That smells like a mixture of, dead cat and fajitas"! (This description *will make sense later in the story)*

"Ohhhhhhh god"

"Abby"

"hhhhhhhhhuuuuhhhhh"! George was on the edge of gagging.

Abby was highly amused, her tail was wagging, and she was squirming around trying to twist herself onto her feet, but because she was wedged between the back of the sofa and George, she was well and truly stuck. George rolled off the sofa onto the floor, immediately followed by Abby who landed on his back. There she found her feet and used George as a springboard to launch herself out of the room. Poor old George was forced giggling into the carpet and looked up just in time to see Abby disappear out of the room.

"That's right you smelly monster, you leave me with your farts!"

All he got back from Abby was a big *"wooooooooof"* as she ran into the kitchen.

"I guess that means you want to go out"? He called after her

"Woooooooof"

"Hang on then, here I come. Jeeeeezzzz, you stink!"

George caught up with Abby, she stood at the back door, wagging her tail still causing her entire body to wag, tongue out, pretending to bark, but not actually making a sound.

"Off you go then" said George opening the door.

He lit up a cigi and followed Abby into the garden. The temperature had really dropped now and he was hoping Abby wouldn't take long to do her business. He most definitely hoped she wouldn't get distracted and go wandering off, after all the garden led straight onto the river Thames.

"Come on Abbs, there's a good girl, I'm freezing!"

She knew her master so well and came running straight over to him doing her best to jump up at him but looked more like one those customised American cars with hydraulic suspension that make the cars bounce up and down.

"Come on girl, it's bloody cold out here."

George headed to the door and Abby was only too keen to follow him, and, headed straight back to the fire and made herself comfy.

"Don't fart here girl, you'll blow the bloody house up".

George turned off the TV and walked over to the fireplace. He poked at the fire to make it smaller, then put the fire guard in front. Kneeling down next to Abby, he began to run his fingers through her fur.

"Hey Abbs, coming to bed with me"?

Abby half opened one eye and looked up at George half-heartedly. She was super comfy where she was and really couldn't be bothered to go upstairs.

"I'll take that as a no then"?

Abby raised both her eyebrows and her big brown eyes looked straight into George's. She was so warm where she was.

"Well, you know where I'll be if you want me, love you babe"

George leaned in, embracing Abby tightly and planting a gentle kiss on her forehead. The hug lingered, a moment of connection. Abby, content with a soft murmur, closed her eyes and drifted back into slumber. George stood up, leaving for bed. As he walked away, Abby opened her eyes, watching him depart. She cherished her master deeply and couldn't imagine life without him.

⟨◆⟩

Chapter Six

Chris still couldn't find anything worthwhile to watch and was frustrated by the same old rubbish on offer by almost all the TV stations. He was considering penning a letter to the lot of them and letting them know exactly what he thought of their pitiful attempt at Christmas entertainment but decided for the better that it would be a complete waste of time and energy, as if any of them would have the slightest interest in what the public thought of their choice of festive entertainment. Die Hard is most definitely not a Christmas movie, just because it's based around Bruce Willis, running around an airport in a vest and no shoes, single-handedly taking on an army of highly trained terrorists, at Christmas.

Chris had found himself looking at old photos, mainly of the holidays he had enjoyed with the boys, laughing at how cool they thought they looked, and how hard Chris was trying to look like his idol, Mr George Michael.

There was a photo of Woody and Andy with blown-up condoms on their heads, how Woody managed to blow his up, was a miracle, and he was laughing so hard on what he did.

There was one of Chris and Woody, Chris wearing his SEX INSTRUCTOR first lesson free T-Shirt, which yes, he did actually have the balls to wear out in Magaluf at night.

Another photo he found had Chris himself, and he was very proud because it depicted a birthday cake, he had received from some girls he had met on holiday. In reality, it was a doughnut with a tampon in the middle, covered in shaving foam, and adorned with a couple of plastic straws posing as candles. However, the highlight was the birthday card behind the doughnut. Although it wasn't very clear in the photo, the card read, *'To George,'* because that's what the girls called him, and he loved it."

One more, with Chris in the middle of two very attractive girls, the blonde one, Chris did have a holiday romance with, they even kept in touch for a while when they got home. Then there was the one of Chris looking very trim and very tanned in his Club Tropicana hat, rubbing oil onto his mate, not in a gay way, more because he was annoying his other mate, Andy.

And then he found one of his mate, Rick. He didn't know Rick long as it turned out, but for the time he did know him, they had some good times. Chris met Rick through Woody, who had started a new job with a swimming pool company and was buddied up with Rick. Obviously, they got on well at work and Woody invited Rick to join the boys on a night out. Chris and Rick hit it off immediately, although it was the most unusual partnership. Chris hardly left the house unless he looked as much like George Michael as possible. Whatever George had been pictured in or what he had worn in one of his videos, that's what Chris was wearing. He particularly liked the look George had in his Monkey video. Chris had the stonewash jeans, the white T-shirt, the black braces, the cowboy boots with the chrome tips, the hat, the Ray Ban Generals, and the huge silver cross hanging from his ear, oh and of course, the designer stubble. In Chris's mind and eyes, he was George Michael, especially when he hit the dancefloor.

Then there was Rick. When they first met, Rick had cropped, bleached-blonde hair, big loops in his ears were very tanned from working outside. He was quite well-built and it had to be said, looked a lot like Billy Idol. It's difficult to imagine George Michael and Billy Idol being drinking buddies but there they were. Rick would turn up at Chris's house at the most bizarre times and as usual it was always down to Chris's dad to answer the door. Chris's dad thought Rick was a bit cocky and didn't think much of him, he didn't like being addressed as Mr H. He would open the door and Rick would say, *"Alright Mr H, is he upstairs"?* before Chris's dad could answer, Rick would have barged past and was halfway up the stairs, leaving Chris's dad at the door. *"Come in Rick, don't mind me Rick, Yes Chris is upstairs Rick, I'll just talk to myself then shall I"?* Although Mr H didn't have a great deal of time for Rick, in time he would surprise Chris beyond belief.

Chris lived just outside High Wycombe and Rick thought nothing of rocking up at 9:30 in the evening with the great idea of heading down to Bournemouth.

"Cmon matey get your George on, let's go down to Bournemouth" announced Rick.

"Bournemouth? It's 9.30? replied Chris.

"That's Alrighhhhht, an hour and half to get down there, the pubs will still be open, then we'll hit a club"

"Really"? asked Chris.

"Cmon George, you know it's the right thing to do"?

"Okay Okay, I'll get changed" replied Chris.

The pair of them bounded down the stairs.

"I'm off out"! Chris shouted as they headed out the door.

"Where you going?" asked Chris's dad

"Bournemouth"! Came the answer.

"Bournemouth"? "it's 9:30"?

But it was too late, the door slammed shut and they were gone.

A year or so later, Chris and Rick had drifted apart. Rick was a very complicated guy, every morning when he woke up, he would put on Vivaldi's Four Seasons to start his day, then he would get his car and put the Smiths on, talk about from one end of the spectrum, to the other. Rick and Woody had left the pool company and got into sales. Unfortunately, it was pyramid sales and Rick wasn't really cut out for the pressure that this would bring. He got into debt and depression took hold of him. Although Chris and Rick hadn't hung out for a while, it was Chris who got the call from Rick's mum telling Rick had taken his own life. This was a massive shock to Chris; he had led a pretty sheltered life and had no idea to handle this sort of news. It was now that Chris's dad was to surprise Chris's more than ever.

"So why did Rick do it mate?" He asked.

"Money seems to be the main reason; it appears he had got himself into quite a bit of debt" Chris replied.

"Why didn't he ask for help"?

"I have no idea!"

"I would have helped him." Replied Chris's dad.

Chris couldn't believe what he was hearing, his dad didn't like Rick. At all.

"But, you didn't like him, right?

"That doesn't mean I wouldn't have helped him. And I didn't hate him, I just found him a bit weird" said Chris's dad.

"Wow that's amazing, I would never have thought to ask you for help, even if Rick had asked me for help."

"Life is more important than money."

"Thanks Dad" Replied Chris, still in a bit of shock at his dad's response.

Chris and his dad didn't hug, even though they had just shared a moment, they never hugged, and the comment *"Life is more important than money"* would come back to haunt Chris. Chris left his dad in the living room; they had just shared a very special moment and Chris had seen a side to his dad that he had never seen before. However, after what had just happened, there was only one person who Chris knew would help settle his mind and his thoughts of confusion. He went into his bedroom, turned on the Hi-Fi, and sat back to be enveloped by his guardian angel, George Michael. His words and velvet voice filled Chris with a soothing sense of comfort. As he closed his eyes, memories of the good times with Rick replayed—a therapeutic embrace, as if George had wrapped his arms around Chris, urging strength. The magical bond left Chris feeling full.

It was probably about a year later, Chris came home from work and as he walked through the door his mum shouted from the Kitchen,

"Andrews been over, you need to go straight down the pins, the boys are all there*!"*

The Pins like "the chad" was short for the Ninepins and it was the boys favourite pub. It wasn't that great but it was local and in crawling distance from home. Considering they had all been drinking there the same amount of time, the rest of the boys knew the landlord and his wife, but for some reason Chris didn't? Chris always thought the landlord should know him after all he was George Michael.

Chris got in his car and went to drive off, but before he could start the car his dad came out.

"It will probably be better if you walk" he said

"Why's that"? Chris enquired

"The boys are waiting for you, you had better get down there". Came the answer.

His dad had a very serious look on his face, but Chris couldn't work out why. He locked the car and walked down the hill, across the main road and ran up the grass bank to the pub. There were two entrances to the pins and Chris never liked going in alone. He knew people knew him, but he just never felt relaxed in there, even though nobody had any reason to have a go at him, unless they took offence at him looking like George? At least it was George Michael and not Boy George.

As he walked in, he looked up and down the pub for his guys. Typically, they were on the raised section with the pool tables, and they weren't looking very happy. Andy came over to Chris,

"What ya drinking"?

"What's going on?" Chris asked

"Go and sit down, I'll get you a larger" replied Andy

Chris went up the stairs and sat down.

"What's going on?" He asked

There was a bit of a silence, then Aggy spoke.

"Woody's dead"

"What"? asked Chris

"Woody is dead" repeated Andy

"For Fuck's sake" sighed Chris

In a heart-wrenching reflection of Rick's path, Woody had also chosen the same tragic end, a hose from the exhaust to the car's cabin. The thought of his family discovering him was unfathomable for Chris. Rick, at least, was found by a stranger in a field, but the shared pain hung heavily in the air that sombre night. The Pins felt the weight of Woody's loss; a well-liked soul who left behind a void of silence and grief. It was about 10:30 when Chris looked up and saw his dad at the bottom of the stairs.

"Come on, it's time to come home." He said calmly.

"It's not late." Chris insisted

"I know, but I want you to come home." He said quietly not wanting to embarrass himself or Chris

"Go on mate, do as ya dad has asked" It was Pete, the pub's landlord.

Chris finished his drink and got up.

"See ya lads." He said quietly.

"See ya mate." Came a chorus from around the tables they had taken over.

"Yeah, I think I'll head home too." Came a voice after Chris.

"Me too." Came another.

"Me too!" Said another.

"See you all tomorrow. And we need to go and see Woody's mum and dad." Said Graham.

"Yeah, we really need to do that." Came an answer.

When Chris got home, he headed straight upstairs to his bedroom. Plugging in his headphones, he turned to the familiar comfort of George Michael on his Hi-fi. Sleep was elusive as thoughts of losing two dear friends lingered. George's music seemed to cradle Chris, providing solace and echoing the support felt during Rick's passing. The bond with George grew stronger, becoming a reassuring presence akin to a caring big brother. Chris found in George a unique peace, a secret keeper, someone he could talk to like no one else. George's influence in Chris's life expanded, a constant companion offering a sense of safety. The emotions were complex, defying easy explanation, and Chris chose to keep them to himself, understanding their indescribable nature.

Woody too had taken his own life, but Chris could never fathom why. Woody was good looking, always happy, always had a girlfriend, if not two. He had a good job, a car from company, no money worries, a stable loving home. And, everybody loved him. What could possibly got into his head to make him do such a thing? It just never made sense. Chris's dad would ask why Mark had done it and Chris couldn't answer, because he himself didn't know the answer. Chris's dad did in fact give his son a hug on this occasion and Chris did think it was as much for himself as it was for Chris, because Chris's dad really liked Woody .

Chris had completely lost track of time with all reminiscing while going over the photos. To lose one of your mates is bad enough, to lose two, is just so disturbing. As Chris fumbled through the photo envelopes, he came across another envelope. It was a square brown one, that had clearly been ripped open what was inside was something of great interest to Chris. He pulled the card file out of the envelope, to discover an old school report.

"This will be interesting" He muttered to himself. As he thumbed through the report, something became very clear to Chris, there was very little content, in fact in one report there was just two and half lines. It was clear from the report that his teachers didn't have a clue who Chris was. The comments were so none descript and completely void of any goals or even complaints. Chris wasn't the front row guy, who'd constantly get the teachers' attention by wanting to answer every question. Nor was he was the guy at the back of the class, the joker, the attention seeker, the social lad and the constant distraction.

Chris felt like the guy stuck in the middle, unnoticed and invisible. As he read the reports, it hit him—they didn't really know him. He wished his teachers had taken the time to understand him better, to see his potential. The problem, as Chris saw it, was that they didn't try; they just wrote their reports and moved on, never really seeing him. He thought about how different things could've been if they had done their job, helping him have a more fulfilling professional life. Instead, Chris drifted through school, and that mindset lingered into his work life. The back page of the report, where his parents should sign, remained blank. Chris chuckled, finding it typical. His mum probably skimmed through it, forgetting it afterward. It likely never occurred to her to question the school about the lack of details about her son. Chris doubted if his dad had ever seen the report; his mum might not have bothered to show him. It dawned on him that this seemingly insignificant report spoke volumes about his journey. Flying under the radar meant his full potential remained hidden—a missed opportunity, indeed.

Chris switched off the telly even though he hadn't paid any attention to it for the last couple of hours. If you had asked him what had been on, he wouldn't have been able to say. He headed over to his grand piano. Although he didn't feel like singing but he did feel the need to play 'A Different Corner', his favourite song of all time and of course it was one of George's. The first time he had heard it was at work. Simon Bates on Radio 1 was due to play George Michaels new single, and Chris couldn't wait. Then with no introduction and considering Chris had never heard the song before, within the first three bars, Chris knew this was the song and it was brilliant. Not a grower, an instant yes!!!! Clearly Simon Bates agreed and played it three times in a row back-to-back, and Chris just stood in the back of the shop where he worked and listened to every second of all three. Luckily enough in the afternoon, either Gary Davis or Steve Wright played it back-to-back twice too, which made Chris very happy, he loved it from the very first second, he heard it and it remains his favourite song today.

So, there he was at his piano playing his favourite song, not singing out loud, but singing silently as he played. This was the extended remix extra-long super mix of 'A Different Corner' that must have lasted at least 20 minutes. Chris finally wounded it up and after a couple more minutes of careful contemplation, he headed up to bed. One last tour of the house to make sure all the doors were locked, even though he hadn't actually opened any of them all day, then up the stairs to bed.

Chris got into bed and quietly lay there in the dark.

"One more sleep till Christmas." He quietly said to himself.

Chapter Seven

<<<<<<<<<< PAUSE >>>>>>>>>>

3.00AM December 25th 2016

"Whoooooahhhhhhh!!!!!!!!" Chris was woken with a start.

"Jeeeeeeezz what the?"

"Brrrrrrrrrrrrrrr"

Chris woke up with a start, the hairs on the back of his neck, arms and legs were standing to attention.

"What the fuck was that?" He asked himself.

"BRRRRRRRRRRRRR did someone just walk across my grave?" Chris muttered to himself.

"That would be me." Came a voice from the corner of the bedroom.

"Whoooooooaaaaahhh!" Yelled Chris.

"Who's that?" Chris followed up with.

"How did you get in my house?" He tried.

"My house is protected; how did you get in?" He repeated.

"What are you doing in my bedroom"? Chris enquired.

"What do you want"? He added.

"I've got a gun! Chris shouted.

"No, you haven't. Came the strangely familiar voice.

"I have and I'm not afraid to use it!!!" Chris Shouted through the dark.

"Of course, you haven't, this isn't America" came the reply. Again, the voice sounded familiar, but Chris couldn't put his finger on it in his panic. As Chris's eyes started to become accustomed to the limited amount of light, he could see that someone was sitting on the sofa on the far side of his bedroom. A ghostly figure was slouched on the sofa, looking very tall, dressed in all black but not moving, not looking like he was about to jump up and attack Chris. It was still.

"I'm going to turn the light on and when I do, I want to know what the fuck you think you're doing in my fucking house? Then I'm going to kick the fucking crap out of you!!!"

"No, you're not" the stranger calmly replied.

"You bet your fucking arse I am!" Chris replied, desperately trying to sound like Jason Statham.

"I bet you don't" came the reply.

Chris leaned over to the bedside light and switched it on. It took a few seconds for his eyes to focus.

"What the fuck are you doing here?" Chris yelled when he saw who was sitting on his sofa.

"Is this some sort of fucking joke or something?"

"Is this some sort of Christmas Carol thing going on?"

"Are you pretending to be the ghost of fucking past, present or fucking future?" Chris was really scared now.

"I honestly haven't got a clue what is going on" Said Chris's Christmas visitor.

"Then why is George Fucking Michael sat in my bedroom at 3,00am on a fucking Christmas morning?!"

Considering the man Chris had idolised for the vast majority of his life was sitting in his bedroom, he certainly was swearing at him a lot.

"My apologies, but I really don't have a fucking clue on what is going on" George replied.

"I have no idea how I got here, or how I ended up sitting in your bedroom mate."

"How did you get in? This place is like Fort Knox." Chris said looking at his watch.

"I don't know!" replied George.

"How did you get here? Is someone playing a prank on you? Were you at a Christmas party at Andrews and got wasted then they dropped you off here?" Chris asked. Andrew Ridgeley doesn't live far from Chris, so this was a plausible possibility.

"No, No and No." "I wasn't anywhere near Andrews tonight." Said George.

"How did you passed the gate?" Asked Chris

"Did you jump over my wall?"

"No, I fucking, didn't." Laughed George.

"This must be a dream". Chris announced. *"I must have eaten too much cheese.."*

"Yes, that's it, you've eaten too much cheese" replied George *"The trouble is that I didn't have any cheese tonight but I'm in the same fucked up dream."*

Chris looked at his watch again, it was still saying 3:00am. The second hand was moving but the time hadn't changed.

"I need a drink" said Chris *"I definitely need a drink, I need a drink now, do you want one?"*

"No thanks, I'm not thirsty". Replied George.

"Okay, whatever."

"I'm going downstairs." And with that Chris got out of bed and headed downstairs.

He could sense that George was behind him and he was racking his brain trying to work out, how George Michael had got into his house? Why George Michael had, got into his house? What did George Michael want? All these questions going around in his head, when actually he should have been over the moon that George Michael was in his house. Chris's house was a security masterpiece, there were sensors on every door and window. If a badger wandered into the garden, the sensors would pick it up and light the garden up like a football stadium, there was no way anyone could have got in uninvited, so how the hell had George got in. Not that he wouldn't be welcome, of course George Michael would be welcome into Chris's house, just not in this spooky way.

"Nice place, you're doing alright for yourself." said George as they came down the stairs.

"Thanks" replied Chris, totally confused at what was going on.

"My staircase isn't as big as this, even in the London house".

"Alright." Replied Chris.

They walked into the kitchen and the first thing Chris did was look at the clock on the wall.

"Still 3.00am and the second hand is still moving" Chris muttered to himself.

"I noticed that too!" said George.

"How did you hear that?" Asked Chris

"*It's a knack.*" Replied George. "Whooaaahh nice kitchen!"

"*Thank you*" replied Chris.

He grabbed a glass and headed off to the drink's cabinet in the living room.

"*Are you sure you don't want a drink George*"? Asked Chris

"*No thanks. Wow you actually used my name.*" Replied George. "*That's an improvement*".

They made their way into the living room, Chris headed for the drinks' cabinet and George took one look at the grand piano and headed straight over to that.

"*Nice Piano, do you play?*" He asked.

"*Ummmmmm, yes*" Replied Chris. Knowing full well George would look at the music sheets.

"*I love the piano, I actually have one of John Lennons pianos, the one he wrote Imagine on*"

Chris already knew this because Chris knew so much more about George than George knew about Chris.

"*I know*" replied Chris "*That must be pretty cool, knowing that Lennon had written 'Imagine' on it and now you're writing your songs on it?*"

"YEAH, It gives…… me a lot of inspiration."

"So, what music do you like to play then?" and with that George started to flick through the music sheets.

"*A different Corner, one my favourites*"

"*Fast Love, cool song.*"

"*Freedom 90, love that one.*"

"*Kissing a fool, nice.*"

"Outside, hell yeah." Laughing while he thought about it.

"Father figure, love it."

"Praying for Time, hmmmm, if only people had listened, the warning is in that one."

"Ummmmm, these are all my songs, right?" enquired George.

"Yepppppppp" replied Chris.

"So, you like my stuff then? Sorry, what is your name?"

"Chris".

"Are you any good Chris?" George asked as he gently started to tinker with the keys.

"Not bad." Replied Chris.

"You'll have to show me." Came back George.

Chris laughed nervously, trying not to think about playing George Michael for George Michael himself. For fuck's sake how critical would he be? On the other hand, he might like it and maybe even offer some advice?

"Yeah perhaps? But don't you think we have slightly more pressing issue to work out"?

"Hmmmmm, yes, we do, don't we?" Replied a very, possibly too calm George.

"Have you noticed the time hasn't changed from the moment you woke me up?" asked Chris, checking his watch again.

"Yes, I had noticed that." George replied. *"Put the telly on, see what the time is on there."*

George continued to tinker with the keys of the piano, he obviously liked it. Meanwhile Chris turned on the telly and started to flick through the channels. Every channel was frozen and every channel was saying 3:00 am. Chris flicked to the news channels, they were frozen and the time on all of them was 3:00am

"*Houston........... We have a problem!*" he said.

George looked up from playing the piano, 'A Different Corner' was the song Chris was playing before going to bed and George had started playing it now too.

"*What's up*"? asked George

"*I'm not sure, but I don't think this is a dream George....*"

Chapter Eight

Chris had poured his second glass, two rather large glasses of whiskey. This wasn't like Chris because he wasn't much of a drinker. He liked a drink at parties and if he was in the mood, he certainly could sink a few. The rest of the time he would drink Diet coke or squash, he wasn't even a big coffee drinker and never touched tea.

George was still playing A Different Corner on the piano, a slightly different version to what Chris was used to, probably something he had been playing around at home on John Lennons piano. George was really in the groove, swaying his head from side to side and humming as he played. He didn't look like someone who was in a stranger's house, with its owner, having no idea how he got there. He actually looked really relaxed.

Chris wondered over to the piano.

"So, George, how do you think you got here, and how do you think you got into my locked house? None of the doors or windows are broken. None of the alarms went off. It's impossible to get in here unless you're invited."

George stopped playing the piano.

"I haven't got a fucking scooby doo". He replied (For any Americans who might someday get to read my story, Scooby Doo is slang for having no clue) *"I've been racking my brain to try and work out what happened, and I'll be honest love, I'm a little bit lost, to say the least".*

"Do you remember anything at all?" Pushed Chris.

"Not really! I had had a pretty normal day apart from having an argument with my partner"

"Fadi"? Chris interrupted.

"Yes. Then I got pissed with my housekeeper, then after packing her off home in a cab I watched some crap Christmas telly. Abby my dog tried to kill me with the most disgusting fart? You have never smelt anything so bad! Ohhh my god it was disgusting, it nearly killed me, then I went to bed" explained George.

There was a brief silence.

"Ohhhhhh my god, Holy fuck!" Said George.

"I remember waking up in agony. I had a massive pain in my chest. I've not been well lately; my whole body feels like it's packing up? I know I've pushed it to its limits over the years, but it seems like I've really screwed it up. I don't know if you've ever felt like your time is up but that's how I've been feeling lately, as if someone is saying, "That's it George, your time is up". I thought it was just really bad acid reflux or heartburn. I've been getting those pretty bad recently, it's nasty, it feels like I had drunk a glass of acid, my god it hurts, it's so uncomfortable. It's not public knowledge, I certainly wasn't going to spill it to the paps, they've done nothing but haunt me my entire career, they were going to be the very last fuckers to find out I was ill, I can only imagine what spin those wankers would put on it? They would probably come out with I had AIDS or something"?

Another silence.

"Then everything went quiet, the pain stopped, and the next thing I remember was sitting on your sofa in your bedroom and you threatening to shoot me."

"I wouldn't have shot you, once I had realised it was you, George!" Replied Chris.

"Nothing to do with the fact that you haven't got a gun then." Asked George.

"You don't know for sure that I haven't got one"

"I think it's a pretty safe bet". Said George sarcastically.

"Hmmmmmmm" mumbled Chris. *"But that doesn't tell us how you got here?"*

"George? Are you sure you can't remember how you got here? And why here? It's a long way from Goring-on-Thames to Cornwall; surely, you would remember the journey or at least some of it? You've been here a while and it's still 3.00am."

"That had crossed my mind." Replied George.

"This is fucked up, isn't it?" Replied Chris. This was going to be the strangest Christmas ever.

"There has to be a reason why I'm here" Said George. *"I mean……. why here, in particular? What is so important to bring our worlds colliding together"?* And how the hell did I get here, it's a complete blank to me, I don't remember anything after the pain stopped."*

"I have no idea!!" Replied Chris.

"There has to be a reason. There has to be something that has brought me to your house, did you get into my house in Goring and drug me? Have you kidnapped me? Are you some sort of freak who thought he would kidnap George Michael on Christmas day as some sort of psycho stunt? Am I the one who needs to be afraid?………… You're the nutter not me! That's how I got into your house without setting off the alarm, you brought me here." Said George, trying to put the pieces together.

"Well, I can tell you for sure George, that definitely didn't happen." Replied Chris.

"Look just let me go and we won't say anything more about it." Tried George who was now actually starting to feel quite nervous about the situation.

"George, I haven't kidnapped you! I woke up to find you in my house, in my bedroom, and you didn't look like a man who had been kidnapped? If I had kidnapped you, wouldn't it have been prudent to tie you up before leaving you in my bedroom while I went to sleep?

"Well, it's the only way that I can see how I got here." Replied George.

"So why have the clocks stopped? Why is time standing still? I must be a genius, not only to kidnap George Michael, but to stop time while I did it. I'm not Dr Evil and you're not Austin Powers."

"Hmmmmm, there is that?" Replied George, now completely bewildered.

"So, have you liked my stuff for quite some time, Chris?" Asked George, trying to change the subject and give himself time to think.

"Yeah, quite a while. I guess I started following you when you released Fantastic".

"Fantastic!!!!!? that's like my whole career"!!!!!!

"Yep"

"You're not a stalker, are you?"

"Hey! We've already agreed, you're the one in my house, uninvited."

"It wasn't planned." Returned George.

"And I'm not a stalker, trust me". Insisted Chris

"*You have to admit, that's a long time to follow someone.*"

"*Are you actually complaining that you have loyal fans George?*"

"*No, of course not.*" Giggled George.

Chris began to ponder George's potential reaction upon discovering that Chris had spent most of that time trying to be him. Would George find it amusing, peculiar, or perhaps question his sexuality? Would he make advances? Unlikely, but that would certainly be unusual. The range of possible reactions was vast, and Chris resolved to navigate that uncertain territory when the time came.

"*This isn't getting us anywhere, is it?*" George sighed.

"*No.*" Replied Chris.

Chris had imagined meeting George all of his life, and now that George was actually in his house, in his living room, sat at his piano, playing A Different Corner, it had to be in the strangest of circumstances? Why had these two been bought together now?

"*Not being funny or anything, but why you?*" Asked George.

"*No offence taken.*" Replied Chris.

"*I'm guessing if you've been a fan of mine for over 30 years, you know a fair bit about my life?*"

Chris couldn't help but laugh. "*Yeah, a fair bit*".

"*It must be related to the fact that you've been a fan for so long, that is why I'm here*"?

"*Oh right, so do you think time is going to stand still while you go round signing autographs?*"

"*Do you think it's that simple?*" Asked George.

"*No George, I don't! There has to be more to it than that.*"

"Yeah, yeah." Replied George.

"*George? Do you think time is going to stand still, until we work out why you are here?*"

"*Fuck! I hope not. Left up to us, time could be standing still for a while if that's the case?*"

"*Do you think the whole world has stopped?*" Asked Chris. "*What if we try to phone someone?*"

"That's ridiculous." Replied George. "*It can only be us, surely everything outside your house is going on as usual? Are you sure you haven't kidnapped me and turned off all the clocks to try and make it look like some sort of weird freak of nature?*" Replied George, again trying to go down his kidnapping theory, which seemed the most obvious at this point. George had no idea who this strange man is, and he certainly seems to have a fascination about George, and he was starting to feel a little bit threatened.

"*But if that's the case, at some point, not long from now, people are going to start waking up, and you're not where you're meant to be, and nobody knows you're here or how you got here. Don't you think the world will find out that, one of its biggest mega stars have gone missing on Christmas Day?*"

"*Hmmmmmm good point! I don't want to brag but I am quite well known.*" Answered George.

"*Understatement?*" Replied Chris

"*Start praying for time, we need it.*" Said Chris.

With that George started the intro of his single, 'Praying for Time'.

"George!!!!!! I didn't mean, start playing the bloody song, I meant start bloody praying for time!"

"Well until that clock starts to move again, I think we have quite a bit of time, right?"

And with that, George continued to play 'Praying for Time' on the piano. Maybe it was helping him to think. Maybe he was playing it because it was only a matter of time before his host got nasty.

"What if we haven't got endless time"? Asked Chris. *"What if we only have a certain amount of time to work out why you are here, in my house and, if we don't work it out, you'll be transported back to your house and it will be as if nothing had happened?"*

"Nothing like putting a positive spin on things, thanks Chris."

"It's just an idea..." Suggested Chris.

"I suppose it's a theory, but only you know how things will turn out". Replied George, now convinced he had been kidnapped, although Chris was doing a very good job of making it look like something very different.

"Why are you here? Why have I been chosen for this bizarre, whatever it is." Asked Chris.

"That's a million-dollar question!" Commented George. *"Maybe I was due for one last shag?"* Trying to put a lighter spin on things and appeal to his possible kidnapper's better side.

"I'm not gay George." George informed.

"Shame." Replied George with a cheeky giggle, trying to lighten the atmosphere.

"Glad you're laughing!" Stated Chris.

"Oh, come on Chris, if we're stuck together, at least have a laugh with me."

"George! We're trying to work out why you're here."

"Maybe it's because I need one last shag and you're the only one available at Christmas?" Tried George.

"It's not happening, George."

One of the downsides to trying to be George Michael was that Chris had received quite a few advances from gay men in clubs. Mainly before the big Beverley Hills Toilet Gate, so Chris found it strange why so many gay men were coming onto him. Obviously, it was common knowledge in the gay community that George was gay and the fact that Chris was trying to emulate George, automatically made Chris, a gay too.

"Is it because I'm gaaaaay?" George said in his best, slightly-weird northern accent, the same one he had used with James Corden on Comic relief.

"UMMMMM? YES!!" Responded Chris.

George was now thinking he had been kidnapped because he was gay. Where Chris was still trying to work out how his idol had got into his house, without setting off any of the alarms. The two of them were on very different trains of thought.

"Well, we can tick, one last shag off the list of why I'm here then?" Asked George.

"Yep" Returned Chris. *"It ain't gonna happen!"*

"Tight arse." Mumbled George.

"And that's the way it's going to be, thank you." Rallied Chris.

"So come on wise arse, you think of something?" Suggested George.

"I'm trying."

"A lot. " Quipped George.

In what must be acknowledged as the strangest of circumstances, two people who had just met were surprisingly starting to connect quite well.

"Not necessary." Told Chris

"Was too" Retorted George, clearly running out of ideas and opting for straightforward playful banter instead.

"So, let's look at your life for a bit." Started George. *"You're obviously quite wealthy. You have a very nice house from what I've seen so far. Possibly single? As there doesn't appear to be anyone else in the house. No wedding photos, no photos of a girlfriend or boyfriend. As clearly, you're not gay, or so you say?*

"I'm not gay." Interrupted Chris.

"Do you have a job?"

"Nope"

"Where do you get all your money from then?"

"I do a George Michael tribute act." Blurted Chris.

"Fuck off!!!!!" Screamed George.

"Hahhhhhhhh!!!!! I won the lottery. But don't tell anyone because only myself, Camelot and the bank know, and now you of course."

"I'm good at keeping secrets." Added George, still thinking that he could come to a sticky end in this very strange situation that he has found himself in.

"It's actually quite a big secret." Clarified Chris.

"Whatever." Laughed George. *"So, what else is there to you that would mean we need to be connected in some way? There must be something we have in common or something we have to do."*

"I can only think of one thing, but I'm too embarrassed to say." Mumbled Chris.

"You said we're not going to shag, is that back on the table?" Laughed George.

"The kitchen table baaaaaabyyyy!" (Obviously taken from the track 'Outside') Chris came in the deepest voice he could manage *"Aaaaaaaaannnnd once again, noooooooooo."*

"So, what's so embarrassing then?" Asked George.

Chris paused and took a long hard sigh before heading back over to his bottle of whiskey for a top up.

"Cmon, it can't be that bad!!" Urged George.

Chris took a big gulp of whiskey, then blurted it out.

"I wanted to be you! I've spent the whole of my adult life trying to be you. There I've said it."

"You've done what?" Gulped George.

"You heard me" Replied Chris.

"Whhhhhyyyyyyy?????????" Exclaimed George.

"I can't explain it! I can't explain it to myself, so how the hell am I going to explain it to you?"

"But whhhhhhhyyyyyy"? Tried George again.

"I have no idea, where to start from." Uttered Chris. *"I love your music, I love your videos, I love your dressing sense, I love your sense of humour."*

"You love me?" Intervened George.

"Maybe, but not in any usual way that you would associate love. It's not sexual, I don't fantasise about shagging you."

"Why not?" Babbled George.

"Because I'm not gaaaaaaaaaaayyyyyyyyyy." Replied Chris.

"He doth protest too much doth he?" Giggled George.

I'mmmmmmmmmm noooooooooooot!!!!!!!!!!"

"I was joking." Laughed George.

"There's just something and I don't know what it is."

"I think we may have found our reason." Said George in a far more serious tone. "So, clearly you don't love me in the normal sense, or in a way that you can put your finger on? Maybe it's that indescribable, un-understandable love, that brought us together? You're not a stalker, we've established that. You're not gay. Are you really, sure about that?"

"Yes, I'm really sure."

"But you have kept an eye on me. You haven't judged me. You've kept your distance and supported me. So, why have we been brought together? Is there something that needs to be finished by us?"

"Maybe" Said Chris, deep in thought.

At that moment, George rose from his seat, a restless energy compelling him to pace the room. It was precisely then that a revelation struck him, a revelation signalling that he might be in substantial trouble, a serious trouble, yet not the kind he had contemplated since encountering his bonkers host. As he strolled past the window, his own reflection took his attention. No longer the bloated figure he remembered from bedtime, he now embodied a slimmer, more polished version of himself, reminiscent of his cool persona from the '90s. Youthful and astonishing, he marvelled at the transformation. Looking at his shadow, he saw brilliance. No aches, no pains; his body wasn't protesting. In that moment, he felt remarkably well.

He spun round quickly in shock, and for the first time since meeting Chris, he was actually in touching distance with him while Chris was stood right behind but instead of bumping into each other, George's arm went straight through Chris.

"*WHOOOOAHHHHHH!!!!!*" George shouted.

"*What just happened there?*" Screamed Chris.

"*I'm not sure.*" Said George.

"*Whatever it was, I didn't like it.*" Replied Chris.

"*Nor me.*" Announced George.

Chris and George stared at each other. This was again, the first time they had really stared at each other. Chris of course knew how George looked like, he had 30 years to get to know him. George on the other hand, didn't know Chris. He looked him up and down, which was weird because Chris was still in his PJs. George noticed that Chris did have some of his characteristics, the designer stubble, trimmed eyebrows, chiselled cheek bones, sun tan, even in December, and George could imagine if Chris didn't have bad head we would have a similar haircut.

"*Did you just see what I saw?*" Enquired George.

"*I think I might have just witnessed something!*" Informed Chris

With that George lurched forward, and took the wildest swing at Chris that he could manage. It was a pretty good right-hook from a left hander, and if it had of landed on Chris's jaw, it would probably have knocked out, or at the very least, sent him flying across the living room. As it happened, Chris didn't feel a thing. Which was just as well, because he certainly wasn't expecting his unexpected, uninvited guest and especially George Michael to suddenly launch a viscous attack on him.

"What did you do that for?" Yelled Chris.

"Just testing." Replied George with a nervous laugh.

"That could have really hurt if it had landed!" Complained Chris.

*"It did land. "*Stated George proudly.

"It didn't, you big girls' blouse". Giggled Chris

"It bloody did." Laughed George who couldn't quite believe Chris had just called him a big girls' blouse.

"So why am I still standing then?" Questioned Chris.

With that George launched another wild right hander.

"Did that miss too?" He laughed.

"What the........." gasped Chris.

Then George went a step further and didn't just take a swing at Chris he ran straight at him. Chris crapped himself, screamed, then ducked.

"AAAAAAAAAARRRRRGGGGHHHHHHH"!!!!!!   Shouted Chris.

"AAAAAAAARRRRRGGGGHHHHHHH"!!!!!   Screamed George as he ran headlong towards Chris.

"AAAAAARRRRRGGGGGGHHHHHHH"!!!!!!!   Roared Chris.

"AAAAAAAAARRRRRGGGGGHHHHHH"!!!!!!!!! Squealed George from behind Chris.

Chris spun round.

"What did you do? What just happened? Are you fucking mad?"

"Did you just see that?" Uttered George.

"I did, but I wish I hadn't." Said Chris, shocked at what had just happened.

Chapter Nine

They both looked at each other very very bewildered, in fact, bewildered would be the understatement of the century. Chris checked himself from head to toe to make sure he was still in one piece. George on the other hand was stood there giggling to himself uncontrollably.

"HAHAHAHAHAHAHA Did you see that? Did you see what I just did?"

"Yep" replied Chris, sitting down before he fell down.

Chris had shifted from the spacious living room near the piano, where his somewhat eccentric house guest had just passed through him like a breeze. Now, he found comfort on one of his three plush, four-seater sofas arranged in a cosy U-shape—the kind that embraces you when you sink into them. They were not just furniture; they were a cherished indulgence, a symbol of comfort he insisted on when making this house his own. When you lean back in them your head is caught by the huge deep back cushion. Chris hated those sofas where you lean back and there's nothing to catch your head, it just keeps going until your neck snaps or you get whiplash. No, these were the ultimate in comfort, long enough to lie down fully, deep enough for two people to snuggle up and spoon while watching a film, proper Netflix and chill equipment. Even though Chris was single, he had thought ahead to when he was ready for a relationship and when he would be able to impress a new girlfriend with his super, sensational comfy sofas.

George came over and sat down opposite, looking directly at Chris.

"Fuck me! How comfy is this?" He exclaimed.

"I know." Replied Chris smugly. George was in fact Chris's first guest in this house and the first person to be treated to the most comfortable sofas in the world. *"You're my first guest to sit on it."*

"No way." Laughed George. *"You're an even bigger recluse than me."*

Chris laughed and looked at his watch, it was still saying 3.00am.

"It's still 3 o'clock, we can't have an infinite amount of time, surely things will have to restart soon? Won't they?" Chris asked.

"You're asking the wrong person, matey." Replied George. *"Oh this is so comfy."*

George was now thinking about the obvious. Chris wasn't a kidnapper, unless he had already done something monstrous. Something horrible had happened at home in Goring-on-Thames, and the reason the clocks weren't working was because something very strange was going on, but exactly what that was, wasn't clear as yet.

"Cheers" Replied Chris. *"Some, thank you that is?"*

"Thank you for what? What have you done?" Asked George.

"I don't know, but there must be a reason we are in this predicament?" Urged Chris.

"You said dick?" Laughed George.

"Behave, we're not on Family Guy." Replied Chris.

"I love Family Guy." Responded George.

"Thought you might."

"Don't you?" Asked George.

"Yes, it's brilliant, and if the TV was working it would probably be on at least one channel and we could have watched that instead of trying to work out what the hell is going on." Said Chris impatiently.

"Well, I'm actually getting quite used to this mysterious malarkey and this sofa is so bloody comfortable I don't feel inclined to worry myself about this, so called predicament that we find ourselves in." Rattled off George.

"Who are you now? Bloody Captain Jack Sparrow?" Yelled Chris.

"Oh, you got that did you? I wasn't sure if I had pulled it off." Giggled George.

"George!!!!!!!! Is this really the time to be showing me your repertoire of voices? No matter how good they are."

"Maybe not!" He giggled. *"But I was impressed that you got it. Love those films."*

George had now really made himself at home and was stretched out on the sofa, all 6 feet of him, his hands were on his stomach linked by his fingers, then he separated them and tapped them on his stomach.

"That's another fine mess you got me into, Stanley." He managed to get out without wetting himself.

"Laurel and Hardy now? It's a good job, whoever sent you here chose me, and not some youngster who wouldn't have a clue what you just did there." Frowned Chris.

(For those of you reading this book who aren't aware of who Laurel and Hardy are; they are a comedy duo that go back as far as silent movies, in fact, I wouldn't be surprised if their first films weren't silent movies.)

"What are we going to do now, Boo Boo?" This was the next one for George, to test Chris with.

"Duuuuuuurrrrrr, I don't know Yogi, maybe we should concentrate on getting the clocks to work"? replied Chris in his best Boo Boo accent.

"Very Good." Commented George.

Chris found a quiet pleasure in the banter with George. The initial panic had melted away, but a lingering sense of curiosity tugged at him. Why was George here? The question hung in the air, unanswered. On the flip side, George, slowly discarding the notion of kidnapping, started feeling a strange safety in this unknown place. How he got here and why remained mysteries, but for the moment, he was focused on the present and the peculiar comfort it offered.

"Are you not concerned about why you're here George?" Chris asked.

"Well of course I am, you numpty, but I'm guessing it has to be for a reason, and I'm guessing the reason will be made clear at some point."

"I hope so..."

"Well clearly, we can't be trusted to work it out for ourselves. So somehow, we have to fall upon a clue at some point."

"And that's why you're a super rich, super successful mega star and I'm not!" Suggested Chris.

"Probably?" Responded George.

It got quiet for a bit. No more George copying voices, no more Chris asking things. Chris thought about asking

George some stuff about his life, especially the last few days, but he didn't want it to feel like an interview. So, he just sat there, wondering why the guy he looked up to his whole life, the one he copied and wanted to be, was sitting right across from him. Why? Why? Why?

"I guess you were sent to me because I've spent the last 30 years wanting to be you." Chris said spontaneously.

"Really Chris, why?" Asked George.

Chris remained silent because he hadn't intended to say that. It was meant to stay in his head, for him alone to hear.

"Well...." Tried George.

"If you're still around, in a few days, you will probably have worked out that I know a fair amount about you. And that might be the reason you are sitting in my living room."

"Hmmmmmmmm". Pondered George. *"What time do you think it is, outside this weird bubble of ours?"*

"It's got to be between 4 and 5 I believe." Answered Chris. *"Hey George, Hey George, you gonna a write a song about this?"* Sang Chris to the tune of George's, 'Happy'.

"I could be so happy!" George sang back.

"I could be so happy..." Followed Chris.

"Oh yeah"!!!! laughed George.

"Maybe that's it?" Questioned Chris. *"Maybe we're meant to do a song together? Maybe you're meant to do that dance album you've been promising for years."*

"By Jove, young man? I do believe you may have stumbled onto something." All of a sudden, George was alert. *"It's the unfinished business, isn't it? I'm here because I haven't finished what I was supposed to do? You fucking genius Chris, you've only fucking gone and worked it out!"*

At that very moment, the TV came back, it was in fact, 6:30am on Christmas day 2016. The usual news loop had just started and the newsreader was introducing the headlines of the day. As was usual on Christmas day, the news was a bit lacking, no Tsunamis, no earthquakes, no wars had broken out and most importantly, no news that George Michael had died.

Chapter Ten

In the quiet, Chris felt a bit puzzled. He had always admired George's lively personality on TV, expecting their time together to be filled with lively chats. But here they were, stuck in an odd silence. Chris had seen George being chatty on interviews and lively on daytime TV, so this quiet atmosphere felt strange. It made Chris wonder if there was some tension or if things were just off. The gap between the TV George and the real-life George was surprising, leaving Chris with a sense of confusion and a shattered expectation of their time together.

The clocks were now working, time had resumed, the world had started to turn again. Not that we were sure that it had stopped turning, it was probably some sort of time warp or bubble of some sort? Who knows, it was impossible to know what had been going on for the last few hours outside the house.

"*So how rich are you then?*" Enquired George out of the blue.

"*I'm probably worth about as much as you, but I don't earn royalties.*" Replied Chris.

"*And nobody knows who you are, right?*" Asked George.

"*Yes. I am completely anonymous.*" Replied Chris.

"*You lucky bastard!*" Chuckled George. "*What I wouldn't give to be anonymous?*"

"Weird, isn't it? We both have similar amounts of wealth and yet you are one of the most well-known people on the planet and want to be anonymous. While I'm anonymous and try to emulate one of the most well-known people on the planet. It's all back to front." Opined Chris.

"Trust me Chris, you might think you want what I have, but after having it a while you would soon want to give it back." Replied George. *"It's not all what it's cracked up to be, I can tell you."*

"I guess it's easier to want something you haven't got, but in your case it's impossible to get rid of it!"

"Don't get me wrong, I am very grateful for what I have been blessed with, let's face it. I've had far more good times than bad, it's just the bad times that seem to be the ones certain people remember and insist on reminding everybody else about."

"Yeah, I can certainly remember more of your bad experiences than the good ones. I doubt I'm wrong in saying, most the good ones will be very private to you. No?"

"Yeah, you're so right! The bloody Paps were so intent on ruining my career; the good times were all a bit of a blur."

"What we need to do is swap." Said Chris, jokingly.

"If only." Replied George. *"Do you really think you would like being me?"*

"Hell yeah! Who wouldn't want to be George Michael?" Laughed Chris.

"Hmmmmmm? I don't think you've really thought it through, have you mate?" Asked George.

"I've pretended to be you on and off, mainly on, for the last 30 years, of course I would love to be you." Replied Chris.

"I've been thinking." Said George with a pause, continuing, *"There's obviously a reason why you were chosen for whatever this is. Maybe in some other Universe, in another dimension, you were meant to be me."*

"Naaaaahhhhhhhhhh" said Chris.

"Think about it? You have lived your life as someone else, certainly most of it. Would it be fair to say that you possibly aren't completely sure who Chris is?" Suggested George. *"I'm confused, what the difference is between Gorgeous Paniotou and George Michael, and I'm the same person. So, how the hell can you truly know who Chris is, if you've also been trying to be George Michael."*

"Valid point." Replied Chris.

The morning light streamed in, defying the weight of Chris's thick, layered curtains. With a swift gesture, Chris reached for an LCD control panel, tapped an icon, and the entire room's curtains gracefully began to open.

George looked over his shoulder towards the windows and remarked, *"Show off."*

"Cool huh?" Chris asked smugly.

"Yeah, really cool!" George replied sarcastically.

"Looks nice out there, difficult to thinks it's Christmas Day." Chris commented.

"Have I said Happy Christmas? I can't remember? Happy Christmas George!!"

"Happy Christmas Chris." Replied George with a huge smile on his face.

George got up and wandered over to the piano and started to tinker away on the keys again. It was kind of a mixup of different songs eventually turning into Cowboys and Angels, it seemed to just be the one that made sense at that moment in time. Chris thought George might suddenly burst into song and start singing Christmas Carols but that didn't happen. In some ways Chris was relieved because he didn't know the words to many of those other songs so, if George had asked him to join in it would have been a blood bath. Cowboys and Angels meshed into Praying for Time and it seemed George had definitely moved into a more thoughtful mood. Chris wandered off for a shower and a change of clothes. He had a decision to make. Would he dress normally and have George laugh at him, or put on something that George would never be seen in and have George laugh at him anyway. He took the easy route and decided on a black T-shirt and jeans, can't go wrong with that!

Chris could hear George in the living room, although didn't recognise what he was playing.

"Something new?" Chris enquired.

"Yeah, it was something I was working on recently. It sounds good on your piano..." Smiled George.

"If you want to freshen up, feel free. I won't come up and spy on you!" Laughed Chris.

"Thanks. It wouldn't bother me if you did as I don't mind other men ogling me." Replied George with a wink.

"Touche" laughed Chris. *"I know for a fact; I am not gay."*

"Yeah yeah. You keep telling yourself that." Quipped George.

"I'm not!" I bet Elton used to wind you up before you came out, didn't' he? Didn't he"?

"Elton is a huge wind-up merchant, but he knew, and yeah, he used to nag me about it and say people wouldn't

care, your fans love you, they won't give a shit, just come out and get it over and done with. We fell out over it a few times because I wasn't ready, mainly because of my folks."

"Must have been tough!"

"So, changing the subject? Why would a multi-millionaire, want to be someone they're not? Someone famous? I'm interested Chris, do tell." Asked George, who had been busy thinking about the situation while Chris was upstairs.

"Well, I haven't always been a multi-millionaire for starters, that part of my life is relatively new."

"But you are now, and yet you still want to be me." Pushed George.

"I guess it's how I've lived my life? I've been living this way for so long now; I don't know any difference."

"I've been thinking while you were upstairs, about trying a little experiment. Are you up for it?" Asked George.

"Depends." Responded Chris.

"If it works, we might be able to make your biggest dream come true!" Hinted George.

"I'm intrigued, what's in your in mind?" Enquired Chris.

"What if you could be me?" Suggested George.

"Awesome!" Replied Chris.

"You say that now Wait till you've been me for a while, then let me know what you think."

"So, what's your plan then?" Enquired Chris.

"We've obviously been brought together for a reason, right?"

"Mhm."

"We're obviously getting closer to that reason, because time has started again, right?"

"Alright…"

"So, here's my idea." Replied George with some trepidation. *"You know I ran through you earlier?"*

"Yeah, that was scary! Replied Chris.

"What if?" Said George before pausing again.

"Yes?" Asked Chris on tender hooks.

"What if?" Another pause.

"Ohhhh get on with it. Spit it out!"

"Patience or I won't tell you." Said George, still trying to delay saying what he had on his mind.

"Hmmmmmmmmm?" Sighed Chris.

"What if……………… Instead of running through you, I stop half way." Broached George.

Chris was silent while he considered exactly what George was suggesting and the repercussions if anything went wrong. After all, neither of them had a clue what was actually going on and neither of them were medically trained. What if something went wrong? Would Chris have to phone 999 and announce he had George Michael stuck inside him? The operator would probably think it was some sort of Christmas idiot wasting her time after too many glasses of bubbly on an empty stomach. Also, George was several inches taller than Chris. Chris was only 5' 8" while, George was over six feet tall. If George stopped halfway way through Chris, would Chris have to stretch to fit George or would George shrink to fit into Chris? If Chris was to be George Michael, he would need to be six foot or people would question why George Michael had suddenly shrunk by four inches.

"*Are you sure about this? What if you get stuck?*" Enquired Chris.

"*Don't you want a bit of George in you?*" Mocked George.

"*I'm being serious. We haven't got a clue what we're doing.*" Replied Chris.

"*Well, I'm already dead, so I've got nothing to lose!*" Said George.

"*Nice.*" Retorted Chris.

"*Don't you think it's worth a shot? It could mean that you could actually get to be me.*"

This was a good argument from George and very difficult for Chris to defend, after all it would be incredible if they actually pulled this off to know what it's like to be George Michael.

"*So, what's your plan then?*" Asked Chris.

"*Well. We know I can run through you, without any damage.*"

"*That we know of?*" Questioned Chris.

"*Do you feel anything?*" Asked George.

"*Do I feel queer, do you mean?*" Commented Chris.

"*Oh, hahahaah I asked for that?*" Returned George. "*No! do you feel that your organs are all in the wrong place?*"

"*No, they all feel fine.*"

"*Right, so the plan is that I am going to do the same but stop halfway through.*"

"*Could you try it from the side? I don't want you coming in me from behind.*" Giggled Chris.

"*You're so gay!!*" Said George.

"*So not!*" Replied Chris.

"*Are we going to do this or not?*" It was George's turn to be impatient this time.

"*Come on then, but if we both end up dead, the coroner is going to have a hell of a job trying to work out what was the cause.*" Replied Chris.

"*So, from where do you want me to come in you?*" Chuckled George.

"*It's a good job, we know you're gay or I'd have serious questions.*" Replied Chris.

"*You're so easy to wind up, I'm actually starting to really like you!*"

"*Oh good, it's only taken 30 years!*"

"*Don't blame me for that! If you were that bothered, you could have come and at least tried to find me? It's not as if the Paps hid my addresses, is it?*"

"*Just what you needed, another stalker?*"

"*Well, if I got to know you and liked you? You wouldn't be a stalker, would you?*" Insisted George.

"*So, if I stand sideways on to you, and then you slide sideways towards me, and we'll see what happens*"? Suggested Chris.

George took a deep long breath, then breathed out, "*Let's go!*"

Chapter Eleven

"*How do you feel?*" Asked George.

"*Not sure.*" Replied Chris. "*I think I'm okay, what about you?*"

"*Well, I'm dead, so honestly, I'm feeling pretty shitty at the moment.*" Retorted George.

"*Why did I agree to do this with you?*" Questioned Chris. "*Don't you take anything seriously at the moment!*"

"*Because you love me, and you know it!*" Laughed George.

"*I had no idea you were this cocky.*" Replied Chris.

"*You know it's true.*" Continued George.

"*We need a mirror, I'm going upstairs.*" Said Chris as he headed towards the living room's door.

It certainly didn't feel any different to walk. All of his organs felt normal. His bones felt normal. His breathing felt normal. Everything totally gave a normal feel. Chris or should I say "they" headed upstairs to his bedroom, where this whole crazy situation first started. It seemed like a decade had passed just to get to this point. It seemed like George had been a part of Chris's life forever. And I guess in a way he had? The walk up the stairs was long, the anticipation of what they were going to see in the mirror was overwhelming. Chris was scared while George was silent, what exactly were they about to witness?

Chris gently pushed the bedroom door ajar, a subtle anticipation lingering within him. He'd tidied up while dressing, an unspoken desire to shield George from any disarray in his personal space. The bed neatly made, clothes tossed into the laundry basket, windows opened to invite the crisp, cold air, and the lingering scent of deodorant adorned him.

Approaching the mirror on the far side, Chris avoided his reflection until he stood right before it. With trepidation, he started lifting his gaze – socks, jeans, belt, and the familiar black T-shirt. Tanned arms, unchanged weight, the reflection echoed a semblance of the past. Yet, in those moments, a silent uncertainty lingered, the mirror unveiling a version of Chris that was both known and unknown.

"Okay, here we go!" As Chris prepared to look himself in the eye. *"Right! Okay then? Okay? Right?"*

Chris was looking at George Michael in the mirror. It would appear, that all of George's features had taken over. George was now the prominent appearance in the mirror.

"George Michael is alive!" Chris uttered.

"Okay." This was the first time George had spoken since leaving the living room.

They were both looking at a single figure in the mirror and that figure was George. Chris was still thinking as if he was Chris, if he closed his eyes, he could visualize what he looked like before George had made his experiment. "Okay" was all George had said since looking in the mirror and Chris was wondering what George was seeing. Was he seeing Chris, as Chris was seeing George? Did it work both ways? Were they each experiencing different things?

"What do you see George?"

"I see me, why? What are you seeing?"

"I'm also seeing you." Responded Chris.

"So, we've done it then. right? I'm still alive and you're going to experience what it's like to be George Michael!" George didn't sound as excited as he did before the experiment, was he regretting what he had done.

As they stood there looking at themselves as one person, they were both thinking very different things. Chris was thinking how much time he had spent trying to look like George with some small pieces of success. He might not have looked just like George, but he had managed to get the effect of looking like George. He knew this, because on so many occasions people had referred to him as George so, he must have looked something like him or people wouldn't have made the comparison, they would have come up with some other celebrity, possibly one Chris had never heard of and that would have been devastating, or if they had come up with someone Chris didn't like, that would have been even worse. Here he was looking just like George Michael, because in fact he was George Michael and although he didn't want to admit it, he had George Michael inside him. That sounded so wrong, there must be another way of imagining their situation. Chris was looking himself up and down, he liked being over six foot tall, obviously it felt good. He loved his new hair line, Chris's natural hair line was much further back than George's, in fact that had been the hardest part of trying to look like George, because George had far better hair than Chris. Their jaw lines were similar and their cheek bones were similar and actually their noses weren't a million miles away from each other. Chris looked at his eyes and they were now dark brown. Chris's eyes had always been one of his best features, he had kind of bluey, grey with yellow on its surround. On video calls, they looked piercing blue. Girls had always complimented Chris on his eyes and how they sparkled, especially in the sun. Chris would always keep his eyes wide open when chatting to girls trying to use them in some sort of hypnotic way.

George saw a transformed reflection, not the worn-out version from hours ago. It wasn't the George in pain or fear but the confident, carefree one admired by fans. He recognized the Patience album cover image—relaxed and unruffled. Despite life's turbulence, George thought of Chris, realizing without him, he could be lying lifeless. Then, a fleeting relief: "Thank God Noom won't find me now."

"So, what now?" Asked George.

"Good question." Replied Chris. *"I'm actually liking what I'm seeing."*

"It can't be that much of a surprise, surely?" Enquired George.

"I suppose not." Sighed Chris.

Chris could actually have stood in front of the mirror for the rest of the day but now that George had taken on a more physical form again, he was feeling like he wanted something to eat and drink.

"I could murder a coffee and something to eat."

"Oh my god. I hadn't thought of that!" Replied Chris. *"I hope I don't have to eat two meals."*

"Hahahahhah, you'll be so fucking fat if you do." Laughed George.

"You don't have some sort of stupid appetite; do you, George?"

"No, you're safe. I like my food, but I'm not a pig."

"Thank god for that." Said Chris with a sigh of relief. Chris didn't have a particularly large appetite and gained weight merely by looking at food, so the thought of eating for two did not excite him one bit.

They turned around and walked away from the mirror, out of the bedroom and down the stairs towards the kitchen.

"Hey what if we need to go to the loo, who's going to hold onto who?" Laughed George.

"Oh crap, I hadn't thought about that!" Replied Chris. *"We'll have to separate."*

"That might not always be possible." Returned George. *"It'll be fine if we're at home, but what about when we're out and about?"*

"Hmmmmmmmmm" said Chris.

"Personally, I don't mind." Said George. *"You're the one with the hang ups who swears he's not gay."*

"Once again George."

George quickly interrupted, *"I'MMMMM NOT GAAAAYYYYYYY!"*

"That's right." Returned Chris.

"Well, you might have to get used to the fact that you're going to have to hold my old fella from time to time while I take a piss."

"You can hold it and I'll close my eyes." Replied Chris.

"That's all well and good Chris, but what if it's not my fella I'm holding? What if it's yours?" George made a huge laugh.

"Oh my god this getting way to complicated......" Sighed Chris.

"You wanted to be me." Said George.

"You turned up at my house!" Replied Chris.

"Mhm, because you've wanted to be me for the last 30 years!" Responded

George.

"Because you haven't finished what you were supposed to finish." Stated Chris.

"Because because because?" Shouted George. *"One of us is going to have to hold the other one's fella at some point. And that stays a FACT!"*

"Coffee?" Asked Chris.

"Yes please, make it a big one, make it huge, so I have to pee for England." Chuckled George.

Chris frowned and put the kettle on. He didn't know why he frowned because George wouldn't be able to see him frown, but would he be able to feel him frown, or just instinctively know that he had frowned?

"Did you see me frown?" Interrogated Chris.

"I didn't see it but somehow, I knew you did it. We are definitely in sync with each other. This is so cool!" Gleamed George.

"How do you take your coffee?" Chris asked.

"Black's fine." Mentioned George.

"Cool, me too." Expressed Chris. *"I was going to have Weetabix too, banana flavour."*

"Banana Weetabix? I've never had those before." Giggled George.

This was going to be a very peculiar Christmas Day, they spent most the day winding each other up, George being the biggest wind-up merchant, he had quickly worked out how to rattle Chris's cage. Despite Chris rolling his eyes and putting up a facade of protest, it was evident that he was genuinely relishing being part of this extraordinary experience. After all, Chris played a crucial role in George's life—without him, George wouldn't be alive. Thanks to Chris, George Michael was alive.

The time had come when one of them would need the loo and it actually was quite easy to block the other out, although they had agreed to go to the loo separately whilst in the house. They had also discussed how George would manifest himself when they weren't in the house, was he a ghost? Did the physical version of George still even exist?

They had decided to go over to Goring on Boxing Day, because of course, poor Abby would be starving by then and probably left several messages on the kitchen floor as a thank you for leaving her on her own all day. There was a fresh bowl of water there on Christmas Eve, George had made sure he had topped it up before he went to bed, he had also left a fresh chew by the bowl so at least she would have had something. How was Abby going to react to them, animals have different instincts to humans, would she see George or Chris? Would Abby have found George's lifeless body in the morning when she went upstairs to see her dad, or would the bed be empty? Surely the creator of this great plan wouldn't have made Abby suffer, thinking her dad had gone for good. What if when we got there, she was howling the house down, crying her eyes out on the bed next to George?

After sitting up and bantering for hours, they began to know each other well. Chris, thinking he knew George inside out from their 30-year friendship, discovered he knew little about the real man behind the George Michael persona. Conversely, George, aside from a few glimpses, knew little about Chris.

Surprisingly, they got along remarkably well, sharing a similar sense of humor—both sarcastic, immature, and adept at playful teasing. Their compatibility hinted they could have been great friends had they met earlier. George playfully probed Chris's protective stance on his sexuality, sensing Chris enjoyed the attention.

It felt like a first date—questions about favourite food, film genre, and music. Unsurprisingly, they both liked George Michael. As they got to know each other, the hours slipped away, and strangely, they forgot the peculiar situation they found themselves in. Maybe, by avoiding the topic, they hoped to stumble upon the answer accidentally.

One of the questions George had asked Chris was 'who he fancied most in the world?' One of George's many attempts at embarrassing Chris during the evening. George was expecting Chris to say "well obviously you, George, even though I'm not gay". Instead, the answer was much simpler and caught George a little off guard, he certainly wasn't expecting such a rapid answer, most people usually have to think for at least a couple of seconds before answering a question like that. But not Chris, he knew exactly who he fancied and didn't have to think about it for a single second. "Jennifer Aniston" he replied spontaneously. George was impressed, and was actually, quiet a big fan of Ms Aniston too, let's face it, she is gorgeous, a goddess, amazingly funny and basically sex on legs, who doesn't fancy Jennifer Aniston? George put that answer in the bank and decided he would investigate that in more detail at any other time.

Eventually they decided they probably have plenty of time to get to know each other, as it would appear they were to be as one for the foreseeable future and so decided to head up to bed.

"*Which room have i got?*" Enquired George.

"*Pick which ever one you like George. They're all en-suit and pretty similar in size, except my room of course which is slightly bigger, and it's my room, therefore, I will be the only one sleeping in it.*" Conveyed Chris.

"*Are you a heavy sleeper Chris?*" Queried George.

"*Nah not really, I don't think. I guess I must go into a deep sleep at some point.*"

"*So, I won't be able to sneak in then?*" Grinned George.

"*I would rather you didn't, George.*" Reported Chris

George headed off to one of the other rooms laughing his head off.

"*You are so easy to take the piss out of Chris. And call me Yog, all my friends call me Yog!*"

"*Idiot*" muttered Chris under his breath. "*Cool I will! Nite Yog*" he called over to George feeling pretty, bloody pleased with himself. George Michael classed him as a friend and says he can call him Yog, life is good, what a Christmas this is turning out to be?

Chapter Twelve

December 26, 2016 Boxing Day morning, Chris woke up slowly thinking to himself whether he had had a very long, very realistic dream that had appeared to have lasted for the whole of Christmas Day. Surely, he hadn't spent the day with George Michael in some sort of alternative world where George seemed to have died and was using Chris as his physical body. Surely, they hadn't spent the day trying to work out between them why their worlds had collided. Surely, they wouldn't have spent the day bickering and winding each other up. It must have been all a dream. Chris must have eaten something strange that had sent him into this hallucinogenic state and his subconscious mind had made up everything in the most minute detail. Chris lay there giggling to himself about how clever the subconscious was, and how it had taken the piano playing from Christmas Eve and played out this weird and quite wonderful piece of theatre in his mind. Obviously because Chris had been thinking about George and playing his music so, his subconscious had devised the entire thing. It was strange though that Chris couldn't remember anything else about Christmas Day, not a single thing that didn't somehow, include George Michael. The entire day was a complete mystery and could only be explained by having slept through the entire day.

"Oiiiiiiiii! Are you up yet?"

In that very second the truth of what had happened on Christmas Day came bursting through the door of Chris's bedroom.

"C'mon matey boy, we need to get up and run to Abby, she'll be going nuts all on her own." Yep, George Michael had come bursting in confirming that the day before was not an hallucination, it was in fact a reality.

"Shit! That's two days running you've come bursting into my room uninvited." Asserted Chris.

"C'mon you grumpy sod, get your arse out of bed and drive me up to Abby!"

"Please?" Replied Chris.

"Just do it, don't be such a grinch." Chuckled George.

"You really know how to get on the good side of me." Replied Chris

"What are you trying to hide? Show your uncle George!" Giggled George as he started to pull the duvet off Chris's bed.

"What are you doing?!" Yelled Chris with a degree of laughter in his voice.

"Who's got morning wood going on?" Shrieked George. Still tugging the duvet.

"If I did, it's gone now you fool!!!!" Shouted Chris as he tried to keep his duvet on the bed.

"YEAH YEAH!!! CHRIS HAS GOT A HARD ON! CHRIS HAS GOT A HARD ON!!!" Chanted George.

"For god's sake Yog!!!!"

"Ohhhhhhh look at you calling me Yog!"

"I did and I liked it! Now get off my fucking duvet"

With that George launched himself onto Chris's bed and started to attempt to wrestle him out of bed.

"Grrrrrrrrrrrrrrrrrr" shouted George.

"Grrrrrrrrrrrrrrrr" shouted Chris

"ONE-A TWO-A THREE-A HE'S OUT!!!!" Shouted George as he got Chris into a headlock.

"Just you wait till I get out of this!!!!" Mumbled Chris through the pillow George had planted his head in.

"What ya gonna do bout it, buddy boy?" Returned George almost in hysterics.

"I'm gonna! I'm gonna! I'm gonna" Mumbled Chris.

"I'm gonna what?" Returned George.

"Kick your frigging arse!!!" Came a muffled answer.

"Yeah yeah yeah!!!! How's that morning wood coming along, has it gone down yet?" Probed George hysterically.

"What do you think you utter nutcase?"

"So, you did have one?"

"Well, if I did? I haven't now! Let me go or I'll give you such a beating!!!!!"

George let go, bounced off the bed and ran for the door, before Chris could lift his head from the pillows George had buried him in.

"Catch me if you can!!!!" Cheered George from the door, in the campest voice he could think of.

"You had better start running Yoggy boy!!!!!" Shouted Chris

"Yoggy boy?" Laughed George. *"That's a bit familiar, isn't it?"*

Then he noticed Chris had escaped from the confines of his pillows and duvet and was now climbing out of bed and clearly intent at launching himself at George.

"Start running!!!!!!!!!" Whooped Chris

George didn't need to be told twice and was on his toes running across the landing and down the stairs laughing his head off as he went.

"You wait till I get hold of you!!!!!!" Came the holla from behind him. George didn't reply, he couldn't he was way too busy giggling to himself.

At the bottom of the stairs, George decided to take the most direct route that didn't include slowing down if he could help it. He turned right at the bottom and headed down the corridor, straight in front of him. He could briefly remember Chris saying that it led to the indoor pool. He hadn't been down there before, and had no idea that there was a door leading from the corridor to the pool, this meant of course stopping to open the door and therefore, giving Chris precious seconds to catch up.

George flung the door open, dashing into the pool area. Yet, in that fleeting moment, it was just enough time for Chris to close the gap. As Chris reached the poolside, he felt the firm grip of his pursuer's arms encircle his waist, lifting him off the ground. Together, they plunged into the water. After a brief scramble and the disorienting swirl of water, they both resurfaced. *"Haaaaaaaaaaa!!!!!!!! Got ya!!!"* Gurgled Chris.

George was still laughing too hard from his attempted escape, and was having way too much fun to bother trying to think of a clever reply, instead, opting to try and swim his way out of trouble.

"That's right Yog, swim away!" Chris liked calling George, Yog a lot.

All he received in response was an unrestrained burst of giggles as George splashed about, attempting to evade. It wasn't a dignified escape but more a blend of doggy paddle and a frenzied man in distress—a sight that might be deemed embarrassing for someone of George Michael's mega-star status. As he reached the opposite side, he scrambled out to the safety of the pool bar, aptly named Club Tropicana.

"You're an idiot Chris!" He laughed as he read the sign across the front of the beach shack style bar.

"Don't you like it?" Asked Chris somewhat hurt by George's comment.

"Club fucking Tropicana." Continued George. *"Are the drinks free?"*

"Of course," replied Chris

"Awesome!" Chuckled George.

"I'm soaked now!" Screamed Chris across the pool.

"Don't blame me, you're the one who rugby tackled me into the water." Countered George.

"Are you going to have breakfast?" Asked Chris. *"What time is it anyway?"*

It was in fact only 6:00am, George was keen to get back to see if Abby was okay.

"6 o'clock, now get your arse in gear and get me up to my beloved Abby!" Yelled George.

Chris pulled himself out of the pool and grabbed one of the bath robes hanging on the wall.

"Bath robes here if you want one." He shouted over to George. *"I'm going to put the kettle on!"*

"I'm good thanks." Replied George. *"Don't be too long!"*

After putting the kettle on, Chris went upstairs and got washed, dressed and tidied up the mess left by George's morning attack. When he got back downstairs, George was sat at the piano tinkering away, playing a tune that Chris didn't recognise but did instantly like, it had a good vibe about it, a nice up beat Mediterranean vibe, the sort of tune that you would expect to hear in somewhere like, Café del Mar whilst chilling out in the sun. It reminded Chris of some of the early wham stuff, like 'Blue' and 'Ray of Sunshine', one of those soft tunes that could warm you up just by listening to them. He went into the kitchen, made a coffee and grabbed a couple of Weetabix, then uncharacteristically took it into the living room.

"*Something new?*" Chris enquired.

"*Maybe!*" Added George. "*Just playing around with some ideas.*"

"*Sounds good, very warm, very summery.*" Acknowledged Chris.

"*Cheers, that was the vibe I wanted!*"

"*Job done then?*" Retorted Chris.

"*You are joking?*" Chuckled George. "*You'll have to come into the studio and see how much work goes into making a record.*"

"*I would love to!*" Replied Chris. "*Let's face it, you can't go in without me now, can you?*"

"*Good point! I hadn't thought of that. Good job, you play the piano or we would have been in a whole world of trouble.*"

"*Hmmmmmm, I'm not as good as you, remember?*"

"*Never mind that now, get that breakky down your throat and let's get going. How long do you reckon it will take to get up there?*"

"*Hopefully not long today, there shouldn't be too much traffic on the road and optimistically, there won't be too*

many police about, so I'll be able to give it some beans."
Replied Chris.

"Cool." Replied George.

"So how long we going for?" Asked Chris

"I don't know, why?" Replied George

"Do I need to pack an overnight bag?"

"Oh right, yeah? Hmmmm we have no idea what is going to happen when we leave these four walls do we?" Said George slightly nervously.

"No, we don't. What will Abby see? What will your housekeeper see? Will she just see you or will she see both of us? I'm guessing she'll just see you, who will actually be me looking like you, because you aren't actually you anymore."

"She can't see you, because if she sees you, then where will I be? And if she does see you then again, where will I be? And what would you be doing in my home if I'm not there?"

"Is your housekeeper due in today?"

"No, she's off for Christmas, but we got pissed on Christmas Eve and I put her in a cab to get home, so I suppose there is a chance she'll come over to pick up her car."

"Well, we're going to have to meet people at some point so maybe it would be best if it was someone like your housekeeper first."

"Her name is Noom, I don't shout "Oi"! housekeeper get me a coffee! I would say something like "Hey my lovely any chance you might make me on those amazing cups of coffee that you're so good at?"'

"Creep!" chuckled Chris.

"At least I have a housekeeper." Replied George.

"At least I have a housekeeper." Mimicked Chris adding, *"I don't need one I'm a recluse."*

"Idiot! You make it sound like it's your profession."

"I liked being a recluse, thank you. I was fine being a recluse until you decided to crash the party."

"Idiot!" Sighed George.

They got ready, Chris had a quick tidy up, he didn't like leaving the house in a mess, George suggested he get a housekeeper but Chris was adamant that recluses don't have housekeepers. Then for the first time, they attempted to leave the house, only to find they couldn't do it as two people. They could only be themselves in the privacy of the house, it would appear everywhere else they went would have to be as one person, namely George.

⸺◈⸺

Chapter Thirteen

Chris flicked the switch on his key fob and the garage door slowly started to open up, revealing his pride and joy, a sparkling Mercedes Benz C63 AMG Coupe. 6.2 litres of V8 Bi-Turbo German engineering in dark blue, looking like it had just left the showroom.

"*Nice car.*" Said George. "*I'm a bit of a fan of Mercs myself.*"

"*And yet you have a Range Rover and a BMW?*" Replied Chris.

"*And you reckon you're not a stalker?*"

"*Thank the Paps for all the photos of you, asleep in your cars.*"

"*Don't you just love the tossers? Can't a man go for a night out or a bit of nooky without a bloody Pap sticking his camera through the window? I never look my best in those shots; they always got my worst side.*"

"*It must be difficult getting another angle when you've got a Happy Snaps store sticking out of the other side of the car?*" Chris was of course referring to George's lapse of concentration behind the wheel and subsequent collision with a Happy Snaps photo shop, which the media were all over like a rash on a baby's bum.

"*Oh, very funny!*" Retorted George. "*I fell asleep, it was a late night.*"

"And didn't they make you pay for it? You must have made the front page of every newspaper and the headlines of every news programme for a least a couple of days."

"Yeah, as usual it was blown right out of proportion. If it had just been a regular guy, like you for instance, nobody except the insurance companies would have known about it." Said George defensively.

"George. What is the status of your driving licence, at the moment?"

"I don't have one at the moment, why?"

"If the police see you driving and they know you don't have a licence, what do you think they're going to do?" Enquired Chris.

"You'll just have to be you. You've spent how many years trying to look like me? You'll just have to tell them you're a big fan and you enjoy looking like me. Or in your case an exact perfect in every way carbon copy of me. I'm sure they'll believe you."

With that, they synchronized their movements and stepped into the car. A press of the START/STOP button brought the V8 engine roaring to life. Chris patiently awaited the seatbelt mechanism to present the belt to him; no need to fumble behind for it in a Mercedes. Slowly maneuvering out of the garage, despite ample space for two cars and the Mercedes centrally parked, Chris wasn't willing to take any chances with his pride and joy. Activating a button on his key fob, the garage door smoothly closed behind them, and with another switch on a separate fob, the gate at the entrance to the drive began its unhurried ascent.

"Jeeeez how many gadgets have you got man?" Asked George.

"*Enough*" replied Chris.

Chris loved the sound of the engine in his Merc, it's subtle, but left no doubt there was a monster of an engine under the bonnet. Chris couldn't stand boy racers with their big bore exhausts that were all noise and no substance. It always amazed him that the sort of people who put these pointless exhausts pipes on their cars, claimed to know something about cars? But if they knew anything about cars, they should know that sticking an exhaust pipe the size of the channel tunnel on a Ford Fiesta made absolutely no difference whatsoever, except to piss off everybody in hearing distance of it.

Chris yearned for the moments when a young hotshot in a small, rev-happy 1.6-liter car dared to challenge him at a traffic light. As they exchanged confident glances, Chris in his commanding 6.2-liter Merc, he couldn't help but chuckle dismissively. Allowing them to zoom ahead initially, he relished in the surprise that awaited them as he effortlessly revealed the true power of a genuine car when the green light signalled the start.

On several occasions while casually driving up the A30, a boy racer with a big bore exhaust would pull alongside him, and when he looked across, he would see three or four spotty teenagers looking back at him with inane grins on their faces as if to say, "we dare you." The driver of the car would be accelerating then taking his foot off the gas pedal so the car would make a pointless popping sound, then back on the gas again. Chris could see that they found this highly amusing. Again, he would wonder why anybody who knew anything about cars, would think for one moment, that a Ford Fiesta with a big bore exhaust, no matter how big the exhaust is, would stand any chance against an AMG C63 Mercedes? The easiest way to get rid of them was to slow down, let them get in front then pull into their lane behind them. The two idiots in the back would be staring out of the rear window while the driver would plant his right foot on the floor. The Fiesta would slowly climb up to the 80s then a while longer if they were lucky, it might hit the 90s but getting to 100mph would be a challenge, not only because of the weight of the big bore exhaust pipe, but the car only had a top speed of just over 100mph when it was new. Compare that to a Merc capable of 170mph and the outcome is obvious. It would be at this point Chris would put on his indicator to let them know he wanted to pass, drop down a couple of gears, then plant his right foot on the floor and leave them spluttering behind in his dust. From that point onward, it became a matter of allowing them to nearly catch up before swiftly vanishing into the distance. Every few minutes, they would inch closer, and he would replay the process until sheer boredom led him to pull so far ahead that catching up became an impossible feat.

Chris wasn't in the mood for these antics today and thankfully there were no boy racers on the A30 that day. Maybe they had all got new big bore exhausts for Christmas and were at home fitting them. They had been on the A30 for about twenty-five minutes, when George thought he would take the opportunity to quiz Chris on the other love of his life.

"So, Jen, what's that all about then?" Asked George.

"Don't you mean Jennifer?" Responded Chris. *"I'm not sure if she prefers Jen or Jennifer."*

"I reckon she's a Jen or Jenny." Suggested George.

"Maybe to her inner circle." Replied Chris

"So, what is it about Jen makes you hot to trot then?"

"*Hot to trot? How old are you?*"

"*You know what I mean.*" Laughed George.

"*You have to admit, she is pretty close, if not perfect.*" Returned Chris.

"*I do concur, she is bloody gorgeous.*" Laughed George

"*She has got everything going on, hasn't she? She's drop dead gorgeous, funny, her body is hmmmmmmm hmmmmmm, seems incredibly down to earth and she has this cute way of using her facial expressions.*"

"*What do you mean?*" Questioned George.

"*Have you seen any of her films George?*"

"*Probably.*" Replied George.

"*I'll show you them, but in, Just Go With It and Murder Mystery, even, We're the Millers, she has this cute way of looking into her man's eyes and her lips kind of quiver. If she's acting fair play to her, but I reckon she would probably do that in the real world. At the end of Just Go With It, with Adam Sandler, when they are looking into each other's eyes, I would definitely want to be Adam, in fact there's a part of the film when they've walked back to Jennifer's room and it's started to sink in for Adam that he fancies her. If you watch his eyes, I'm sure he's checking out her boobs, and she's definitely not wearing a bra.*"

"*You definitely pay a lot of attention to the details, don't you? I have a feeling I have seen that one.*" Stated George. "*I have definitely seen the Break Up.*"

"*Yeah, I've seen that but I'm not a huge fan of Vince Vaughn, especially as this involves him being a prat towards Jen.*"

"*It's only a film Chris! Didn't they date for a while?*" Asked George.

"I wish that was only a rumour, but I've seen pics of them together." Retaliated Chris.

"Touchy." Giggled George.

"I just don't like him." Replied Chris, defensively.

"Was he nasty to your Jen?" Giggled George.

"Yes!" Exclaimed Chris.

"So how did you plan to meet the love of your life then?" Asked George. *"We both know you're not into stalking."*

"No idea! I figured she would come looking for me." Laughed Chris

"Yeah right." Clarified George.

"It worked with you, didn't it?" Retorted Chris.

"Oh right. So, you want Jen to die before you, possibly get to meet her?" Asked George.

"No, of course not!"

"It was alright for me though." Complained George.

"This isn't about you George! And let's face it, Jen takes a little bit more care of herself than you did."

"Touchee." Laughed George. *"So come on Einstein, how you gonna make one of the most famous and most beautiful women in the world fall in love with you?"*

"I don't know!!!!!!" Wined Chris.

"I figure we need to come up with a plan my lovely." Suggested George.

"That would be amazing George!" Responded Chris.

"Leave it with me, I'll come up with a plan." Laughed George.

"You presume you're gonna get Jennifer Aniston, to go out with me?" Demanded Chris.

"Where there's a will there's a way!" George affirmatively replied. *"I always said I was going to be a mega star and I did it. I set up Martin Kemp and Shirlie Holliman, and they've been together ever since. I am a miracle worker."*

"I'll leave it on you then, shall I George?"

"You leave it to your uncle George; I'll get Jennifer Aniston to fall in love with you." Replied a very over confident George. *"What can you offer Ms Aniston then, Chrissy boy?"*

"Well, I won't be after her money, will I?"

"Don't make it about money mate, Jen is better than that. She's going to go out with you for you, not your money. What are you going to give her?" Quizzed George.

"It's tough George, I'm not famous, but that might be a good thing. But it might also make her suspicious, no? I couldn't be less famous even if I tried.

"Being a recluse is a bit strange. What is it with you Chrissy boy? You want to be reclusive but you pretend to be one of the most recognised men in the world and you want to date one of the most recognised women in the world. I don't get you?" Said George.

"What can I say George, I like to be different!" Replied Chris.

"Whatever." Laughed George.

As George thought about how to introduce Chris to Ms. Aniston, Chris was excited to hear about George's school days with his old friend, Andrew Ridgeley. It's widely known that they became friends when Andrew decided to take care of George, the new kid. But what if things had turned out differently? What if Andrew hadn't volunteered? What if they didn't get along and actually disliked each other? What if Andrew wasn't paying attention or didn't want to be friends with the nerdy new kid? The world of music could have been totally changed by these "what if" moments in their school days.

As time went by, the boys started to experiment with music and although, George went along with it for a bit of fun, it was Andrew who was starting to dream big about being the biggest duo of all time and what that would bring, such as loads of money and girls, so many girls. Talk about the perfect chat up line "Hi my name is Andrew and I'm one half of." (Band name still to be decided) Little did either of them know, they wouldn't need chat up lines and the girls would literally be throwing themselves at them. Little did they know that they would have their faces postered on almost every bedroom wall of every girl in the country. How many of those girls went to sleep each night fantasizing what they would do to the boys given half a chance.

The boys became renowned locally in Bushey North London, for their antics and certainly weren't associated with taking life too seriously, and why should they? They were young, it was the eighties and life was meant to be fun. Mrs Thatcher, the Prime Minister at the time, was making sure the boys had all the material they needed to start writing their first lyrics that would make up the album Wham Fantastic.

George's parents, especially his father began exhibiting signs of dissatisfaction with George's lack of ambition in anything other than music. After all, he pondered, being a pop star doesn't guarantee financial security, and the path to becoming one, let alone a mega star, seemed uncertain. Most of them produce a handful of songs, possibly an album, then disappear never to be heard of ever again.

Hardly any of them make it big. What a great idea for an album title? Oh yeah George and Andrew did just that with album number two, followed up by the one of the bestselling songs of all time, which stayed at number one for thirteen weeks and constantly wins the converted accolade of being the population's favourite single of all time, Careless Whisper of course. Not bad for a couple of jokers from Bushey. George was slightly envious of Andrew because his plan was to make a shed load of money as quickly as possible, be part of one of the biggest bands of the 80s, meet and bang as many girls as possible Andrew wanted to have the time of his life and that's exactly what he got, probably way more than he and George could have ever had imagined as they chatted about their dreams for world domination. What George was most envious about Andrew, was that he was able to walk away, they both knew that Wham was about two young lads, living life to the max and that as they got older, they wouldn't be able sell that image.

Andrew likely wished the ride had lasted a bit longer than it did and felt thoroughly disappointed. when the decision to call time on Wham, came when it did, but he always knew it wouldn't last forever. He was of course after a very short solo career, able to go off and live life totally on his terms. George knew all too well, he couldn't have done what Andrew did, music was in his blood and he had so much more to give, but a part of him wished he had been able to walk away.

Time had been passing swiftly as they chatted away, and the miles were being eaten up pretty quickly in the Mercedes, Chris was not exactly breaking the sound barrier but he was just on the edge of driving ban territory if they had been stopped. He was hoping that if they had been stopped, the police would have given him a bollocking, wished him a safe and happy Christmas and told him he could carry on, but a little bit slower. Fortunately, they weren't pulled over, in fact they didn't see a single police car. Before they knew it, they were pulling off the M5 motorway and heading onto the M4 and a little closer to of course, Abby.

George had spent most the journey scrolling through Chris's play list on the in-car entertainment system. Being a Mercedes Benz, the sound system was excellent and George seemed happy to play with the touch screen. As he scrolled through the list, he made his likes and dislikes very clear and on a couple of occasions, he deleted tracks he really really didn't like, much to Chris's annoyance. But George knew, now that when Chris made a fuss or showed annoyance towards him, it was all an act and if he didn't like something, Chris would probably follow suit.

"I can't believe you listen to some of this crap Chris? What were you thinking when you downloaded that shit?" Laughed George. *"It has to go."*

"Hey I liked that!" Replied Chris.

"Bollocks, did you? It's rubbish." Chuckled George.

"It's okay."

"It's rubbish and it has to go! Going, and gone!"

"Did you actually delete it?"

"It had to go Chris; it was an insult on the ears." Laughed George.

"I liked it." Responded Chris.

"You must need your ears cleaning out then." Counteracted George, who was still laughing. *"Let's see who else you've got on here then"*

"Don't delete anymore!"

"I might, if they deserve to be deleted."

"Please don't!!"

"Can't promise! If it's shit, it has to go." Stated George.

Chris's second favourite band is Coldplay, and pretty much everything they have done is on his playlist after George.

"You've got a lot of Coldplay on here, must be catching up with my stuff?" Asked George.

"Yeah, I like Coldplay, they've got something extra about them." Replied Chris

"No, I agree." Replied George. *"I love their stuff and I love their concerts as they bring so much energy to them. Chris is a nutcase; I have no idea where he gets his energy from!"*

"The crowd probably?" Replied Chris.

"Oh, for sure. I love how he throws himself around, and rolls all over the floor, and just laughs when he fucks up or forgets the words. A true professional and a craftsman."

"Have you ever met them?" Enquired Chris.

"Yeah, I've bumped into them occasionally, at an award ceremony or something like that ." Returned George.

"Never thought of collaborating with them then?" Sought Chris

"I'd love to, they have a really big fun vibe about them, I bet we could come up with something awesome. Chris seems to like collaborating with the women though."

"And you don't? Whitney, Mary J Blige, Bloody Aretha, Beyonce, Mutya? Anyone else I haven't mentioned?"

"Yeah, I know I know, but they are bloody hot girls aren't they?"

"You certainly know how to pick them!"

"Hey! They picked me too, you know?"

"I'm sure they did!" Teased Chris *"You never thought to do a duet with Geri? She clearly fancied the pants off you."*

"Nah, I love Geri to bits but we could never sync our schedules to make it into the studio."

"You couldn't you mean?"

"There's nothing wrong with Geri, she's a lovely girl, she's got a heart of gold." Protested George.

"I used to fancy Geri" Bantered Chris. *"Up until she hooked up with Christian Horner, what does she see in him?"* Complained Chris.

"I did notice you have a fair bit of Miss Halliwell on here? I've met Christian, he's alright. Totally obsessed with Formula 1, but that's his business so he has to be. They're good together, Geri's happy and that's the main thing. I think Christian has levelled her, she's in a good place now and that's cool. Anyway, you fancy Jen, you can't have Geri too, and Geri is married. You better not be a marriage wrecker, alright? I won't introduce you to Geri if you're going to try and cop off with her." Tittered George.

George and Geri are great friends and have spent many a fun time together, George used to let Geri stay at his home in St Tropez in the South of France. On one occasion, Geri had a crash in George's Mercedes Benz SL, which no doubt he was annoyed about, but instead of having a go at her, he bought Geri a Mercedes of her own, which she loved to bits. When Geri wanted to get a dog, it was George who accompanied her to Battersea Dogs Home in London, to find one. Imagine being on duty that day and George Michael and Geri Halliwell walk in asking to have a look at the dogs. When Geri was invited to sing happy birthday to

Prince Charles, George was back stage with some words of encouragement. Clearly the pair of them were very close and Geri made no apologies for admitting she fancied the pants off George.

"I wouldn't do that, although I bet it would be a good night, I bet she's great fun between the sheets, if you know what I mean?" Chuckled Chris. *"Hey George, did you ever"* ....

"I know exactly where you're going with this and a gentleman never tells." Stated George.

"So, you did then?" Pushed Chris.

"I'm not telling you!"

"That's definitely a yes, isn't it George? You shagged Geri, didn't you?" Snickered Chris.

"Shut up, I'm not saying nuffing! Geri and me are good friends and that's all you need to know."

"George shagged Geeeerrriiiiii!!! George shagged Geeerrriiiiii!!!!" Chanted Chris.

"Idiot" was George's short and sweet response.

"George Shhhhhhhhh" ....

"Stop it!!!!!" Shouted George.

"Hit a nerve, did I?" Confirmed Chris.

"My lips are sealed." Protested George. *"Are we nearly there yet?"* Asked George trying to change the subject.

"It would probably be easier if you guide me from here, after all I'm not a stalker, so I don't actually know where Mill Cottage is."

George laughed. *"You're just saying that, so you don't look like a stalker, aren't you?"*

"No, I honestly don't know where your house is. I did think about coming over and looking for it but thought you

would probably be inundated with star spotters and didn't want or need another one." Replied Chris.

"Ahhhh thanks." Said George sarcastically.

"I bet you had a fair few in the pub, looking across at you trying to have a quiet drink or pretending to bump into you at the bar."

"Yeah, one or two." Laughed George. *"But I didn't mind as long as it didn't get silly. My local should be a place of refuge away from star spotters."*

"I totally agree, hence why I decided not to come over, you should be allowed some peace and quiet." Replied Chris.

George stopped playing with the playlist and guided Chris straight to the house and onto the driveway.

"Right then here we go! I wonder what we're gonna find..." Said George.

Chapter Fourteen

As they climbed out of the car and started to walk towards the house, George could hear Abby barking, which he thought was amazing as there is no way she could have recognised the sound of Chris's car, after all it sounded nothing like anything George drives. George was listening hard, twisting his head in a way his right ear was directed straight at the house, trying to work out if Abby sounded happy or distressed. As George approached the house, the deep bark resonated in the air, sending shivers down his spine. Yet, amidst the uncertainty, a surge of warmth filled his chest. The familiar tone reassured him, weaving a tapestry of comfort and familiarity. Each step toward the door intensified the anticipation, transforming the seemingly endless walk into a journey of reunion. Confidence welled within him, convinced that behind the door awaited not just a loyal companion, but an exuberant Abby, radiating joy at the recognition of her cherished friend.

"*That must be Abby?*" Asked Chris.

"*Certainly is.*" Replied George.

"*How does she sound to you?*" Enquired Chris.

"*I think she sounds okay, a little excited, but also a little angry.*" Returned George

"*So would be you if you had been locked indoors for 24 hours.*" Suggested Chris.

"Alright!" Retorted George.

As George opened the door, relief and joy washed over him at the sight of Abby bounding towards him. Her cheerfulness, in a vigorous tail wag and body wobble, resonated with infectious happiness. Eager to express affection, Abby tried to leap, her hefty frame anchoring her. George crouched down, met with hilarity as Abby playfully toppled him over. Amidst laughter, George's heart swelled with delight as Abby showered him with affection. Her antics painted the room with shared joy and friendship.

"Hello baby.......... are you pleased .... to see me......... did you....... miss me?" Gasped George.

"Wooooooooof............. wooooooooof...........woooooof!" Replied Abby.

"I missed you so much my lovely."

"woooooooooof......... woooooooof"

Suddenly, like a starting signal, Abby raced out the door, swiftly locating an open area. Without delay, she gleefully squatted down, releasing a burst of energy with unbridled enthusiasm. If you have never seen a dog look so relieved this was the moment. She kept going and going and going, the poor girl must have been holding it all in, hoping George wasn't far from home. George pulled himself off the floor and stood up watching Abby like a proud dad. From Chris's point of view, it seemed weird to watch this mega star looking so proud of a dog having a pee. It just goes to show, no matter how big a mega star you are, it's always a proud moment watching your dog pee.

Once Abby had eventually finished her business, she came running back to the house and straight to George's side.

"I guess I had better have a look around." Stated George with some trepidation.

"Yeah." Replied Chris who was pretty nervous about what they may find.

"Do you want to go alone?"

"Ummmmmm? No, I think I would like you to come with me." Replied George. *"Can we go separately? Though, I want to see if Abby reacts at all."*

"Sure, good plan!" Answered Chris.

Abby had gone into the kitchen, probably hoping George would follow her and feed her, this was the perfect time for the boys to separate. George stepped to one side and Chris to the other. They looked at each other, had a quick look, up and down and then followed Abby into the Kitchen.

"Abby! Do you want some food? Are you starving?....... You poor thing? I'm sorry you've been alone for so long."

Chris stepped back and oddly enough, Abby didn't seem to notice his presence— she didn't even look in his direction. Okay she was definitely starving, so probably was more interested in food than Chris, the complete lack of response felt peculiar.

"Come on then." Invited George as he left Abby to her food. *"I'll give you a tour later, for now I need to check upstairs".*

"Yeah, yeah that's fine." Responded Chris.

George led the way out of the kitchen and down the hall to the stairs.

"How easy am I? You didn't even have to try to get me upstairs." Joked Chris.

"Shut up Chris, this isn't the time, can't you tell I'm crapping myself?"

"Sorry."

"Come on, this is it." Said George, ignoring Chris's apology.

As they stood at the door to George's bedroom, they were both having very different thoughts. Chris was thinking "Oh my god I'm going into George Michael's bedroom and I'm not even gay." Whereas, George was thinking "Fuck, I feel sick, what the fuck! What am I going to find behind that door?" And from nowhere, Abby came tearing up the stairs, barged past them, still ignoring Chris, almost knocked the door down, and disappeared into the bedroom. Chris put his hand on George's shoulder, following him through the door into the bedroom.

As they got in, they saw Abby sat on floor with her tail wagging reverberating through her body, certainly not looking sad or distressed in any way. George and Chris looked from a wobbling Abby up to the bed, almost in complete unison, neither of them wanting to see anything out of place.

George sighed the biggest sigh of relief in his entire life, the bed was fully made as if it had just been prepared in a five-star hotel. George was used to this level of preparation because Noom took great pride in making George's bed. Chris looked across to him as if to ask, is everything okay.

"What do you think?" Enquired Chris.

"I think everything is okay." Responded George.

In that moment, Abby joyfully circuited the room, leaping onto the meticulously made bed. Soon, she sprawled on her back, legs in the air, tongue out, tail wagging – a delightful display of pure canine bliss.

Suddenly, George appeared, diving onto the bed to engage in a playful wrestling match. Laughter echoed as they rolled, barked, and growled, their connection evident in the shared excitement. Abby, at times, would playfully pounce and then gracefully yield, letting George envelop her in a bear hug. Mock growls harmonized in their game, echoing a unique understanding between them. Like the best of friends, they revelled in a dance of shared moments, each move anticipated, each connection a testament to their unspoken bond.

"I'll leave you guys to it." Announced Chris as he turned to leave the room.

There was no reply from George nor from Abby, so Chris left them to their game, and went back downstairs. He didn't feel that he should wander around George's house until he was invited to, so he went straight to the kitchen, sitting quietly, hoping nobody would turn up at the house out of the blue and start asking awkward questions as to who he was and why he was sat in George's kitchen. It didn't take long before Chris heard the sound of Abby tumbling down the stairs followed by the obvious sound of George chasing her down the stairs giggling his head off. The two of them came flying into the kitchen, Abby, being a dog was not designed for slippery floors and was doing the dog equivalent of a wheel spin as she tried to steer herself around the kitchen and George was doing a sort of crouched style run in hysterics which reminded Chris of Woody.

"I'm coming to get you!" Laughed George hysterically as he chased Abby.

"I'm coming to get you"

"Here I come"

"I'm coming"

As he cornered Abby by the back door, she crouched down as if she was getting ready to pounce. Her tail wagging, body swaying, tongue hanging out, dribbling all over the floor,

"Woooooooooooof!"

"Here I come!" Chuckled George.

"Woooooooof.." Replied Abby and then sprinted underneath George and off into the house.

George twisted around and watched her vanish from the kitchen, then, catching his breath, he stood up, pausing halfway to rest his hands on his knees.

"Having fun?" Asked Chris.

"Ha ha Yeah, it's great to see her." Answered George.

"Does everything seem okay in the house?" Questioned Chris

"So far." Replied George. *"Abby doesn't seem distressed at all?"*

"She certainly does seem happy to see her dad." Stated Chris

"Yeah." Replied a very out of breath George.

"Does she normally ignore strangers?" Queried Chris

"What do you mean?" Demanded George.

"She hasn't shown any interest in me whatsoever, it's as if I'm not here." Came Chris.

"Are you feeling left out?" Teased George in his usual sarcastic manner.

"No." Replied Chris defensively, but actually he was feeling left out.

"Come on then, let's see if we can introduce you to her." Suggested George

"Abby! Abby!"

It didn't take long before Abby waddled through the door of the kitchen and straight over to her beloved dad.

"Who's this then?" Asked George as he directed Abby over to Chris.

Abby sniffed the air around Chris and momentarily looked a little confused, in a dog sort of way. Abby could sense that someone or something was there, but not being able to see anything, lost interest almost instantly.

"Abby!" Called Chris.

Abby stopped in her tracks, looked towards Chris but because she couldn't see anything, she went back to nuzzling George.

"Who's this Abby?" Said George, trying again to get a response from her while patting Chris on the leg to see if this would make any difference.

"Abby." Added Chris.

She stopped again, looked in Chris's general direction, but that was it. She showed no signs that she could see Chris.

"She can't see you, can she?" Stated George.

"Doesn't look like it." Retorted Chris.

"Hmmmmm." Replied George.

"But at least she can see you." Said Chris, trying to put a positive spin on things. *"It doesn't matter if she can't see me really does it?"*

"No, but it would be nice." Replied George.

Chris didn't reply but silently agreed with George.

All of a sudden there was a vibration in Chris's pocket, followed by Father Figure muffled, but obviously Father Figure, Chris rushed to his pocket to see who was at the other end of the phone and George and Abby looked across, George in amusement and Abby in confusement, she heard the phone and probably recognised her master's voice, she must have heard that song plenty of times.

"HAHAHAHHAAH! You're so sad." Laughed George.

Chris looked across at him and frowned, somewhat embarrassed as he swiped the answer button on the screen, then hit the speaker icon. Chris hated mobiles he could never hear the other person unless he had the speaker on.

"Hi." Said Chris answering his phone.

It was his mum.

"Hi Chris, I'm glad I caught you, how are you, happy Boxing Day!"

"Yeah fine, how are you?" He replied.

"How's your Boxing Day, what are you up to today, any plans?" Asked his mum.

"Just taking it easy I think, nothing really planned." Answered Chris

"HAPPY CHRISTMAS MRS H!" Shouted George from across the room.

Chris put his hand over the mouth piece and mouthed silently in a shouty fashion

"WHAT ARE YOU DOING?"

"Who was that?" Enquired Chris's mum.

"Just a friend." Responded Chris.

"IT'S GEORGE MRS H!" Shouted George.

Chris covered the phone again.

"*WHAT ARE YOU DOING?*" He mouthed.

"*Hello?*" Replied Chris's mum somewhat confused.

"*It's my friend George.*" Ensured Chris.

"*Oh right, are you spending the day together?*" Asked his mum.

George couldn't contain himself any longer, he rushed over the room and grabbed the phone out of Chris's hand without stopping, then heading off in the opposite direction before Chris had a chance to move.

"*Hello my lovely, it's George, Chris obviously wasn't going to introduce me. I've not been feeling very well, and Chris has been keeping me company.*" Said George with a big grin on his face.

Chris hadn't moved, he just sat there bemused at what was going on.

"*AGAIN..... WHAT ARE YOU DOING?*" He mouthed at George.

George just shrugged his shoulders and winked at Chris.

"*Oh right that's nice of him.*" Spoke Chris's mum, still oblivious to who she was talking to.

"*Have you had a good Christmas so far Mrs H?*" Queried George.

"*Ummm thank you lovely.*" Came a confused reply.

"*Chris has been great, I'm feeling much better, thanks to him.*" Continued George.

"*Oh, that's nice, he's a good boy*". Replied Chris's mum, still trying to work out who she was talking to.

"We've spent all Christmas together, two guys hanging out, having fun." Continued George.

Chris was on the other side of the table waving his arms around and mouthing at George.

"WHAT ARE YOU DOING!!"

George was trying not to laugh and carried on.

"He was quite shy to start with, but he soon got in to it."

"Oh, that's nice." Acknowledged Chris's mum, not having a clue at the inuendo that George was revelling in.

"I can't believe it's taken us so long to meet!" Said George.

With that Chris launched himself at George and grabbed his phone back.

"So how was yesterday?" He asked him mum.

"Oh, it was fine, I went over to Claire's (Chris's sister) for the day, did the present thing, which took hours as usual, then had a lovely lunch, Charles (Claire's husband) put on a super spread, far too much food, but I'm sure they'll make use of it. What did you do?"

"Ummmm well George and I just hung out. We had some stuff to sort out." Chris replied.

"I don't think I know George, do I?" Interrogated his mum.

George was now in hysterics, waiting to see how Chris would climb out of the massive hole George had dug for him.

"Well, you do, and you don't." Answered Chris.

"His voice sounded familiar." Told his mum.

"It was George, George Michael." Replied Chris

"*Oh right?* "Came the answer, the penny still not having dropped.

"*George Michael mum.*" Repeated Chris.

"*Oh, that's nice.*" Replied his mum, clearly still not aware what Chris had just said. Old age was catching up on her and it took a while for things to sink in these days. Either that or she didn't listen to a word Chris said or maybe her hearing wasn't great and hadn't really heard what Chris had said.

"*George Michael mum, you do know who I mean by George Michael, don't you?*" Asked Chris.

"*Yes of course I do.*" She replied.

"*Who is it then*"? Asked Chris

"*Your friend George and Michael.*" Came the answer.

"*No mum. George Michael, Just George Michael, not George and Michael.*" Stressed Chris.

"*What? The George Michael you're always listening to?*" She emphasised.

"*Yes, that George Michael.*". Replied Chris

"*HELLOOOOOOOO MRS H!*" Yelled George.

"*How do you know him? I didn't know you knew each other? How come you're spending Christmas together? Isn't he gay?*

George was in total hysterics now, seeing Chris squirm as the questions came flooding through the phone.

"*Long story!*" Replied Chris

"*IT'S ALRIGHT MY LOVELY, HE ISN'T GAY, HE'S ASSURED ME OF THAT!!!*" Shouted George from across the room.

"*Oh, that's okay then.*" Replied Chris's mum, now completely bewildered at what was playing out in front her.

"What are you doing for the rest of the day?" Asked Chris, trying to change the subject.

"I'm going over to Claire's for lunch and supper and I think she's got something planned for the afternoon as well." She replied in complete confusion, desperately trying to take in what was going on.

"Cool, have fun." Said Chris

"WE'RE GOING TO SET HIM UP WITH JENNIFER ANISTON MRS H!!" Shouted George.

"That's nice." Replied Chris's mum, who probably didn't have a clue who Jennifer Aniston is. Chris's mom acts knowledgeable, but it's mostly just a front. Her knowledge extends only as far as recent news or the Daily Telegraph. Jennifer Aniston's name might ring a bell, but beyond that, the tapestry of her roles, even in "Friends," eludes her grasp

"I'll let you go then, have fun." Said Chris

"SEE YOU MRS H, HAVE A GREAT DAY!!" Exclaimed George.

"Thanks, you too. Bye George.". Replied Chris's mum before hanging up.

"Well, that wasn't awkward at all, no?" Said Chris.

"That was so funny, from the second your phone went off with Father Figure and then your mum not having a clue what was going on." Replied George still struggling to contain his belly laughs.

"And you enjoyed every second of it." Winged Chris.

"Sorry, I couldn't resist and once I started, I couldn't stop." Added George, still holding in the giggles.

"You're incorrigible George! You are actually a child, aren't you?" Probed Chris.

"You asked for it, you should have told your mum what you were doing. Didn't you want her to know you were with me? Is it because I'm gaaaaaayyyyyyyyyy?" Teased George in his northern accent again.

"No, it has nothing to do with that, I doubt she even knows you're gay, she didn't realise it was you I was with, until I made it crystal clear."

"I know that was so funny. She doesn't know who Jen is either, does she?" Asked George.

"Not a clue." Replied Chris.

The phone call from Chris's mum was all George needed to go and check any messages on his answer machine. He wandered away, leaving Chris to ponder what George had initiated. Wondering if his mom would recall the talk or dismiss it as a peculiar dream, Chris couldn't shake the intrigue of what might unfold.

The answer machine was flashing and George hit the play button.

"You have seven new messages, message one:"

"Hi yorg it's your dad, I haven't heard from you today, I'm worried, call me to let me know you are okay. Speak to you soon. I hope you are okay. Call me as soon as you can yorgous."

"Press one to repeat. Press Two to save. Press Three to delete. Press four to return the call."

George pressed four and waited for the phone to start ringing. George's dad knew the true state of George's health and had every reason to be afraid for his son and the fact that he hadn't heard from him.

"Yorgous. Is that you? Are you okay? I didn't hear from you yesterday, I was worried!"

"*Hi dad, yeah it's me, everything is fine, I'm fine, no need to worry.*" Replied George.

"*Yorgous it is so good to hear your voice. I was worried sick because you didn't phone me; you always phone me.*"

- where were you yesterday-

"*Sorry dad, something came up which kind of took me away for the day but we're getting it sorted now.*"

"*Was it to do with that Fazi guy Yorgous? You know I don't like that man; did he cause you trouble again Yorg? You know I don't want him upsetting you Yorg, you need to look after yourself.*"

"*Fadi dad, and no it wasn't him, I haven't seen him since Christmas Eve, we had a row and he stormed off, I haven't heard from him since.*"

"*Good I don't like him Yorg, I hope you never see him again Yorg.*"

"*Okay dad.*"

"*What did you do then that kept you so busy that you couldn't phone your father? You know I worry about you Yorg.*"

"*I know dad, I'm sorry, I'll fill you in with everything in the new year, but don't worry about me dad, I'm feeling great.*"

"You say you are feeling great Yorg but you know I worry about you, my boy. I am your father and it's my job to worry about you."

"*I know dad, but I promise I'm feeling better than I have for a long time.*"

"*You do sound okay, I must admit, you have something in your voice. Have you been drinking Yorg, are you drunk?*"

"*No dad I'm not drunk, I'm just feeling good.*"

"Okay Yorg, but take it easy, don't wear yourself out, you need to take care of yourself Yorg."

"I will dad, I promise."

"Okay well phone me tomorrow, don't make me worry Yorg".

"I will dad, enjoy today, speak to you tomorrow. Bye"

"To listen to the message again press one, to save this message press two, to delete the message press three, to listen to your next message press four."

George pressed four to get his next message.

"Hi Yog it's Mel, just wishing you a merry Christmas, hope you're feeling okay, call me, love you."

"To listen to the message again press one, to save this message press two, to delete the message press three, to listen to your next message press four."

George made a mental note to phone his sister, Melanie back, then pushed four.

"Yog, it's Andrew, (Andrew Ridgeley) how you doing buddy, hope you're having a good Christmas matey, call me when you get a minute. Later buddy. It's Andrew."

"To listen to the message again press one, to save this message press two, to delete the message press three, to listen to your next message press four."

"Happpppppppyyyyyyyy Christmas buddy, hope you're good, call me."

George made another mental note, this time to call David, one of his best friends ever.

"To listen to the message again press one, to save this message press two, to delete the message press three, to listen to your next message press four."

"Hello lover boy, it's Geri, just phoning to wish you a happy Christmas, hope you're having a good one, speak to you in the new year, love you, call me!"

"To listen to the message again press one, to save this message press two, to delete the message press three, to listen to your next message press four."

"It's Fadi, you really pissed me off yesterday. Obviously, you are busy, I guess I will have to wait for you to call me when you've chilled out a bit? I'm fine by the way, as if you care!"

"To listen to the message again press one, to save this message press two, to delete the message press three, to listen to your next message press four."

"Hi George, it's Roman, just phoning to say "Hi" and happy Christmas. Mum and Dad send their love, speak to soon buddy, take care, speak soon."

Roman is George's Godson and one of Martin and Shirlie Kemps boys. Martin Kemp from Spandau Ballet, and Shirlie from Wham, who George got together. He actually went on their first date until they told him to make himself invisible.

"You have no more messages."

George hung up and went back into the kitchen where Chris was sitting alone, Abby had disappeared from the lounge and was asleep in front of the fire, which still had a little bit of warmth coming off it.

"Everything okay?" Asked Chris

"Yes, thank you, had a chat with my dad." Answered George.

"Jack?"

"Yeah."

"How is he?"

"He's fine, he worries about me."

"Understandable."

"Yeah, I know." Sighed George as if everything had come flooding back to him. Chris had been able to take his mind off things for a while, but he had suddenly had a reality check and it hurt.

Chapter Fifteen

Chris's mum pulled up outside Claire's house, grabbed her handbag and got out of the car. She wondered up the drive and knocked on the front door. She couldn't help thinking about the strange conversation she just had with Chris and possibly George Michael. Was Chris really spending Christmas with George? She thought. It really shouldn't be that surprising, after all Chris had been following George for as long as she could remember. The only thing she ever heard coming out of his bedroom when he lived at home, was George. Even though she didn't class herself as a George Michael fan as such, but whenever she heard a George Michael song, she knew who it was, even if it was a song that George had released after Chris had moved out. She always thought George had a very individual and beautiful, unique voice, not like the other rubbish you hear on the radio these days, there was something very special about George's voice and she totally understood why Chris was so obsessed with him.

Charles, Claire's husband opened the door, nothing changes, it's always the man of the house who has to open the door.

"Hello Margaret, come in, come in, let me take your coat." Charles lent forward and gave Chris's mum a kiss on the cheek. *"They're all in the kitchen."*

"Morning Charles, thank you." Replied Chris's mum handing Charles her coat.

They made their way through the hall and dining room into the kitchen where they found Claire, her two daughters, Sophie and Layla, Chris's Aunt, Stella and her daughter Sarah, with her husband Andrew.

"Hello Margaret." Yelled Stella

"Hello." She replied

"Hi." Said Claire from the other side of the huge island in the middle of the kitchen.

"Hello." She replied again.

"Did you get home okay last night?" Asked Stella.

"Yes, thank you, it was fine, the roads were very quiet."

"Can I get you a drink Margaret?" Requested Charles

"Oh yes please Charles." She replied

"What would you like?"

"What have you got?"

"Tea, Coffee, wine, champagne, G and T, anything you want?"

"Could I have a wine please?"

"Of course, you can, red or white?"

"Ummmm red please, that would be lovely."

"It's on its way." Replied Charles

"Everything okay mum?" Asked Claire

Charles handed Margaret a large glass of red wine.

"There you go."

"Oh, that looks lovely Charles, thank you."

"You look like you needed that!" Said Stella

"You okay mum?" Claire again enquired.

"Yes yes, I just had a very strange phone call with your brother this morning."

"What's he been up to? Happy being 'Billy no mates', spending Christmas on his own?"

"No, not this year. This time, it appears he's spending Christmas with his friend George"?

"Oh right." Responded Claire.

"That's what I thought until I found out which George."

"Which George is he spending it with then?" Queried Claire, sarcastically.

"George Michael." Replied Margaret.

"Yeah right," laughed Claire. *"As if?"*

"No, I spoke to him myself." Replied Margaret.

"You spoke to George Michael?" Asked Chris's cousin, Sarah, Stella's daughter.

"I think so!" Replied Margaret

"Sounds like they're playing a Christmas joke on you mum." Suggested Claire.

"Yeah, I don't think Chris actually knows George Michael." Chipped in Charles

"I don't think he knows him either." Chipped in Layla, then she turned to her elder sister, Sophie and asked, *"Who's George Michael?"*

"Really?" Replied Sophie in disbelief. *"Go and google him or something."*

"Give him a call." Suggested Charles to Claire.

"I suppose I could, I can pretend I haven't spoken to mum, how's that?" Returned Claire.

Chris used to adore Christmas in his youth, a time when family gatherings felt like scenes from heart-warming films. The winters were colder, more festive, with abundant snow. However, as Chris entered his 20s, the magic dwindled, and he grew disenchanted. Nowadays, mild and damp winters reflect the looming reality of global warming, though some remain skeptical.

Despite his evolving feelings towards the season, Chris's dad had a unique talent for fulfilling his every Christmas wish. Oblivious at the time, Chris later realized his dad's seemingly indifferent demeanour masked a deep attentiveness. Christmas in Chris's family was a well-orchestrated tradition, featuring Aunt Stella's leisurely journey in her old Citroen 2CV. Despite its lack of heating and stereo, Stella's visits were cherished, especially for the haircuts she gave Chris and the trendsetting styles he requested, inspired by George Michael.

Sadly, Stella and Sarah ceased their quirky Christmas visits, leaving a void in the festive traditions. Despite the mere age gap between Stella and Chris's mom, their personalities were starkly different, with Stella inheriting an extra dose of humor. Recently, the tradition was revived, with Stella, Sarah, and Sarah's husband returning to celebrate Christmas at Claire's, complete with a car equipped with heating and a stereo.

For Chris, Christmas lost its enchantment, transforming into a commercial frenzy and a gluttonous feast. The once-magical time now concluded with a mad rush to the Boxing Day sales. The iconic Christmas songs of Wham, Mariah Carey, Slade, and Band Aid were replaced by uninspiring tunes, with talents like David Bowie and Bing Crosby no longer gracing the charts. Instead, the number one spot was seized by Lad baby, symbolizing a shift in Christmas culture that felt like another nail in the festive coffin.

The real reason that Chris no longer looked forward to Christmas, was because of what happened in 1991. It had been the new style of Christmas, Stella and Sarah hadn't come up from Bristol, it was just the four of them. Chris's mum and dad weren't in a good place and the whole Christmas was a bit of a quiet one. On Boxing Day, Chris had decided to go over to his mate, Dave's house in the afternoon, the TV was on and there were plenty of snacks to munch on. Dave's mum made some sandwiches out of leftover turkey from their Christmas lunch and the crisps kept flowing.

Chris got back home just after midnight, which to be fair, wasn't particularly late, for a 24-year-old. He could hear the television on in the living room, so he wandered in to see who was there. As he walked through the door, he found it was just his dad sat there on his own.

"You *alright?*" Asked Chris.

"*What time do you call this?*" Returned his dad.

Chris checked his watch. "*It's just gone 12, why?*"

"*Your mum has been worried sick about you, don't you know what day it is?*"

"*It's only 12 o'clock, I'm a big boy now.*" Replied Chris, a little surprised by his dad's attitude. Not thinking too much about the situation, Chris made his way across the room and sat down in the chair next to where his dad was sitting.

"*What you watching?*" Chris asked thinking everything was okay.

"*Well, where have you been?*" Asked his dad, his voice now was not friendly.

"*I've been around Dave's, watching a film, no biggy.*" Replied Chris

"Well, it's a biggy to your mum!!"

"She didn't say anything when I left, I didn't think she was expecting me home at any particular time."

"Well, she did!"

"I didn't know that. Is this any good?" Asked Chris, referring to the film his dad was watching, and clearly having no idea why his dad was making such a big deal of the time.

As Chris settled into the chair, an uncomfortable sensation prompted him to check his back pocket. Retrieving his little red Swiss army knife, a multifaceted penknife with corkscrews, screwdrivers, hoof pics, bottle openers, scissors, and various-sized blades, he marveled at the multitude of gadgets crammed into its compact design. Reflecting on the challenge of navigating through the array of tools, Chris considered the need for a separate penknife with more attachments or exceptionally strong nails to avoid snapping while opening the desired gadget. Perhaps it had been rolling around in the car, and Chris decided to bring it indoors to avoid losing it. Placing the penknife on the chair's arm, Chris nonchalantly returned to watching TV, considering his dad's rant concluded.

"I suppose you're going to stab me with that, are you?" Raged his dad.

Before Chris had a chance to respond and tell his dad that he had no intention of stabbing him, after all, in Chris's mind there was no reason to, Chris's dad lifted himself from the sofa, leaned across and punched Chris in the face as hard as he could. Chris couldn't believe what had just happened as he stretched his jaw making sure nothing was broken.

"What was that for dad?" He asked in a awe.

"You were going to stab me with your silly little knife!!" Replied his dad.

"No, I wasn't!" Replied Chris as he stood up to leave the room, he has had enough of his dad's strange mood so thought he would remove himself from the situation before it got any worse, he certainly didn't think his dad's reaction was called for. Chris leant down to pick up his penknife with an intention of heading to bed, at which point his dad jumped up from the sofa and started shouting at him.

"Come on then Mr hard man, you don't scare me!!"

"What's up with you?" Asked Chris.

"Come on! Come on! I'll wipe the floor with you!!" Shouted his dad.

This was a brave move from Chris's dad because Chris had been practicing Lau Gar Kung Fu, a form of kick boxing, and was getting quite good at it, certainly good enough to hurt his dad. Chris also thought the last person on earth he would ever have to defend himself against was his own dad.

"Come on then!!!" Shouted Chris's dad before pushing Chris in the chest.

Chris didn't answer, he just pushed his dad back so he fell onto the sofa behind him, then leaning in he let fly a few punches, a couple in his dad's ribs and a couple in the kidneys before standing back up.

"I'm going to bed, don't make this any worse." Chris calmly said to his dad. Even in the heat of the moment Chris had too much respect for his dad to punch him anywhere visible. Leaving his dad lying on the sofa, Chris made his way to the door and as he crossed the hall to the stairs, he heard his dad's final words.

"I want you out first thing in the morning, you are no longer welcomed under my roof!!!"

Chris didn't reply, it was pointless, everything had gone way too far over something so minor and all he could think about was where he was going to go. Chris headed upstairs to his room, his safe zone, and he knew who would be able to help him think about what had just happened. As he entered his room he hit the power button on his tower system, made sure his headphones were plugged in, ramped up the volume and hit PLAY. Boom there he was in his safe place with the one person he trusted most in the world, his guardian angel, George Michael.

In the morning, Chris got up early and headed out to see if he could find somewhere to stay short term while he found something more permanent. A couple of his friends shared a house and said they were okay with him crashing on their sofa for a few days. With that sorted, he headed home to pack his things and move out. His car was filling up quickly, everything those days had to be big, he had a Sony tower system with turntable, twin audio cassette decks, graphic equalizer, FM radio and best of all a 5 CD multi disc player. He had also upgraded his speakers to a pair of Jamo 380s, which stood about four feet tall and left nothing to the imagination. He also had a huge TV, there was no such thing as flat screens then, or if there was, Chris certainly wouldn't have been able to afford one, early Plasma TVs cost thousands of pounds. The massive TV was the last thing to go in the car and as Chris made his way down the stairs with the monstrosity in his arms and at the bottom was his dad stood, blocking his way, snarling at Chris. His mum was stood in the kitchen doorway, watching him move his stuff out.

Chris hadn't spoken to his mum since the day before and she had made no attempt to ask him his side of the events from the previous night. Having had time to think about what had happened, Chris did think it was strange how defensive his dad had been, considering he hardly spoke to Chris's mum these days and the next logical step for them was a divorce.

"Get him out of my way or I will drop this TV on his head!" Chris told his mum.

"Come on Peter, come in the living room, let him go past." Chris's mum took his dad's arm and pulled him towards the living room's door. He didn't put up any resistance and Chris was able to come down the last few stairs and out to the car. That was one of the last times Chris ever spoke to his dad.

On New Year's Eve, Chris went out with his new house mates, they headed over to a hotel close to the house, apparently there was a New Year's Eve event going on and it was crawling distance from the house, so nobody needed to drive. Chris was feeling pretty chilled out and of course had dressed accordingly, once again he was George Michael, let's face it, of course George Michael would be spending New Year's Eve in a hotel in High Wycombe, why would someone of George's stature want to be anywhere else? Of course, that didn't occur to Chris, nor did it seem to matter, he was happy in his weird mixed up imaginary world.

As the evening went on, Chris spotted a girl at the bar, and made his way over to see if there was any chance of getting lucky. Chris didn't have chat up lines, he relied completely on the fact that he was George Michael, and therefore, didn't need chat up lines. He stood at the bar and when the girl looked over, he gave her a cheeky little grin.

She grinned back then looked away, Chris looked over to his mates who were all laughing their heads off, but when Chris turned back, she was stood right next to him.

"Hello, you gonna buy me a drink, or just stand there staring all night?" Asked this beauty.

In close proximity, she was even more gorgeous than he had realized — with amazing skin, large eyes, a beautiful smile, and an incredible body.

"Errrrrrrr yeah, what are you drinking?" Replied Chris.

"I'll have a white wine please, dry." She replied.

"Cool." Chris grabbed the bar girl's attention and ordered the drink.

"Aren't you going to ask my name?" The girl enquired while she waited for her drink to be poured.

"Of course, yes, how rude of me to buy you a drink before asking you your name." Grinned Chris.

"That's a cheeky smile, you're going to be trouble, aren't you?" She replied without actually giving her name.

"Me? Trouble? Never!" Replied Chris

"Well..." She asked

"Well, what?" Asked Chris.

"Name." She replied.

"Oh right, yes, Chris." Came the reply.

"Not yours." She retorted.

"Oh yeah, sorry, so what's your name?" Asked Chris, handing her the glass of wine.

"At last, thank you for the drink, Rubina by the way." She giggled in a flirtatious way.

"Like the drink?" Replied Chris in cocky sort of way.

"No not like the bloody drink, cheeky." She giggled.

"Only joking." Laughed Chris.

They spent the rest of the night giggling and flirting, and Chris's mates looked on gobsmacked that he had pulled it off. At the end of the evening, they exchanged numbers and arranged to meet up for a second date. They did actually keep seeing each other for a while, but Chris couldn't get Denise out of his head, and felt Rubina deserved more and that he just wasn't in the right place to give her that.

A couple of weeks after moving out, Chris secured a room in a friend's house in a nearby village. After a few months there, he had an unexpected visit from his dad. Informed by Chris's mom about his financial struggles, his dad arrived with a cheque book, eager to assist. However, Chris wasn't ready to welcome him or accept the offered help. Filled with fury, Chris launched into a vehement rant, demanding his dad's immediate departure before he was forcibly thrown out.

After Chris's dad left, his mom called, revealing how his dad returned home pale and uncontrollably shaking. Chris had made his point. Once again, Chris found solace in music, but this wasn't the time for soothing tunes like "A Different Corner" or "One More Try." It was a moment for "Hand to Mouth," "Hard Day," and "Monkey." Chris cranked up the Jamo Speakers, letting the entire street feel the intensity of his release.

Chris stayed in his new home for about four years until an incident forced him to move out and move back home. His dad was no longer living in the family home, he had left Chris's mum and moved to Northampton, where he had set up a business.

A couple of weeks after moving back home, Chris had arranged with Ade, who owned the house he had just left, and Pete, a chap that also lived at the house for about a year, to meet up for a drink. For the time that Pete was at the house there was an amazing atmosphere, unfortunately, when Pete moved out, the new guy that replaced him was a bit of a pratt, and he was the reason for the incident leading to Chris's decision to move out. The three of them had a fun evening, reminiscing about the fun times they have had, and slagging off the new guy, just a regular night with three good friends. Chris used the evening to confess to a small, yet, what he thought was a quite amusing discretion with the new guy's girlfriend. She stayed at the house quite regularly and when the idiot wasn't home, Chris would have some fun with his girlfriend. He may have thought he got away with ripping Chris off with a few pounds for his share of the phone bill, but Chris made sure he got paid in another way. Funnily enough, Ade wasn't overly surprised, and Pete thought it was highly amusing, but they both wanted to know if she was any good between the sheets. At the end of the night, they went their separate ways as if nothing out of the ordinary had happened.

When Chris got home and pulled into the driveway, he was greeted by a police car in the driveway, this is never a good sign. He pulled alongside it, switched off his car, got out and headed for the front door. Before he was able to get his key in the door, the door swung open and he was met by a hot looking policewoman.

"Christopher?" She asked calmly.

"Urrrrr yeah, what's going on?" Replied Chris.

"You had better come inside; I have some news for you." She answered.

Before Chris was halfway up the hall, the police officer turned around to look at Chris.

"I'm afraid to tell you that your father has taken his own life, he was found earlier today, it's taken a while to trace you and your mother."

"What?" Asked Chris in a surprise.

"Come in the living room, sit down." She said quietly

Chris followed her into the living room, where his mum was sat on the sofa silently, Chris looked across at her and she just looked back, clearly upset, Chris had no idea how long the police had been waiting with her for him to come home.

"How?" Chris asked.

"Carbon monoxide poisoning, do you know what that is?" She replied.

"Yes." Answered Chris. Of course, he knew what it was he had lost two of his best friends because of it.

"I'll leave you with your mum, we were just keeping your mum company until you got home. You haven't been drinking and driving, have you, Chris?" She asked then added, *"We won't bother with that tonight."*

"Really?" Chris asked. *"And no, I haven't been drinking and driving."*

"I could smell lager on your breath." She said quietly.

"I had one lager shandy, then went onto soft drinks." Replied Chris.

"Okay, good, sorry I mentioned it." She said apologetically.

"No problem." Replied Chris.

"I'll see myself out, look after your mum." Said the officer as she backed out of the room.

"Okay, yes I will, thank you, thank you for waiting with mum." Stated Chris.

"That's okay, so sorry." Said the officer.

With that, she was gone leaving Chris and his mum just to look at each other in disbelief, and all Chris could think about was that he would never ever be able to patch things up with his dad. They had fallen out over something so ridiculous, so pointless, all the arguments they had ever had, this was one of the smallest, even including the punch Chris's dad had landed on Chris's jaw.

For a long time, Chris was angry with his dad for what he had done, especially when Chris found out the root of the problem was money. He remembered what his dad had said to him when he found out about Chris's friend Rik, taking his life because of money, and how he would have helped Rik if he had known. Maybe that's why he came round to see Chris with his cheque book, even though they hadn't spoken in ages, he didn't want to risk Chris copying his friend. But things were so bad between them he didn't feel he could talk to his own son, maybe he didn't think Chris would be able to or offer to help? As the years have passed by, the anger had been replaced with love again and Chris found a way to forgive, and understand, his dad for what he had done. He grew to miss his dad and wished that such a small argument had never ruined their relationship. But during the recovery years there was one constant, one person that Chris was able to turn to, his guardian angel who was always there, ready to listen, ready with words of advice, and that one person was George Michael. Although George didn't actually know, just how important he was, how critical he was, it was George Michael who helped Chris through the loss of his dad, just as he had when Chris lost Rik and Woody, George was always there at Chris's beck and call. Whenever Chris felt down, and took time out to think about his dad and how he should have heeled the wounds, he had no doubt, if he had approached his dad and made the effort to repair their relationship, his dad would have taken that chance, because Chris believed his dad wouldn't have wanted to be so detached from his one and only son.

That was the catalyst for why Chris no longer treated Christmas with any great affection, it had definitely lost it's magic. Christmas to Chris, was a reminder of the night he fell out with his dad so badly and so pointlessly, that they would never really ever speak again. On top of that, even though Chris was a multi-millionaire, the whole commercialism of Christmas had gone too far, the magic had been lost and Chris pitied those generations that would never experience a proper Christmas.

"I'll give him a call, shall I?" Claire asked the room.

"Go on!" Jumped in Stella.

"Why not!" Asked Charles.

"I want to know if he's actually with George Michael." Rallied Sophie

"Me too." Added Sarah.

Claire picked up the phone and scrolled through her contacts for Chris's number.

"Home or Mobile?" She asked.

"I think he was on his mobile." Said Margaret.

Claire picked his mobile number, pushed the green icon and waited for the phone to start ringing.

"Hi" came the answer from Chris.

"Hi ya, just phoning to wish you a merry Christmas and see what you're up to."

"Oh right, thanks." Replied Chris, unenthusiastically.

"How have you been?" Asked Claire.

"Fine thanks, how was your day?" Replied Chris.

"Lovely, thank you, it was a shame you didn't feel inclined to join us."

"Ahhh well, maybe next year?"

"So, what have you been doing?" Asked Claire.

"Keeping busy," mentioned Chris.

"Have you spent Christmas with anyone we should know about?"

At Chris's end of the phone the penny dropped, mum had blabbed and now Claire was on the phone digging.

"Who's on the phone?" Shouted George, across the kitchen where Chris had taken the call.

Chris put his finger to his lips to shhhh George, but it was too late, George was up to his tricks and wasn't going to be silenced.

"Hey Chris, wish them a happy Christmas from me, whoever it is!!"

"Who was that?" Came Claire's voice down the phone.

"Nobody." Replied Chris.

"Nobody?" Questioned George.

"Doesn't sound like nobody." Retorted Claire.

As usual Chris's phone was on speaker, so George could hear every word his sister was saying.

"I'm definitely NOT! a nobody," laughed George.

"Who is it?" Pushed Claire.

"A friend of mine." Replied Chris

"Just a friend?" Claire asked.

"Yep." Replied Chris, frowning at George.

"I'm more than a friend caller, I'm the love of his life." Giggled George. "Who *is it?*" He whispered to Chris.

"My sister." Whispered Chris back.

"Really?" Whispered George.

"Yes." Whispered Chris.

"Hello Chris's sister!!" Shouted George.

"Who's that!?" Laughed Claire.

"I'm George, apparently I'm just a friend of your brother."

"Oh right, I didn't know Chris knew anyone called George."

"We have only met recently." Replied George as he grabbed the phone out of Chris's hands again.

"That would explain it then." Answered a somewhat confused Claire.

"Have you had a good Christmas?" Asked George.

"Lovely thank you." Claire was obviously a little flustered, as now that she was talking to George, she started to recognise his voice.

"Your brother is so tightly wound, isn't he?" Asked George trying his hardest to keep a straight face.

"Nice." Said Chris.

"What? I'm bonding with your family!" Protested George.

"Really?" Asked Chris.

"So what do you do for living then, George?" Investigated Claire.

George was now in absolute hysterics again, holding his stomach which was aching from belly laughs.

"What's this? A Spanish inquisition? I don't think Chris is planning on marrying me, are you Chris?"

Chris shook his head.

"He says no." Continued George. *"Anyway, he fancies a girrrrrrl"* carried on George, like a little boy in the school playground.

"Oh right, who does he fancy then?" Interrogated Claire

"Jennifer Aniston. Can you believe it? Jennifer bloody Aniston."

"Of course, he does." Replied Claire.

"I'm going to come with a plan to get them together." Returned George.

"Oh, are you? I take it, you know Jennifer?"

"Not personally, but I have contacts, don't you know?" Responded George.

"So, what is it you do George, you didn't say?" Claire tried again.

"I'm in the music industry." Was the vaguest he could think of, wanting to keep the suspense going.

The questions were coming thick and fast from everyone in the kitchen, Stella and Sarah were googling George Michael interviews to see if they could match the voice on the end of the phone and general consensus was that it did sound exactly like George Michael. If it wasn't George Michael, he was doing a bloody good impression of him. Sophie was showing her younger sister, Layla, who George Michael was on her laptop, and it turned out Layla did recognise him. Charles and Sarah's husband were listening intently, surprised that it could actually be George Michael at the other end of the phone.

"What do you do in the music industry then, George?" Claire pressed.

"Oh, I make music. Abby No! No! ABBY!!! Sorry my dog looks like she's just about to have a crap on the floor, here's Chris. Abby, outside, come on girl, let's take that outside…… Lets go outside, in the sunshine." He sang as he passed the phone back to Chris. As it happened, Abby wasn't even in the room, she was fast asleep in front of the fire.

"Hello." Said Chris.

"Who was that nutcase?" Claire asked.

"George." Replied Chris

"George who?" Asked Claire.

"George Michael." Replied Chris.

"Seriously?" Asked Claire.

"Yep." Replied Chris in a cocky sort of way. *"I'm dying to go to the loo, I needed to go while you were talking to George, but I was nervous about what he might say. I have to go I'm bursting. I'll speak to you soon."* Chris hung up before his sister could ask another question.

As George wandered aimlessly around the garden, Chris, peering through the kitchen window, felt a mix of curiosity and concern. He pondered whether others could see George or if he was the sole witness to his friend's presence. Questions swirled in Chris's mind about the dynamics of visibility. Amidst these thoughts, he observed George's carefree movements, wondering about the emotions concealed behind his friend's exterior. Was George content or perhaps a bit mischievous in his newfound freedom? The uncertainty lingered, adding a subtle layer of intrigue to the scene.

While George was heading back towards the house, he saw Chris watching him from the window and started making rude gestures at him, sticking two fingers up at him, blowing him kisses, doing stupid walks. Was this the real George, the George that Chris had always wanted to see, to get to know? This ridiculously immature man who loved to be a pain in the arse, no pun intended, or was this a George, a Yog, who was revelling in the fact that he had been given yet another chance to live? For someone who had died just over 24 hours ago, he certainly was high on life right now. His smile was running from one side of his face to the other. His walk was tall, and confident with a bounce about it, he was oozing life, and he looked so happy. This was the person Chris expected, imagined, the real George Michael would be like, maybe not quite so immature, but somewhere close to what he was witnessing. How was Chris supposed to feel watching this larger-than-life mega star doing the most ridiculous walk towards him as if nothing was wrong? Had George forgotten what had happened only 24 hours ago? Surely not.

As George got closer to the house, he could see Chris standing at the window watching him and laughing at his silly antics, which to be fair, just encouraged George to do even more stupid walks. As George looked at Chris, Chris wondered what was going through his head, and whether he was getting what he expected from the George Michael he had spent most of his life following, or had he bitten of more than he could chew. George trusted Chris, after all, it was George who gate crashed Chris's life, and there was no way that Chris could have engineered that. He certainly wasn't some sort of undercover pap, looking for some in depth story. George thought about how difficult it was for him to come out of the closet and he knew who he was and was crystal clear about his sexuality. He felt sorry, in a way, for this weird little chap that he had been landed with, because he doesn't have a clue who he is. He was certain, he wanted to be a recluse and yet when he did leave the house, he did his utmost to be recognised as one the most well-known men on the planet. On top of that, he was in love with one of the most famous women in the world. If George ever thought he felt mixed up and confused in years gone by, he was beginning to think this guy was off the scale. He actually was starting to like Chris, his quirks made him different, his honesty was refreshing and his positivity was starting to rub off on George. As George swapped into yet another ridiculous walk and another outburst of excessive gesturing at Chris, he thought about how happy he felt.

George opened the kitchen door and almost fell into the kitchen.

"*Alright?*" He asked.

"*Good, you?*" Replied Chris.

"*You look deep in thought.*" Asked George.

"*Nahhhh, just wondering, watching you if you suffered some sort of brain damage whilst being delivered to my bedroom.*"

"*Hahahahahaha, sorry was that too much?*" Replied George.

"*Nahh it was funny, it was good to see you being a prat, sorry did I say being a prat? I meant having fun.*"

"*Good one, Mr Serious.*"

"*My bad, it was just weird seeing George Michael doing walks from the Monty Python school of silly walks.*"

"That's me, better get used to it, you're stuck with me now buddy boy, and there's nothing you can do about it. Nothing nothing nothing, Chris…. Is…. Stuck…. With… George! Chris…. Is…… stuck…. with …George!"

"Well, I had better get used to it then? It's going to be tough, spending so much time and having so many laughs with George bloody Michael."

"You idiot, your opinion of me is way too high." Replied George.

"Where's Abby?" Asked Chris, changing the subject.

"Not sure. She didn't follow me outside." "ABBY! ABBBBBBBYYYYY!"

A few seconds later, Abby peeped around the door of the kitchen as if to say. *"What?"*

"Here's my girl!" Shouted George. *"Hello girl, hello my lovely, hello my beautiful Abby."*

Abby padded over to George, and leant her whole body against his legs with her tail wagging and looking adoringly up at her master.

"Who's a beautiful girl then? Who's daddy's favourite girl?"

"Woooooooooooooof"

"That's my girl."

George looked over to Chris,

"She hasn't got a clue you're here, has she?"

"Doesn't look like it? You would think an animal, especially a dog, would pick up on something?"

"Yeah, that is weird." Replied George.

George understood Chris's struggles, having created the persona of George Michael to embody the person he aspired to be. Andrew Ridgeley, George's friend and Wham's fashion-forward half, exuded confidence and charm. For a while, George played the role of Andrew's understudy, learning the ropes of coolness. A head injury in his early teens marked a transformation for George. Formerly a geek fascinated by insects, the bump turned him into a Pop icon enthusiast. His mornings shifted from insect hunting to immersing himself in the music of Elton John, Roxy Music, and Queen. Who would have thought that the insect enthusiast would later flawlessly perform his heroes' songs, such as Elton's "Don't Let the Sun Go Down on Me" and "Tonight," along with a note-perfect rendition of "Somebody to Love" at the Freddie Mercury Tribute concert?.

Yog had crafted George Michael as an alter ego for himself, and it wasn't until George began receiving more attention than Andrew that Yog truly started to believe in his creation. Sure, his talent shone through, he was without doubt, one of the most talented musicians of all time, but what made him the complete product, was that he became a sex symbol as well, fancied, dreamed about, lusted after by millions of girls around the world.

What Chris was doing was piggy backing on the image that George created. The way Chris looked at it, was that women must have found George Michael attractive and therefore, if Chris could copy George, they would find him attractive and fancy him too. What in fact the cosmic difference between George and Chris was, that George was a mega star, brimming with talent. Yes, women fancied him and thought he was very good looking, but it wasn't just his looks it was the whole package that is George Michael, and this is what Chris could never attain, no matter how hard he tried. This eventually led Chris to believe if he added some secrecy to his own life, to become a recluse, people might think that the new guy in the big house who never came out, was George Michael.

It was these insecurities that ran deep through the veins of the two men that probably had brought them together now in this bizarre scenario that they were now going through. At the end of the day, they are much more closely aligned than they could have thought. It was because of this subconscious connection that "the powers that be", "the Universe", had bought their worlds crashing together.

Chapter Sixteen

In the ensuing days, George and Chris developed a unique bond, discovering each other's vulnerabilities in the pursuit of amusement. Their dynamic mirrored that of Inspector Clouseau and Cato from the Pink Panther movies, engaging in a playful game that left them both in fits of laughter. Amidst the laughter, there were moments of silent companionship, where words were unnecessary, deepening their connection. Their shared love for the piano became a source of joy, with George seeking Chris's input on new songs and Chris yearning for validation. George, amused by Chris's self-consciousness, encouraged him to play freely. The blend of laughter, music, and unspoken understanding formed the foundation of their evolving friendship.

New Year's Eve came and went without event to the relief of Chris. Chris had never liked New Year's Eve for some reason, he had always been wary of it. Although it was really like most Saturday nights where you go out and the chance of trouble is just around the corner, New Year's Eve to Chris had an even higher risk. Whenever Chris went into a club or pub the first thing he did was scope out where he thought the highest risk of trouble was and then make sure he was as far away from it as possible. The tactic had served him well as he had never been involved in a fight or had any need to defend himself in any way.

Strange, as he always went out hoping to be recognised as someone he wasn't, while at the same time remain anonymous, which were two very different characteristics for the same person, how can you have a desire to be noticed, while going completely unnoticed? It was the most confusing trait of Chris's personality, and one that he was left to cope with all on his own, as none of his friends seemed to pick up on the constant internal confliction he was going through. Chris would be stood there, most of the time pretending to enjoy himself, while actually he was constantly on the lookout for something about to breakout. He would also be scoping the venue for any girls who took his fancy and seemed to be single. The very same Chris who was always suspicious of trouble, was also the same Chris who would leave the safety of his group and go have a good look around for someone to catch his eye, or who he could catch theirs. Chris didn't believe in chat up lines, not because he thought they were corny, but because he couldn't think of any. Chris totally depended on his smile, hoping they liked George Michael and therefore, would find him attractive too. Not the best technique ever developed to pick up girls, pretending to be somebody else has its exceptions, and for Chris, being George Michael was a good exception.

Over the years, it transpired most of his girlfriends weren't that into George and declared that they went out with Chris because they fancied Chris and not George. This didn't stop him from quietly continuing to try to look and dress like George. After all, this had become a major part of his identity now, and almost impossible to change. Chris's wife actually thought George's music was depressing and self-indulgent, clearly, she didn't understand George. How can you say, Freedom, Fast Love, Freeek or Star People to name a few are depressing? Chris's first love also wasn't over complimentary about George and desperately tried to find the real Chris, who had probably been lost forever and he was only 21 then.

"*So, come on then! Who was your biggest love?*" Enquired George. "*Not including myself, Jen or Geri.*"

"*Hahahaha funny.*" Replied Chris.

"*I suppose it would have to be my very first love.*" He said after a pause for thought.

"*Who was that then?*" Asked George.

"*A girl called Denise; she was gorgeous. A complete pain in the arse, she had me wrapped around her little finger.*"

"*Hahahaaa! Isn't that always the way?*" Returned George. "*So, what was it about Dennis?*"

"*Denise?*" Replied Chris.

"*Whatever!*" Giggled George.

"*She was gorgeous for starters, she always looked amazing, she was quite funny, very focused and ambitious, she was always working. I think I took her to Mr Jacks, I'm sure I took her Mr Jacks (George's parents' restaurant) although I don't think it might have meant as much to her as it did to me. It would have been funny for your mum and dad to see a copy of their son walk in with Janet Jackson on his arm.*"

"*She looked like Janet Jackson?*" Interrogated George.

"*I thought so, but I don't think she was aiming to do so, Denise was very confident in herself.*"

"*She looked like Janet Jackson???*" George repeated.

"*Yes.*"

"*No wonder she was your first love. You lucky dog!*" Smirked George.

"*She wasn't that keen on me trying to be you, she was always trying to find the real me, maybe that's why we didn't work out in the end, she gave up trying to find Chris.*"

"*You idiot! You let go of Janet Jackson to be me?*"

"*She wasn't actually Janet Jackson, nor did she want to be, I just thought she looked similar.*"

"*Janet Jackson is hot, and I'm guessing around that time Janet was on fire, right?*"

"*Yeah.*" Replied Chris smugly.

"*So, let me get this straight. You went out, not wanting to be noticed, dressed as me with Janet Jackson on your arm? Are you fucking stupid or what?*"

"*Steady on!*" Replied Chris.

"*How can you expect to go out and not be noticed in those circumstances?*" Stressed George. "*So I'm guessing she was black?*"

"*Of course, she was, is, she looked like Janet Jackson!*"

"*Okay? so you go out desperately trying to look like me, and you have a black girl on your arm and a gorgeous one, who looks like Janet Bloody Jackson? You're going to draw attention to yourself buddy.*"

"*That's kind of what I wanted though, wasn't it? I wanted to be noticed without the fuss.*"

"*Oh, I bet you got noticed alright?*" Laughed George.

"*Hahahahaa, shame I never noticed it, I was always so wrapped in wondering if I was being noticed to notice if I had actually been noticed.*"

"*Fuck me, I thought I was mixed up.*" Sighed George. "*I have nothing on you. You are on a completely different level; you take being messed up to a professional level.*" Laughed George.

"Thanks." Replied Chris.

"No! I mean it, you are really screwed up." Replied George. *"So, what happened with you and Janet then?"*

"She said she didn't want to go out with me anymore. No big argument, no fall out, just the end."

"And I'm guessing you didn't take that well?" Enquired George.

"What do you think?" Responded Chris.

"I know your pain, trust me." Replied George.

"I've got a photo of the two of us, I'll show you and you can see how she looks like. It's in a restaurant, but I can't remember if it was your mum and dad's restaurant, maybe you'll recognise the décor?" Recalled Chris.

"Hey that would be weird if you were sat in mum and dad's place, we would have come so close to crossing paths." Replied George.

"Yeah, you would have looked across and laughed at the bloke trying to look like you with a super-hot girlfriend." Giggled Chris.

"I would probably have wondered, why a hot 'Janet Jackson lookalike' was going out with a mentalist like you." Retorted George.

"Unnecessary." Replied Chris.

Chris had struggled to get over the break up, after all he did love Denise. He was young, they both were, probably too young to consider they would spend the rest of their lives together, although Chris wasn't thinking that far ahead, he just knew that he was in love and didn't want it to end. Chris remembered the fear of telling his parents well, that he was dating a black girl and imagined how similar it must have been for George to announce to his parents that he was gay. Chris could remember waiting for them both to be in the room at the same time and for his dad to be in a good mood. He didn't worry about his mum; she was always saying she worked with an Indian woman so she couldn't possibly have a problem. Chris was more worried about how his dad would take the news, he wasn't sure at all where he stood, as far as Chris was aware his dad didn't know any black people. It was a Friday evening, Chris and Denise had been dating a few weeks and it was only a matter of time before his mum and dad would expect to meet this girl who had knocked their son for six. They had never seen Chris so blown away by a relationship.

"Are you seeing Denise this weekend?" Asked Chris's mum.

"Yeah, we're going out tonight for drinks." Replied Chris.

"When we going to meet her then?" Teased his dad.

"Soon." Answered Chris.

"What? Has she got two heads? Is she huge?" Joked his dad.

"No." Protested Chris

"Come on there must be something wrong with her if she's going out with you?" Continued his dad.

"Nope, she's stunning actually." Retorted Chris.

"Oh Peter, don't be mean." Chipped in his mum.

"She's black." Announced Chris out of the blue.

His mum who was always bragging about working with an Indian lady fell silent.

"Seriously?" Asked his dad.

"Yeah." Replied Chris.

"You legend, how the hell did you meet her? When are you going to introduce us?" Asked his dad.

This was completely the opposite reaction to what Chris was expecting and he wasn't really prepared for it. As it turned out once he had introduced Denise, both his mum and dad became very fond of her, his dad in particular. Whenever Denise came over, he was as usual the one left to open the door, but he never seemed to mind when it was Denise. He would take her into the living room and chat away to her, he was always very happy to see Denise. When Chris and his dad would go into town on Saturday, his dad would always want to know how Denise was and how they were getting on. He used to pull Chris's leg about when he was married to Denise that they wouldn't be able to do their Saturday morning jaunt into the town. He was just as devastated as Chris when Denise decided she didn't want to date Chris anymore. On all these years, Denise is still the only ex-girlfriend Chris is connected with on social media. Occasionally they touch base with each other and extraordinarily Denise is still single, she never married, maybe she never found anybody good enough to replace Chris? Or at least that's what Chris thought, not in a vindictive way because Denise still held a special place in his heart, but because maybe just a little bit, it helped him deal with it.

"Sounds like she hit you hard mate." Asked George.

"Yeah, I lost a good few years, getting over her. I think I spent a damn site longer getting over her than I was actually with her." Replied Chris *"I always think of Denise when I hear Waiting for the Day, even now, whenever I play it, I think of Denise, she really did a job on me."*

Every part of Chris's life was somehow, linked with George, or George somehow managed to become a part of it. Of course, George had no idea he was involved, but they must have been destined to meet at some point and George's early demise put a huge dent in that plan of fate.

"It's tough, when I lost Anselmo, I thought I would never find anyone to replace him, he was my first real love." Returned George. *"Your first black girlfriend, my first gay love!"* He continued.

"Hmmmmm?" Replied Chris thoughtfully, obviously transported back to his time with Denise.

"Hey! Don't go all morbid on me." Laughed George.

"Sorry." Replied Chris. *"So, how the hell did you keep Anselmo secret, you hadn't been outed then?"* Enquired Chris.

"It wasn't easy I can tell you, we had to be very careful when we went out just to look like a couple of mates in order to not draw attention to ourselves. Not easy when one of us was George Michael and the Paps were always hiding around one corner or another waiting to catch me out for something. They were so obsessed by my sexuality, I reckon they knew the truth, they were just waiting for proof." Replied George.

"Jeeeez and I thought telling my mum and dad I was dating a black girl was tough."

"They probably both had their risks?" Replied George. *"What was she like in bed then?"* He asked changing the gear of the conversation.

"Nosey?" Replied Chris.

"Do tell!!" Pushed George.

"You're so lucky I don't want to hear about your bedroom antics." Replied Chris.

"Don't change the subject Chrissy boy!"

"I'm not going to tell you George, no matter how much you push me." Stated Chris.

"Go on, tell me tell me tell me." Shrieked George tickling Chris to try and torture him into submission.

"It won't work!" Shouted Chris as he tried to escape the latest onslaught from George.

"Hahahahahha! Maybe some other time! I do want to know."

"Maybe if you're good, I'll introduce you to her and you can ask her yourself. I'm sure she would be only too pleased to give you all the details."

"Of course, you're still in touch with her, you could introduce us!" Exclaimed George.

"Possibly." Replied Chris.

"Make it happen, you have to make it happen, I want to meet her, I want to know what you were like back then." Pushed a now, very excited George.

"We'll see." Replied Chris.

"Oh my god, I'm actually going to meet your first girlfriend?" Laughed George.

"She wasn't my first girlfriend!" Replied Chris.

"You know what I mean. Does she still look like Janet?" Enquired George.

"I can't believe how excited you are!" Replied Chris in disbelief.

"I'm interested and she sounds like she'll tell me truth about young Chrissy Boy and you know I like the truth?" Replied George with a wink.

Chris and Denise's enduring friendship endured, marked by regular outings and occasional reunions.

Even in those moments when they briefly rekindled their romance, Chris nurtured a flicker of hope that perhaps a lasting connection could be resurrected. After the passing of Chris's father, a small windfall came his way, which he decided to invest in his first home. This significant decision, kept secret from Denise during the two-month house purchase process, was fueled by a mix of excitement and nervous anticipation. Taking precious time off work, Chris poured his emotions into redecorating the house, creating an intimate space he hoped to share with Denise. However, the unveiling didn't unfold as romantically as he had envisioned. Despite their non-committal status at the time, the disappointment in Denise's eyes was evident. She felt a sense of exclusion, a pang of hurt for not being part of Chris's homebuying journey, leading her to adamantly refused entry into the house. The dream of a shared future seemed to slip away in that moment, leaving behind a complex tapestry of emotions.

Denise did come to the house once and only once and the pair of them had a long chat about their future or lack of. It was on that occasion that Chris grew some balls and told Denise if they weren't going to get back together, he didn't see any point in them continuing to see each other, his second gamble that backfired in his face and Denise left, agreeing they shouldn't see each other anymore. Chris did what Chris did best, and went straight to his CD player. Some people go for a drive when they're down, others go to the pub, Chris goes to his Hi-Fi and leans on his guardian angel, George.

The remainder of the evening unfolded in solitude, the ambiance filled by the melodies emanating from Chris's cherished CDs and the soothing waves of the radio. Sleep eluded him, leaving him wide awake in the quiet hours of the morning. As Capital FM ushered in the love hour, the tranquil atmosphere was shattered by a sudden interruption—a gripping news story from the streets of Paris, France. A car chase, a crash in the tunnel beneath Paris, and the revelation that the pursued vehicle belonged to none other than Diana, the once-beloved Princess of Wales. Chris, an ardent admirer of Diana, had sensed an impending tragedy in the air leading up to this moment, given the relentless media frenzy surrounding her and her boyfriend, Dodi Fayed.

Dodi's life ended at the crash site, and Diana succumbed to the aftermath a few hours later. The news struck a chord with Chris, whose empathy for Diana had only deepened over time. Unbeknownst to him, George Michael, Diana's close friend, shared a profound connection with her. Their camaraderie was evident at concerts and restaurants, and George's participation in Diana's Concert of Hope for AIDS research was a testament to their bond. George found in Diana a rare understanding and a sense of normalcy that transcended his celebrity status.

Amidst the global mourning, the grand funeral at Westminster Abbey brought the UK and vast parts of the world to a standstill. George, accompanied by his close friend Elton John, paid his respects. While Chris's sympathy for Diana and George's friendship with her were not directly intertwined, a peculiar synchronicity unfolded—as if George, in some ethereal form, stood there as a guardian angel. In the complex tapestry of life, connections and coincidences converged, making the ordinary extraordinary and the extraordinary almost ordinary.

"I'm not being rude by not asking you about Anselmo, it's just that I've heard you talk about him and how much you

loved him, and I didn't want to sound like I was interviewing you or something. I also didn't want to upset you, it must still be very painful for you."

"That's okay and thank you." Replied George. *"I don't mind talking about him, he was a huge part of my life and it's good that I can talk about him openly now."*

"Yeah, I hadn't thought of that, you can shout it from the trees now. Hey George, is 'Secret Love' from your songs of the 20th Century album, something to do with Anselmo?"

"You'd turn into a very good detective Chris. You are very astute." Replied George returning to his sarcastic best.

"I thought so?" Nodded Chris knowingly, feeling pretty pleased with himself.

"No hiding anything from you, is there?" Giggled George.

"Not strictly true!" Replied Chris. *"Right up until the point you got arrested in a Beverly's Hill's toilet, I was convinced you were straight?"*

"No way?" Laughed George. *"And I thought you were one of my mega fans who knew everything about me hahahhahahahaha."*

"Obviously not everything." Replied a slightly embarrassed Chris.

Chapter Seventeen

Time had been moving on swiftly, the boys had been swapping between the houses in Goring, London and now Cornwall. George was keen to try and keep some normality going, Noom didn't suspect anything and nor had any of George's friends who they had met up with. Something had been on George's mind though and that was the task he had set for himself to set Chris up with Jennifer Aniston.

"So, you and Jen? How are we going to get you two together?" Asked George inquisitively.

"That's your project, George, you said you're the master of bringing people together!" Replied Chris.

"Yes, I did, didn't I?" Replied George. *"We need to decide which one of us is going to meet her first."*

"Well, I fancy her and you're gay." Laughed Chris. *"You do realise what we're going to have to do, don't you, George?"* Giggled Chris.

"What's that then?" Asked George nervously.

"We're going to have to put you back in the closet." Laughed Chris.

"You are fucking joking, aren't you?" Replied a shocked George.

"Yep! We're going to have to stage another Beverley Hills Toilet but with a girl." Insisted Chris.

"You're crazy!!"

"Nope! George is going back in the closet." Laughed Chris.

"That's not fair, it took me ages to find my way out." Said George.

"Yep, and now miraculously, George Michael is going to have an epiphany and decide that actually you prefer the ladies."

"You're mad, you're off your friggin head, why am I listening to this crazy idea?"

"Because it's the truth, and you know I speak the truth." Responded Chris.

"Have you been quietly planning this?" Interrogated George.

"Nope, just thought of it, but it's bloody brilliant, isn't it?" Chuckled Chris.

"It's not bad." Smiled George.

"So, you're up for it then?" Questioned Chris

"I'll think about it." Laughed George.

"You know it's the only way we can pull this off, don't you?" Replied Chris.

"It's a way, but I'm not sure it's the only way?" Laughed George.

"Got another plan?" Asked Chris.

"Not at the moment, but I'm going to keep thinking, not sure I'm ready to go straight."

"HHAHAHAHAHHA, you know you really want to?" Replied Chris.

"Idiot." Laughed George.

The boys continued to throw ideas around, and George, in particular, was keen to move away from the idea of going back in the closet. The idea of being arrested again was not filling him with excitement, although the thought of knowing it would be all staged did make him have a bit of a smile of satisfaction.

"*George!?*" Shouted Chris out of the blue.

"What, please don't tell me you've come up with another ridiculous idea?"

"*How come you never did Top Gear?*"

"*They wouldn't have me, I really wanted to do it.*" Laughed George.

"*Really?*"

"*Yeah, I think the BBC were afraid I would crash the car.*"

"*But loads of people crashed, Tom Cruise took Gambon corner on two wheels.*"

"*I know right? I think they were scared that they nearly killed Mr Cruise and I was a risk too far.*" Laughed George.

"*Would you have been any good?*" Asked Chris.

"*Bloody right I would.*" Laughed George.

"*It would have been worthwhile to see you in a crash helmet.*" Laughed Chris.

"*What you trying to say?*" Grinned George. "*I would make the crash helmet look cool.*"

"*Hahahahahahahahahhaahaha, the trouble is, George, you probably would.*" Replied Chris

"*Damn right I would!*"

"*So where do you reckon you would come on the board?*" Asked Chris.

George paused to think for a moment where he thought he might be on the leader board, whether he was honest or whether he was being a bit optimistic.

"*You had better beat JK and Cowl?*" Interrupted Chris.

"*Why's that?*" Asked George.

"*Put them in their place, they would both be livid if you beat them.*" Smirked Chris.

"You're probably right." Returned George.

George went quiet again for a few minutes, as if he was contemplating one of the few things he hadn't managed to do. It was a simple thing, but something he really wanted to have a go at.

"*Let's have a go!*" Said Chris.

"*What do you mean?*" Retaliated George.

"*Let's get on Top Gear.*" Said Chris.

"*Seriously?*" Demanded George.

"*Yeah, why not.*" Replied Chris. "*It won't be Jezza and Co, but we can get you on the board.*"

"*I like it!*" Replied George.

"*I'm a pretty good driver, we can see which one of us is the fastest on the practise laps, and he can drive, and nobody will be any the wiser.*" Said Chris.

"*I really like it.*" Explained George. "*You do sometimes come up with some good ideas.*"

"*George, I always have good ideas, and I want to wipe the floor of Simon Cowell.*" Replied Chris in a devious, Dr Evil type of way.

"*Don't you like Simon then, Chrissy boy?*" Enquired George.

"*Not a massive fan.*" Responded Chris.

"You never wanted to be Simon Cowell then?" Joked George.

"No, I only ever wanted to be you, George. Happy?" Retorted Chris.

"Very." Laughed George. *"It makes me feel special."* He followed giggling.

"Spastic." Replied Chris.

"That's not very PC." Laughed George.

"I don't care." Giggled Chris.

"You rebel." Continued George.

"That's me. Rebel without a cause and Cowell is a twat."

George nearly choked on his own laughter at Chris's last retort. A mix of amusement and bewilderment washed over him. He hadn't known anyone like Chris before, who had such a singular outlook on life. If it wasn't connected to George Michael, it wasn't worth the steam off his pee. George felt a peculiar blend of amusement and incredulity, wondering how anyone could navigate life with such a limited view of the world. Yet, he wasn't complaining; he strangely appreciated how outspoken Chris was. It was oddly refreshing that Chris didn't care if people liked him or not; it didn't seem to affect him at all. As far as Chris was concerned, if someone didn't like him, so what? As long as they didn't invade his space, he couldn't care less. George had always craved the love of others, and Chris didn't give a toss. Yet, he spent most of his life trying to be a man who wanted to be loved. George could not figure Chris out in the slightest.

"You really don't care about other people, do you Chris?" Asked George.

"That's not strictly true George, I am a caring person, I just don't care about people who don't deserve my time."

"Very philosophical!" Replied George. *"I'm one of the privileged few?"*

"Yep." Responded Chris.

George looked at Chris, attempting to understand him, trying to unravel the enigma inside his head, wishing he could discover what had shaped this complex guy. A sense of curiosity and concern filled George as he wondered if Chris was entirely messed up or if he was simply fully attuned to life, impervious to outside influences, except for George, that is. Apparently, George couldn't put a foot wrong.

Chapter Eighteen

January and February went by, and for obvious reasons the boys were inseparable, but let's face it, without Chris, there was no George. They had spent a lot of their time playing music, Chris loved George's entire back catalogue and fortunately so did George.

It was the first night of the tour, and the atmosphere was electric, more than electric, much more, the air was fuzzing with excitement. The media had been going mad, hailing that it was going to be the best tour of George's career, even better than the Faith tour. Tickets had been sold out in minutes of going on sale. If you weren't online at the exact time, you had no chance of getting one. The opening night could only be held in one place and that place was of course Wembley Stadium, in fact it had been sold as opening week, because opening night sold out so quickly. Even with the roof open, the stadium felt claustrophobic as the fans poured in, the lucky ones at the front holding onto their position for dear life.

The stage came right out into the audience in a sort of runway, so George could get as close to as many of his fans as possible. It didn't look that long on paper, but in reality, he was going to be covering a lot of ground if he was going to make good use of the stage, and George intended to make very good use of it. The band could be heard warming up, sound checks were given the last tests to be sure everything was perfect. Occasionally, a stage hand would come onto the stage and move something or plug something in or place a cold bottle of water. There would be intermittent teasers of one of George's intros, and the audience would start to scream; then it would go quiet, and the screaming would stop. Was it the band teasing the audience or George? Were they sat backstage laughing while they gently got the audience ready for the actual beginning? In the midst of the anticipation, excitement lingered, building with each pause, and the air vibrated with the shared energy between the performer and his eager audience.

Suddenly, the lights went out, the stage was silent, the audience was silent, Wembley Stadium was in a silent bubble. Nothing happened, nothing at all. There wasn't a power cut because you could see the small LEDs of various bits of equipment waiting to burst into life. You could see the ghostly shadows of the band moving around in what little light there was, and then, from the darkness came.

DUM DEE DUM ..... DUM DIDDY DUM

DUM DEE DUM ..... DUM DIDDY DUM

DUM DEE DUM ..... DUM DIDDY DUM

DUM DEE DUM ..... DUM DIDDY DUM

DUM DEE DUM ..... DUM DIDDY DUM

DUM DEE DUM ..... DUM DIDDY DUM

DUM DEE DUM ..... DUM DIDDY DUM

This went on for several minutes, and the audience clapped along the beat of the bongos, everybody in the audience with their arms in the air clapping. Periodically, some of them would lower their arms to let the blood flow back to their hands and then raise them back up in the air and join in the clapping.

DUM DEE DUM ….. DUM DIDDY DUM
DUM DEE DUM ….. DUM DIDDY DUM
DUM DEE DUM ….. DUM DIDDY DUM

"I WANNA HEAR ALL YOUR VOICES OKAY!!!!!" It was George.

DUM DEE DUM ….. DUM DIDDY DUM
DUM DEE DUM ….. DUM DIDDY DUM
DUM DEE DUM ….. DUM DIDDY DUM

George strutted around the stage, arms in the air, clapping with the audience, moving off in different directions, occasionally pausing to look out into the crowd. He looked amazing, mega-slim in a black pair of jeans and black T-shirt, emphasising his new in shape physique.

"I WANNA HEAR THE WHOLE PLACE SINGING!"

"EVERY SINGLE ONE OF YOU, BEAUTIFUL PEOPLE!"

With that he positioned himself in the middle of the stage and……..

"FREEEEEEDOM!"

"FREEEEEEDOM!"

"FREEEEDOM!"

"YOU GOTTA GIVE WHAT YOU TAKE!"

"CMON!"

"FREEEEEEDOM!"

"FREEEEDOM!"

"FREEEEDOM!" George raised his arms and everybody sang along with him.

"YOU GOTTA GIVE WHAT YOU TAKE!"

"HEAVEN KNOWS, I WAS JUST A YOUNG BOY!"

"DIDN'T KNOW WHAT I WANTED TO BE!"

"DIDN'T KNOW WHAT I WANTED TO BE!" Backing singers

George was moving around the stage with the spot light following his every move, making sure he made eye contact with as many people in the audience, as he possibly could. He was almost like a wild cat prowling the stage, looking for the tastiest member of the audience to pounce on.

"I WAS EVERY LITTLE HUNGRY SCHOOL GIRLS PRIDE AND JOY!"

"AND I GUESS IT WAS ENOUGH ME!"

"GUESS IT WAS ENOUGH FOR ME!" Backing singers.

"TO WIN THE RACE A PRETTIER FACE!"

"BRAND NEW CLOTHES, AND A BIG FAT PLACE!"

"ON YOUR ROCK AND ROLL TV!"

"ROCK AND ROLL TV!" Backing singers.

"BUT TODAY THE WAY, I PLAY THE GAME!"

"IS NOT THE SAME!"

"THINK I'M GONNA GET ME SOME HAPPY!"

"GONNA GET ME SOME HAPPY!" Backing singers.

"I THINK THERE'S SOMETHING YOU SHOULD KNOW!"

"I THINK IT'S TIME I TOLD YOU SO!" Backing singers.

"THERE'S SOMETHING DEEP INSIDE OF ME!"

"THERE'S SOMEONE ELSE, I'VE GOT TO BE!" Backing singers.

"TAKE BACK YOUR PICTURE IN A FRAME!"

"TAKE BACK YOUR, SINGING IN THE RAIN!" Backing singers.

"I JUST HOPE YOU UNDERSTAND!"

"SOMETIMES THE CLOTHES, DO NOT MAKE THE MAN!"

George was going from side to side, and up and down the stage. He moved with a confident swagger; the sort of swagger that only a very confident man can do in front of thousands of adoring fans, clapping their hands and singing along with him. Intermittently, he would direct his microphone towards the crowd to encourage them to sing even louder.

"ALL WE HAVE TO DO NOW!"

"IS TAKE THESE LIES!"

"AND MAKE THEM TRUE SOME HOW!"

"ALL WE HAVE TO SEE!" Backing singers.

"IS THAT I DON'T, BELONG TO YOU!"

"AND YOU DON'T, BELONG TO ME!"

"EVERYONE!!!"

"FREEEEEEDOM!"

"FREEEEEEDOM!"

"FREEEEEEDOM!"

"YOU'VE GOTTA GIVE, WHAT YOU TAKE!"

"FREEEEEDOM!"

"FREEEEDOM!"

"FREEEEEEDOM!"

"YOU'VE GOTTA GIVE, WHAT YOU TAKE!"

"HEAVEN KNOWS WE SURE HAD SOME FUN, BOY!" "WHY CAN'T JUST MY BUDDY, AND ME!"

"WHY CAN'T JUST MY BUDDY AND ME!" Backing singers.

"WE HAD EVERY SINGLE, BIG SHOT GOOD TIME BAND, ON THE RUN BOY!"

"WE WERE LIVING IN A FANTASY!"

"LIVING IN A FANTASY!" Backing singers.

"WE WON THE RACE!"

"GOT OUTTER THE PLACE!"

"I WENT BACK HOME!"

"GOT A BRAND NEW, FACE!"

"FOR THE BOYS ON MTV!"

"BOYS ON MTV!" Backing singers.

"BUT TODAY THE WAY I PLAY THE GAME!"

"HAS GOT TO CHANGE!"

"OHHHHH YEAH!" Backing singers.

"GONNA GET ME SOME HAPPY!"

"NOW I'M GONNA GET ME SOME HAPPY!" Backing singers.

George went running into the centre of the stage as the tempo started to rise, and the track started to move into a faster pace.

"I THINK THERE'S SOMETHING YOU SHOULD KNOW!"

"I THINK IT'S TIME I STOPPED THE SHOW!" Backing singers.

"THERE'S SOMETHING DEEP INSIDE OF ME!"

"THERE'S SOMEONE I FORGOT TO BE!" Backing singers.

"TAKE BACK YOUR PICTURE IN A FRAME!"

"DON'T THINK THAT I'LL BE BACK AGAIN!" Backing singers.

"AND I JUST HOPE YOU UNDERSTAND!"

"SOMETIMES THE CLOTHES DO NOT MAKE THE MAN!"

"ALL WE HAVE TO DO NOW!" George and the backing singers.

"EVERYONE!"

"IS TAKE THESE LIES!" Backing singers and the crowd.

"AND MAKE THEM TRUE SOME HOW!"

"ALL WE HAVE TO SEE, YEAHHHH!"

"IS THAT I DON'T BELONG TO YOU!"

"AND YOU DON'T BELONG TO ME!"

"CMON!"

"FREEEEEEDOM!"

"YEAH!"

"FREEEEDOM!"

"FREEEEEDOM!"

"YOU GOTTA GIVE, WHAT YOU TAKE!"

"FREEEEEEDOM!"

"FREEEEEEDOM!"

George moved back to the centre of the stage, raised both arms up into the air.

"CMON!"

"FREEEEEDOM!" Audience.

"YEAH!"

"YOU GOTTA GIVE, WHAT YOU TAKE!"

George moved in among the backing singers.

"OW OW OW OW!"

"OW OW OW OW!"

"OW OW OW OW!"

George moved back to the centre of the stage to a raised platform.

"OW OW OW OW!"

"HEYYYYY!" Backing singers.

"OW OW OW OW!"

"HEYYYYY!" Backing singers.

George was doing his signature dance on the raised platform.

"YEAHHHHHH!"!

"HEYYYYYYYYY!" Backing singers.

"YEAHHHHH!"

"HEYYYYYYYY!" Backing singers

"YEAH YEAH YEAH!"

"HEYYYYYY!" Backing singers

"YEAH YEAH YEAH!"

"HEYYYY!" Backing singers.

"WELL IT LOOKS LIKE THE ROAD TO HEAVEN!"

"BUT IT FEELS LIKE THE ROAD TO HELL!"

"WHEN I KNEW WHICH SIDE MY BREAD WAS BUTTERED!"

"I TOOK THE KNIFE AS WELL!"

"YEAH YEAH YEAH!" Backing singers.

"POSING FOR ANOTHER PICTURE!"

"EVERYONE TRIES TO SELL!"

Then the moment the audience had been waiting for, finally happened, George stood dead in the centre, on the raised platform and gave a shake of his arse and the crowd went wild.

"WHEN YOU SHAKE YOUR ARSE!"

"THEY NOTICE FAST!"

"SOME MISTAKES WERE BUILT TO LAST!"

"THAT'S WHAT YOU GET!" Backing singers.

"THAT'S WHAT YOU GET!"

"CMON!"

"THAT'S WHAT YOU GET!"

"THAT'S WHAT YOU GET!" Backing singers.

"FOR CHANGING YOUR MIND!"

"THAT'S WHAT YOU GET!"

"FOR CHANGING YOUR MIND!"

George bought his intro to an end, and the lights went out leaving the stadium in complete darkness again. The audience were clapping and screaming for more, just one song in, and George had every single one of them in the palm of his hand. George played to the audience and let them continue to clap and shout.

"We love you George"! Could be heard from all over the stadium.

Eventually the audience started to calm down a little and that was the cue for song number two.

"WE'VE GOT TO EXPAND, THE WHOLE OPERATION!"

"DISTRIBUTION HEHEHEHEEHEHHE!"

"NEW YORK, CHICAGO!"

The whole stage was lit up in white, white strobe lights, white lasers, white lights everywhere.

"RANG DANG DIGIDY DANG DE DANG!" George.

"ROCK!" Backing singers.

"RANG DANG DIGIDY DANG DE DANG!" George.

"FREEEZE!" Backing singers.

"RANG DANG DIGIDY DANG DE DANG!" George.

"ROCK!" Backing singers.

"RANG DANG DIGIDY DANG DE DANG!" George.

"FREEZE!" Backing singers.

"RANG DANG DIGIDY DANG DE DANG!" George.

"ROCK!" Backing singers.

""RANG DANG DIGIDY DANG DE DANG DIGIDY DANG DE DANG DIGIDY DANG DE DANG!" George.

"AHHHHHHHHHHHHH AHHHHHHHHHHHH AHHHHHHHHH AHHHHHHHHH!" George and backing singers.

DUM DUM DUM DE DUM DE DUM from the bass guitar and drums.

"WHITE, OOOOOOOO AHHHHHHHH WHITE!" George.

"WHITE OOOOOOOOO WHITE!" George.

"WHITE OOOOOOOOOO WHITE!" George.

"OOOOOOOOOOO WHITE LINES!" George.

"VISION DREAMS OF PASSION!"

"GOING THROUGH MY MIND!" Backing singers.

"AND ALL THE WHILE I THINK OF YOU!"

"PIPELINE!" Backing singers.

"A VERY STRANGE REACTION!"

"YOURS TO UNWIND!" Backing singers.

"THE MORE I SEE, THEMORE I DO!"

"SOMETHING OF A PHENOMENON!" George and backing singers.

"TELLING YOUR BODY TO COME ALONG!"

"CAUSE WHITE LINES, BLOW AWAY!" George and backing singers.

"BLOW!"

"ROCK!"

"BLOW!"

"TICKET TO RIDE A WHITE LINE HIGHWAY!"

"TELL ALL YOUR FRIENDS THEY CAN GO MY WAY!"

"PAY YOUR TOLL, SELL YOUR SOUL!"

"POUND FOR POUND, IT COSTS MORE THAN GOLD!"

"THE LONGER YOU STAY, THE MORE YOU PAY!"

"MY WHITE LINES, GO A LONG WAY!"

"EITHER UP YOUR NOSE, OR THROUGH YOUR VEIN!"

"WITH NOTHING TO GAIN, EXCEPT KILLING YOUR BRAIN!"

"FREEZE!" Backing singers.

"SAY ROCK, COME ON Y'ALL!"

"ROCK!" Backing singers.

"FREEZE, SAY ROCK COME ON Y'ALL!"

"ROCK, SAY FREEZE, COME ON Y'ALL!" George and backing singers.

"FREEZE, SAY ROCK, COME ON Y'ALL!"

"ROCK, SAY FREEZE, COME ON Y'ALL!" George and backing singers.

"FREEZE, SAY ROCK, COME ON Y'ALL!"

"ROCK, SAY FREEZE, COME ON Y'ALL!" George and backing singers.

"PUT EM UP, PUT EM UP, PUT EM UP!"

"AHHHHHHHHHHHHH!" Backing singers.

"HIGHER BABY!"

"AHHHHHHHHHHHHH!" Backing singers.

"GET HIGHER BABY!"

"AHHHHHHHHHHHHH!" Backing singers.

"GET HIGHER BAY!"

"AND DON'T EVER COME DOWN, FREE BASE!"

The guitarists went wild unloading on the audience, the stage turns into a mass of white lights and George dressed in black, strutting around, covering as much of the stage as possible.

"RANG DANG DIGIDY DANG DE DANG!" "RANG DANG DIGIDY DANG DE DANG!" Backing singers.

"RANG DANG DIGIDY DANG DE DANG DIGIDY DE DANG DIGIDY DE DANG!" Backing singers.

"RANG DANG DIGIDY DANG DE DANG DIGIDY DANG DE DANG DE DANG!" Backing singers.

"WHITE LINES!" Backing singers.

"PIPELINE!" Backing singers.

"AS PURE AS DRIVEN SNOW!"

"CONNECTED TO MY MIND!" Backing singers.

"AND NOW I'M HAVING FUN BABY!"

"HIGHRISE!" Backing singers.

"IT'S GETTING KIND OF LOW!"

"CAUSE IT MAKES YOU FEEL SO NICE!" Backing singers.

"I NEED SOME ONE ON ONE, BABY!"

"SOMETHING OF A PHENOMENON!" Backing singers.

"BABY!"

"SOMETHING OF A PHENOMENOM!" Backing singers.

"BABY!"

"CAUSE WHITE LINES!" Backing singers.

"WHAT DO WHITE LINES DO!"

"BLOW AWAY!" Backing singers.

"BLOW!"

"ROCK!" Backing singers.

"BLOW!"

"A MILLION MAGIC CRYSTALS, PAINTED PURE AND WHITE!"

"A MILLION-DOLLARS, ALMOST OVERNIGHT!"

"TWICE A SWEET AS SUGAR, TWICE AS BITTER AS SALT!"

"AND IF YOU GET HOOKED BABY!"

"IT'S NOBODY ELSE'S FAULT, SO DON'T DO IT!"

"FREEZE!" Backing singers.

"SAY ROCK, COME ON Y'ALL!"

"ROCK!" Backing singers.

"SAY FREEZE, COME ON!"

"FREEZE!" Backing singers.

"SAY ROCK, COME ON Y'ALL!"

"ROCK!" Backing singers.

"SAY FREEZE, COME ON!"

"FREEZE!" Backing singers.

"SAY ROCK, COME ON Y'ALL!"

"ROCK!" Backing singers.

"PUT EM UP, PUT EM UP, PUT EM UP!"

"AAAAAAHHHHHHHHHH!" Backing singers.

"HIGHER BABY!"

"AAAAAAAAAHHHHHHHH!" Backing singers.

"GET HIGHER BABY!"

"AAAAAAAAAHHHHHHHH!" Backing singers.

"GET HIGHER BABY!"

"DON'T NEVER COME DOWN!"

George grabbed his microphone and went on another swagger around the stage, leaving the band to go ballistic on the instruments, bringing the audience to a frenzy. Every single person had their hands in the air doing a pushing movement.

"SOMETHING OF A PHENOMENON!"

"SOMETHING OF A PHENONENOM!"

"DON'T YOU GET TOO HIGH!" Backing singers.

"DON'T YOU GET TOO HIGH BABY!"

"IT TURNS ME ON!" Backing singers.

"YOU REALLY TURN ME ON AND ON!"

"CAN'T YOU EVER COME DOWN!" Backing singers.

"MY TEMPERATURE IS RISING!"

"TIL THE THRILL IS GONE!" Backing singers.

"NO I DON'T WANT YOU TO GO!"

"A STREET KID GETS ARRESTED, GONNA DO SOME TIME!"

"HE GOT OUT THREE YEARS FROM NOW!"

"JUST TO COMMIT, MORE CRIME!"

"A BUSNESSMAN IS CAUGHT WITH TWENTY-FOUR KILOS!"

"HE'S OUT ON BAIL, AND OUT OF JAIL!"

"AND THAT'S THE WAY IT GOES!"

"CANE, SUGAR, CANE, SUGAR, CANE!"

"ATHLETES REJECT IT, GOVERNORS CORRECT IT!"

"GANGSTERS, PUNKS, AND SMUGGLERS, ARE THOROUGHLY RESPECTED!"

"THE MONEY GETS DIVIDED; THE WOMEN GET EXCITED!"

"NOW I'M BROKE AND IT'S NO JOKE!"

"IT'S HARD AS HELL TO FIGHT IT, DON'T BUY IT!"

"FREEEZE!" Backing singers.

"SAY ROCK, COME ON Y'ALL!"

"ROCK!" Backing singers.

"SAY FREEZE, COME ON!"

"FREEEZE!" Backing singers.

"SAY ROCK, COME ON Y'ALL!"

"ROCK!" Backing singers.

"SAY FREEZE, COME ON!"

"FREEEZE!" Backing singers.

"SAY ROCK, COME ON Y'ALL!"

"ROCK!" Backing singers.

"SAY FREEZE, COME ON!"

"FREEEZE!" Backing singers

"SAY ROCK. COME ON Y'ALL!"

"ROCK!" Backing singers.

"ROCK, FREEZE, ROCK, FREEEZE, ROCK, FREEEEZE, ROCK, FREEZE!" George and backing singers.

"A A A A A A A A A A A A A A A H H H H H H H H , AAAAAAAAAAAHHHHH, AAAAAAAAAHHHHHH!" Backing singers.

DUM DUM! DUM DUM! DUM DUM ! DUM DUM!

The audience went wild as George took centre stage, and once again ended the song with his obligatory shake of the ass to please the crowd in perfect timing with the drummer.

George was moving around the stage like a teenager, his dance moves were off the scale and the pace of the show was like nothing he had done before. It was a more fast track energetic extravaganza and the audience were loving every second. Chris was totally knackered. George had been pacing around the stage like a teenager on steroids. Every bone in Chris's body felt shattered, every muscle was on fire, his heart was pounding out of his chest and his lungs were gasping for air. George on the other hand looked like he had been for a stroll around his garden. George had zapped every last bit of energy out of Chris and looked amazing, while Chris wanted to throw up and faint. How could anyone strut around stage for so long and still look so good.

You could see in the eyes of every member of George's fans how amazed they were at his athletic mobility, he was unstoppable, covering every inch of the vast stage and no matter how much energy he exerted, he didn't drop a note. Not only were his physical levels incredible, his voice was the best it had ever been. Even George was staggered by how much energy he was using and still feeling fantastic, and as he put his vocals to the test, he started to push them further and further, holding notes for longer, going higher, then lower, everything he tried was perfect.

By the time the show started to come to an end the audience were totally knackered, even though they didn't want it to end. George had given them an unmissable performance covering so many of his huge back catalogue along with some of the new tracks from his new album, which were instant successes.

Fast Love, with a twist

Amazing, was amazing.

I'm your man.

Freek

Too funky

I want your sex

Father figure

Cowboys and Angels

Star People

Killer/Papa was a rolling stone

Back to life

A different corner

Blue armed with love

This is not real love

Outside

Wham Rap

New life (from the new album) full on dance track

On a roll (from the new album) full on dance track

Where have you been (from the new album) slow track

Careless whisper

Nearly three hours later and the lights went down for the final time, and the audience were able to breath and relax for the first time. They felt like they had ran a marathon and as the started to make their way to the exits, all you could hear from them was. "That was amazing" "George was incredible" "I can't believe how good that was, I'm knackered" "Oh my god that was awesome, George was on fire, how does he do it" "George is so fit, he was like a professional athlete moving around the stage" "George was super human, how could he run around and dance like a mad man and still stay note perfect" "George didn't drop a note and had so much energy"

All in all they all concurred the show was a magnificent success, nobody should be able to exert that much energy and still sing so perfectly.

Chapter Nineteen

Amidst their frequent journeys from Cornwall to Goring and London, the boys cherished these moments, delving into each other's lives. It was a precious quality time, filled with camaraderie, laughter, and good-natured teasing, strengthening the bonds of their friendship.

"So, come on then, what else should I know about you?" Asked George.

"Like what?" Asked Chris.

"I don't know! Make me laugh?" Stated George.

"I don't know. Your life is far more interesting than mine, why are you so intrigued by mine?"

"Because you're even more messed up than me, but you deal with it in such a cool way."

"I'm not messed up, George."

"Oh, I think you are, no, I know you are." Laughed George.

"Thanks for that, George."

"Hahahahahhahahah." Laughed George. *"C'mon, you must have a funny story for your uncle George."*

"Shut up!" Laughed Chris.

"C'mon!!" Insisted George.

Chris went quiet while he thought of something he thought might make George laugh.

"So, when did you start hanging out in gay clubs?" Asked Chris.

"What's that got to do with anything?" Enquired George.

"I was curious." Replied Chris.

"Curious about gay clubs?" Confirmed George.

"No, not the clubs, I'm not bothered about them, just about when you started going to them?"

"You're curious about gay clubs? Chris is curious?" Chuckled George.

"I'm not curious about gay clubs, George!" Protested Chris.

"So why all the questions?" Insisted George.

"Because in the early days of being you, I never got approached by guys, which was what I expected. The girls got it. They knew I wasn't you, obviously, but I think they probably liked the idea that it might be you."

"Jeeeeez you're screwed up!" Teased George.

"I started working in this pub and made some pretty good friends there. So I had my regular friends and the pub friends. I was used to going on holiday with my regular mates and pulling girls pretending to be you."

"I don't think it was actually because you were dressed as me, they must have liked something about you too, or do you really think they dropped their pants, closed their eyes and thought they were shagging me?"

"Something like that..." Laughed Chris

"Once you got your kit off, you were just you. You weren't hiding behind a pair of boots and some sunglasses, right? Please tell me you took your boots and Ray Bans off when you had sex!" Giggled George.

"Of course, I did." Giggled Chris. *"I still had the stubble and the earring."*

"Tosser!" Laughed George.

"Are you going to let me finish?" Asked Chris sarcastically.

"I'm sorry, continue." Giggled George.

"So anyway, before I was so rudely interrupted."

"Whatever!" Sighed George.

"The guys at the pub were organising a trip to Tenerife, over the new year and asked if I wanted to join them, to which I said yes. It was actually on that holiday I bought my Ray Ban Generals. Up until that point I had a pair of cheap copies from Boots."

"Fuck me, you do like to witter on?" Yawned George.

"You asked." Retorted Chris

"My bad, go on." Giggled George.

"So, I went out in my favourite look of that time, my cowboy boots with the Chrome tips."

"I loved those, such a good look!" Agreed George.

"Even if you say so yourself." Teased Chris.

"Maybe." Replied George with a wink.

"So, cowboy boots with chrome tips on toes and heals, stone washed jeans, white shirt or T-shirt, black braces, designer stubble, big cross earing and either my black hat to perfect hair, and of course, the new Ray Bans."

"Good look, no wonder you pulled!" Laughed George.

"It worked for me." Laughed Chris.

"Of course, it did." Replied George.

"Don't talk too soon cocky!" Retorted Chris. *"So, I'm on the dancefloor strutting my stuff, shaking my arse, in your own words. When you shake your arse, they notice fast."*

"You're truly not for real, are you? Did you take everything I said literally?" Laughed George.

"So, I'm dancing away, I had learnt all the top 'George' moves, and this arm comes over my right shoulder, then a moment later, an arm comes over my left shoulder. I thought it was a bit weird so moved over a bit and then it happened again. Obviously, it was being done on purpose so I moved again, this time moving a little closer to the wall. Even though I reduced the room behind me it happened again, if I had made another move, there would have been so little room I would have been dry humped on the dancefloor, so I left and sat at the bar."

"That doesn't sound so bad!" Laughed George.

"It gets better." Replied Chris.

"I hope so." Replied George.

"So, I'm sat at the bar and this guy comes over and says, "Ooooh I do like your boots!" So, I said thanks, thinking it was the end of the conversation. Then he asked where I got them from."

"Chelsea" I replied.

"Whereabouts?" Came from him.

"Kings Road." I replied, then he put his hand on my leg and started to run his finger down my leg."

"Whhhhaaaaatttttt, blatant!" Laughed George.

"Then he says he would like a pair of those. So, I tell him if he doesn't take his hand off my leg, he'll be eating mine.

To which he flicked his head and stropped off with his tail between his legs."

"What's all this got to do with me going to gay clubs?" Asked George.

"Well, I reckon the gay community must have known you were gay, even if the rest of us didn't. Although, I wasn't prepared to be hit on by guys. "

"Hahahahhahahahah, what are you like?" Laughed George.

"It was a bit of a shock, I was used to the girls liking the look and getting a bit of George between the sheets, and now guys were coming onto me too?"

"Getting a bit of George between the sheets?" Shrieked George "What part of me were they getting? I don't remember being between the sheets with any of those 'horny-for-George' ladies?"

"You know what I mean." Exclaimed Chris.

"I'm sorry, but I really don't have a fucking clue on what you mean. I've said it before and I'm going to say it again, and I'm going to keep saying it. You are one very mixed-up guy, living in a world full of fantasy that has absolutely no resemblance of reality what so ever. I can't believe you thought the girls thought they were sleeping with me."

"You don't understand, George." Pressed Chris.

"Damn right, I don't. I made George Michael up for me, not you."

"So, you have a patent on George Michael, do you?"

"Yes, I think I have dibs on George Michael, because I invented him and he's all mine."

"Well, that's just being greedy." Laughed Chris

"What can I say? I'm a greedy man." Laughed George.

"Well, I can't change it now, what's done is done."

"I should charge you royalties for using my dick to have sex."

"Well, that's not going to happen!" Laughed Chris

"I hope you did me proud."

"I reckon I did okay." Laughed Chris.

"You did okay? Okay isn't good enough. Sex with George Michael should be amazing, every single time."

"HAHAHAHHAHAHAHA! Of course, it should. Well, I hope they all enjoyed their shag with George, maybe I should have taken a satisfactory survey afterwards."

"You didn't take a survey? You're an amateur, aren't you?"

"Oh, shut up!"

"I don't want my dick used in vain, Christopher".

"Shut up, George."

"Christopher?" Laughed George.

Anybody in earshot of these two squabbling idiots would have easily come to the conclusion that they had been friends forever, it really was incredible because they had only known each other for such a short time. Was this the reason why Chris was chosen to be the person George was to find in his moment of need? Were they meant to be friends all along? They were so well connected and completely in sync with each other.

Chapter Twenty

Now that the tour was over, and George was keen to get back onto his other project - of getting Chris hooked up with the other love of his life, Jennifer Aniston. The idea that had been broached by Chris, about George getting back in the closet, was playing on George's mind continuously. Although, he wasn't convinced it was a brilliant idea, he did think or agree that it might be the only way forward. The problem being, that even if George was outed as a straight man, how was he going to get Chris in front of Jennifer, as only one of them could be seen by Jen in one go. George may be able to arrange a meeting with Jennifer, but when George was not around, how would Jennifer react to this totally screwed up nutcase that is Chris? Would Jennifer give Chris the time of day? Would Jennifer give George the time of day? There is no proof that Jennifer even likes George, his music, his persona, his style or anything about George? As far as George was aware, Jennifer was into her rock music and showed no real interest in R & B.

George was in a bind, trying to keep a promise of setting Chris up with Jen. He figured this challenge might be even trickier than his dream of becoming big star. It wasn't just about reaching Jen; it was about introducing the quirky Chris without ruining George's street cred. George wondered if Chris would just be himself or go all

George, worried it might scare off Jen. As he dealt with this social puzzle, George thought maybe their dreams of stardom were a catwalk compared to this matchmaking mess.

George had been racking his brain on how he could possibly test the water and see if there was any chance of Jennifer taking the bait.

"So, Christopher?" Asked George.

Chris frowned at George. *"Please don't call me that."* Replied Chris.

"Okay is it Chris or George 2?" Giggled George.

"Chris is fine." Replied Chris. *"George 2? You're an idiot."*

"Touchy." Laughed George. *"So, this whole closet thing? How's that going to work?"*

"Well, we're going to have to wedge you back in the closet, and bring you back out as a straight man, a very, very straight man, who's in love with Jen."

"Nobody is going to believe that." Why can't I just be caught dating her? Do I have to go through the whole straight thing?"*

"Jen will never go out with you if she thinks you're still gay, will she?" Insisted Chris.

"Who says she's going to go out with me at all?" Questioned George.

"Because you're George Michael and now you're a straight George Michael."

"I do appreciate your positivity that I can get any girl on the planet to go out with, but you are, fucking delusional Christopher. Just because you fancy the pants off me, doesn't mean everybody else does, and it certainly doesn't mean that Jennifer Aniston will."

"I do not fancy the pants off you, George, I've explained that to you!"

"Yeah Yeah, and all of that made perfect sense." Replied George.

"You're getting off the point, George. What about Jen?"

"Okay okay, we'll have to find a girl to be caught with, by the paps. We know they'll be all over it, they love digging up the dirt on me."

"Oh, and that's going to be difficult? Finding a girl to sleep with George Michael? How the hell are we going to do that?" Returned Chris.

"Again, not all women want to sleep with me." Insisted George.

"But lots do, and we only need one, unless you're planning on getting caught in a threesome." Suggested Chris.

"Now you're talking." Giggled George.

"Whatever." Replied Chris.

"What? If we're going to do this, why not do it big? Go big or go home." Came George.

"And you think I'm messed up?" Replied Chris.

"Hey! Do you want my help or not? It's my reputation on the line here!" Complained George.

"Jennifer! Can we get back to Jennifer, George?" Asked Chris.

"Okay! Okay!" Laughed George. *"So, we need to sow the seed and see if we get a reaction, we need to see if Jennifer is even the slightest bit interested in meeting up, and then comes the easy part, how the hell do we introduce you into this whole crazy mixed up plan to introduce one of the most famous, beautiful women in the world to you?"* Described

George while looking Chris up and down from head to foot with a large portion of doubt in his voice and eyes.

"This isn't going to work, is it?" Asked Chris.

"Probably not, but obviously, we were bought together for a reason and maybe in the weirdest of weird, we might just pull it off."

"You think." Asked Chris with a, now huge amount of doubt in his voice.

"No." Replied George.

Chapter Twenty-One

"Hello and good evening, everybody, what a show I have for you tonight? I have one of the biggest stars on the planet and someone who I like to call a friend. And I have some awesome news for you all, that will blow your minds. My name is James Cordon, and this is The Late Show, so let's get started. Please welcome my first guest, I love this man, he is an icon in the music industry and he is here tonight to talk to me about something very special. Please put your hands together for one of the biggest names on the planet, I can't believe he's on my show, Mr George Michael!"

With the intro of Freedom 90, booming into the studio, George stepped out onto the stage and made his way over to James, while nervously looking out into the audience with his cheeky smile and giving a wave. The audience were clapping and screaming as he made his way over to James and George couldn't help but notice the women were making more noise than the guys. "Maybe Chris was right about women still fancying him? Maybe Chris was right? Maybe they might just pull this crazy idea off?" Thought George to himself as he got to James.

James had made his way to the centre of the stage to meet George half way.

"*Hi George.*" Greeted James. "*I can't believe you're here.*"

"*Hi James, it's always good to see you.*" Replied George.

"Ladies and Gentlemen, Mr George Michael!" Announced James as the two of them stood in the centre of the stage soaking up the applause, before making their way to their seats.

"George George George, I can't believe you're here, it's fantastic to see you, you know I'm a huge fan of yours." Began James

"Hahaha thank you James, it's great to be here, I always tune into the show when I'm in the States" Replied George. *"You're looking very well."*

"Thank you, George, you're looking pretty damn fine yourself." Returned James. *"So, it's been a while since we've heard from you George, what have you been up to?"*

"Ummmmm I've been keeping busy, a little bit of rediscovery, a bit of self-reflection."

"What does that mean, George? You have things pretty good, don't you?"

"I can't deny it James, I have had a very privileged career, and I have been blessed with some of the greatest fans in the world." With that comment, the audience erupted into screams and applause.

"I guess that's because you keep on giving, George and you always show your appreciation for your fans."

"Of course, James, I love my fans, some of them have been with me from Wham, and it's amazing that the younger generations are finding my music and they seem to like it too." Another huge eruption from the audience and with that George stood up and gave them a courteous bow to acknowledge them.

"You sound surprised that the younger generation like your music? Personally, I think your music is timeless so it would be a travesty if generation Z didn't like you."

"*Thank you, James, flattery will get you everywhere.*" Laughed George.

"*You've just completed a tour and the new album is classic, George Michael with a real upbeat sound, almost going back to a Wham feel, was that what you were trying to achieve?*"

"*Ummmm, yeah, it kind of happened accidentally, but I love the result, it rekindled a bit of my youthful days, and I think that's what has resonated with the younger listeners.*"

"*Is it true, George, that Andrew was involved in the new album?*"

"*Hahaha, you've done your research well, James.*"

"*Of course, George, I'm a fan and I love the Wham days.*" Replied James.

"*Andrew was, and is involved in this album. He's amazing and I love working with Andrew, and he didn't need much convincing to get involved. He had some great ideas and he brought the Wham feel back to the sound.*"

"*You've been spending a lot of time in Cornwall recently, George, is there a particular reason for that?*"

"*Oh My God! James, have you been stalking me?*" Laughed George.

"*Yes George, I have your house and car bugged, and follow you everywhere.*" Laughed James.

"*Is there something interesting taking you down there?*"

"*Hmmmm, Ahhhhhhh.*" George sighed in a shy way. "*I have met someone from Cornwall who has played an important part in my life recently and has shown me something different.*"

"*Have you found love again, George? You certainly deserve too.*"

"Haha, I actually find myself in a very strange position, and that single question James, has actually just made so much sense. Up until you asking that question James, I couldn't understand something I was told at the beginning of this year, but it has literally just made perfect sense".

"That's very cryptic, no, George?" Asked James.

"It wouldn't make sense if I told you, and I'm not even going to try and explain it, but the penny has just dropped."

"So, have you found a new love then, George?" Tried James again.

George took a moment, and in a flash, all the conversations with Chris raced through his mind. What Chris had shared about his feelings for George suddenly made perfect sense. Finally, George grasped with crystal-clear clarity how Chris felt about him—a moment that would stay etched in his memory.

George snapped out of his trance like state. He had only paused for a few seconds but it felt like a lifetime. The audience and James only saw George pause for a few seconds, while George felt like he had checked out for hours. *"It's impossible to explain James, but I have met someone, yes, and he is amazing, but not in a way that I could possibly explain."*

"Wow, that sounds amazing, he's a lucky guy."

"Ummmmm, actually James, I'm the lucky one." Replied George, who had momentarily lost his train of thought. James unknowingly had opened George up to what had been happening over the last few months.

"Wow I feel like I've stumbled upon a headline, George!" Exclaimed James.

"*Hahahahaaha, maybe you have, but probably not the one you were expecting.*" Replied George.

"*So how does it feel to be back in love? Has it bought new light into your world?*" Interrogated James.

There was another long pause from George as he realised this was the moment for him to sow the seed to Jennifer. Maybe she watched the show? Jennifer would almost definitely have someone who knows her well watching and they would get in touch with her.

George used his famous, shy pause tactic to buy himself some time. "*Well, it's tough when you fancy the pants off one of the most famous women in the world, and you haven't got a clue how to tell her.*" Replied George.

"*Woah woah woah George, back up a bit. Woman? You're in love with a woman, my god, have I stumbled upon something?*" Questioned a surprised James.

"*Arrrrrrrgh. Yes James, you heard me right, I am totally smitten with an extremely beautiful and talented and hilarious girl, who I can't get out of my mind.*" Replied George.

"*You say she's one of the most famous women in the world, I guess that means I, we, must have heard of her, George?*"

"*Ummmm yes, you most definitely have heard of her, you've probably interviewed her at some point.*"

"*Ohhh my god George! What's going on, I can't believe you telling me this, I certainly had no idea this was going to come up. George, you can't leave me, and the audience hanging, you have to tell us who she is, does she know?*" Asked a now very excited James.

There was another long pause from George, then James interrupted.

"We're going to go for a break, we'll be right back and I have a feeling you will definitely want to join us for what I think, is going to be an absolute bombshell announcement from George."

Intermission-

The floor director frantically tried to grab James and George's attention, signalling that the adverts were concluding. The audience buzzed with speculation about the mystery woman George was about to reveal. No one could fathom that George Michael was on the brink of professing his love on such a global stage. News of this revelation was likely spreading worldwide at an astonishing speed. This moment carried more weight than George's outing in Beverly Hills. The studio atmosphere was not just electric; it was nuclear. Who the mystery woman was and whether she had any inkling of what was about to unfold remained a gripping question, adding an extra layer of suspense to the already charged atmosphere.

The floor manager was now almost wetting himself trying to get their attention. James was looking directly at George.

"Are you seriously going to drop a bombshell on my show, George?" Asked James.

"This could be quite big." Giggled George nervously.

"Go for it" whispered Chris, who was obviously on the same stage but not visible to anyone else.

"Ohhhhhh Myyyyyy Goddddd!" Proclaimed James. *"I'm going to wet myself."*

"Me too." Said George.

"*Me too.*" Said Chris.

The floor manager raised his hand and did the silent countdown before going back on air.

"*Welcome back!*" Announced James. "*Before the break we were just about to hear something massive from my very special guest, George Michael.*"

"*Oh my god!*" Whispered George. "*What am I doing here????*"

"George" Long pause from James, "George, you were just about to tell us something quite extraordinary. Is it fair to say that George"?

"*Ummmmm, yes, I think it's fair to say that, James.*" Replied George.

"*Oh my god I can't wait to hear what, who, it is you're about to tell us.*" Gulped James.

For George, time had almost stood still. The weight of impending deception hung heavy as he prepared to broadcast a colossal lie to the world for a guy, he'd only known a few months. The prospect of putting himself in an excruciatingly awkward position for this confused and mixed-up man loomed large. This seemed like a potentially ridiculous mistake, one that could cast a long shadow over him indefinitely. Yet, the thought of living without this eccentric individual felt equally unfathomable, feeling both nervous and kind of stuck with this quirky guy..

George laughed nervously as the time had come to set in motion the crazy plan concocted by Chris and himself. A plan that had such a small chance of succeeding, he couldn't believe he was actually going to go through with it.

"Well for a very long time now, I've had a crush on this girl, and I haven't been able to get her out of my mind, she's always there, she's impossible to avoid and, well, I guess I would be fooling myself if I didn't see if there was any possible chance of my feelings being reciprocated."

"George!!! Who is it?" Screamed James.

"This is so difficult James, I feel like a school kid in the playground, trying to ask the girl he fancies to go out with him." Replied George.

"We've all been there George, I bet even you have been there once?"

"A long time ago, James." Laughed a now very nervous George.

"George! You can't keep me, the audience, and the people at home in suspense any longer, the show isn't long enough!" Pleaded James.

"Is there another ad break due yet?" Asked George.

"No George, there isn't, you're going to have to tell us." Laughed James, knowing full well he was sitting on, not just TV gold, but career gold, this was going to be massive.

"Come on George, don't be nervous, she probably isn't watching, well she might be?" Laughed James, leaning across his desk getting as close as possible to George for when he'll spill the news.

"Oh, thanks James, that makes me feel so much better." George's voice was now full of nerves. In fact, George couldn't remember ever feeling this nervous, ever.

"George, you're amongst friends, we won't tell anyone, will we?" Jested James looking out at the audience, and the audience responded with a "NO!!!! "

"*Hahahahhaha very funny, Jennifer Aniston.*" Replied George.

The studio remained enveloped in a profound silence, a shared astonishment that connected every person present. James, with his usual charismatic demeanor, sat next to George, both of them rendered speechless by the unexpected turn of events. The camera man, floor manager, and crew in the sound booth, usually adept at navigating the chaos of live television, now wore expressions of genuine surprise.

The audience, both in the screen illuminating studio and those watching from the comfort of their homes, sat frozen in their seats, faces etched with disbelief. Jennifer Aniston's phone, usually an unassuming accessory, suddenly became a beacon of activity, its screen illuminating the studio with a flurry of notifications. As George surveyed the stunned faces around him, it became clear that this was more than a fleeting moment of surprise; it was a collective pause, an unspoken question hanging in the air, waiting for someone to break the silence and unravel the mystery that had left everyone in a state of awe. "*George?*" Gasped James "*Say that again, I'm not* shaw *I heard that?*"

George paused briefly, "*Jennifer Aniston.*"

"*Uhhh Uhh Uhhh Jennifer Aniston?*" Repeated James.

George looked out into the stunned audience, hoping to get a reaction from them, hoping to see if it was safe to carry on with this crazy cause of his now silent, new friend, Chris. Why wasn't Chris in his head encouraging him, applauding him, giving him the thumbs up, where was Chris right now?

"*Yep!*" Grinned George.

With that, the audience erupted into screams and applause. The girls in the audience were in tears thinking that George Michael was a straight man again. Then one by one each member of the audience began to stand up and give George a standing ovation. James and George looked at each other in amazement at what was going on in the studio. The news went out around the world that one of music's most eligible bachelors was available again. News stations started reporting it almost instantly and newspapers scrapped their front pages to replace them with the news that George Michael was in love with Jennifer Aniston. What had he done? Why did he let Chris talk him into this madness?

The phone in the producer's office started to ring and over the noise in the studio he picked it up and answered it.

The voice at the other end said *"Hi, I've got Jennifer Aniston on the line, shall I put her through?"*

"Umm oh my god, yes put her through, yes I'll speak to her, yes yes put her through."

"Hello?" He softly enquired.

"Oh hi, it's me Jennifer, is George serious or is this a prank set up between James and George?" Asked Jennifer.

"Hello Jennifer. Umm I'm as shocked as you, by George's announcement, we had no idea that he was going to do that, we were completely unprepared for the news."

"Oh, my godd, George Michael fancies me, that's crazy, I can't believe it, that's so funny, George Michael fancies me, I can't stop giggling, George Michael fancies me, that's crazy I can't believe it!"

"You can't believe in a good way or a bad way Jennifer?"

"Hahahahhaha in a good way! George Michael bloody fancies me, that's hilarious." Replied Jennifer. *"Can you put me through to the studio? I want to talk to George."*

"Umm let me see what I can do, give me a second, Jennifer."

With that the producer went into overdrive, getting Jennifer put through to George in the studio.

"Let James know we have Jennifer on the phone, and she wants to talk to George."

On the studio floor, the message came through James's earpiece to tell him that Jennifer was on the phone and wanted to talk to George.

"Please, please people calm down, calm down! I need to speak to George." Shouted James.

George was still looking completely stunned by the reaction and trying not to laugh. He was looking directly into the audience and seeing the love come back like a wave, the atmosphere was electric.

"Thank you, thank you" grinned George.

"George! George!" Shouted James over the audience. *"I've Jennifer on the line and she wants to talk to you!"*

The audience went silent, there were gasps of surprise and you could hear. "Jennifer's on the phone" whispered amongst them all.

"No way?" Laughed George. *"She wants to talk to me?"*

"Yes George, Jennifer is on the phone and she wants to talk to you." Explained James.

"Holy crap, that didn't take long!" Laughed George very nervously.

"Shall I put her through, George?" Asked James.

"*It would be rude not to*" giggled George.

James put his finger to his ear and quietly said, "Put Jennifer through."

"*Putting her through*". Came the reply.

"Hi Jennifer," said a very nervous James.

"*Hi James, hello George.*" Came the voice of Jennifer Aniston.

"*Hi Jen*" replied James and George at the same time.

"*So, I heard someone over there, fancies me, George?*" Giggled Jennifer

"*Hahaha, Umm, yeah, I think that's safe to say*" returned George as he looked nervously out at the audience then straight down the camera.

"*Oh my god!!!*" Screamed Jennifer down the phone. "*Seriously George?*" "*I can't believe it; this is a joke? It must be a joke?*"

"*Uhhhh no Jen, I was being real*" replied George.

"AAAAAAAAAAAAAAHHHHHHHHHHHHHHHH"! Came the scream down the phone. "*I'm so sorry, I don't believe this is happening, George Michael fancies me, CRAZZZZZZZYYYY!*" Screamed Jennifer.

James looked at George, George looked at James then the audience, then the audience erupted again as they listened to Jennifer Aniston get so excited over the phone. George grinned at the audience then piped up. "*That was a pretty positive response.*" The audience screamed with delight.

A very excited Jennifer Aniston came back on the line. "*So, George? I'm not sure this is the best place to have our first date. Maybe we should meet up somewhere less public?*"

"*That sounds like a good idea, this is a little bit public!*" Giggled George.

"A little bit public George? I think the whole world is listening, this is so bizarre, I can't believe it's happening. Listen, give me a call when you've finished with James, I'm sure he will have lots of questions for you now." Laughed Jennifer.

"I certainly will Jen, James will have to hurry up with his questions." Laughed George.

"George, you're not going anywhere, I have so many questions!" Announced James.

"Hands off." Interrupted Jennifer. *"He's mine now, don't you dare hold him up."*

George looked out into the audience in total surprise and they erupted into more applause.

"I think she likes me?" Proposed George.

"Don't be long George, I'm waiting and you don't want to keep me waiting" giggled Jennifer down the phone line.

George looked out to the audience again, his mouth hanging wide open, and right on cue, they erupted into applause and screams of delight. The crazy plan by George's idiotic new friend was now in full flow. Amidst the excitement, Jennifer appeared genuinely thrilled by George's announcement. Yet, a gnawing worry lingered – how on earth would they not only introduce Jennifer to Chris, but more dauntingly, convince her to choose a reclusive George Michael wannabe lottery winner over the charismatic, super-talented mega-star George Michael? George found himself entangled in a web of uncertainty, questioning the choices he had made and bracing for the unpredictable unravelling ahead.

Chapter Twenty-Two

The time had come, it was 1:30 and Jennifer pulled up at Marix Tex Mex Café, in West Hollywood, Jennifer loves Mexican food and knew she could get one hell of a Margarita there to calm her nerves. As she walked in, she could feel her hands shaking a little bit and a bit of a nervous rumble in her stomach. As she breezed through the door, she was met by a member of the staff. They knew Jennifer there, and were always very relaxed to see her, as she was always lovely to the team, and they were able to treat her with a level of normality, which she really enjoyed.

"Afternoon Ms Aniston, my name is Andy, can I take you to your table." Announced the welcome staff.

"Hello Andy, that would be lovely, thank you." Replied Jennifer whilst desperately scoping the restaurant, looking for someone she might know and most importantly, George Michael.

Andy gracefully led Jennifer through the restaurant, and as their gazes met, guests looked up with smiles, silently mouthing greetings to the beloved actress. Graciously, Jennifer reciprocated, her face lighting up with a beaming smile. However, amidst the bustle, she couldn't help but notice the absence of George. Wondering if he was running late or had momentarily stepped away, she kept her expectations in check. Yet, her attention was drawn to another man lurking near a table, his striking resemblance to George impossible to ignore. From his dress sense to his mannerisms, everything about him seemed intentionally reminiscent of the iconic singer. A mixture of curiosity and melancholy washed over Jennifer, longing for her dear friend's presence and hoping he would soon join their gathering.

Andy stopped right next to the George Michael lookalike, and turned to Jennifer. *"Your table Ms Aniston, I'll pop back in a minute."*

"Oh okay." Paused Jennifer. *"Andy, are you sure this is the right table?"* Whispered Jennifer.

"Sorry Jennifer, can I introduce myself? I'm Chris, George had to rush off to Europe. He has this terrible back condition that he's had for years and he won't let anyone other than his Osteopath in Austria go near him when it's playing up. He didn't want to let you down, so he asked me to entertain over lunch rather than have you turn up and nobody was here." Blurted Chris.

George was there however, he stood right next to Chris, looking straight at Jennifer and even as a gay man thinking to himself how gorgeous she is and how he totally understood why Chris fancied her. George was actually thinking that he could get Chris to go to the loo and take over his body so George could enjoy lunch with the little beauty. Jennifer is shorter in real life, but undoubtably, still incredibly gorgeous and incredibly sexy. George had to pinch himself, he was actually starting to fancy Jennifer himself, this lady had some mysterious powers that he wasn't able to defend himself against.

"She's bloody stunning mate." Whispered George in Chris's ear.

"Ohhh okay, that's weird, I wasn't expecting that, but I guess he's made an effort to not let me down, even though you're not George." Replied a very confused Jennifer.

"I'm right here Jen." Whispered George, wishing it was him stood in front of her.

"I totally get that, you must be wondering what's going on, it must be very peculiar, the whole announcement on James's show, and now rushed of off to Austria when he should be here having lunch with you. Let me get you a drink, while you decide if you want to stay or not." Replied Chris.

"I have never had this happen, ever, it's very strange. If it wasn't George Michael, I would definitely done an about turn and walked straight out the door. They do make a really good Margarita here, and I've been thinking about what I was going to have to eat all morning." Reluctantly replied Jennifer.

"Please stay Jen, I just want to watch you for as long as possible." Came another announcement from the invisible George.

Andy had been prewarned of George's none appearance and had been hovering to see how Jennifer would react to the news, just in case he had to escort her back through the restaurant which would have been highly embarrassing for both of them.

"Andy, can Jennifer have one of your amazing Margaritas? And for me, a bottle of larger please." Asked Chris.

"You not joining me for a Margarita, they do make a bloody good one here!" Intervened Jennifer.

"Oh umm, I suppose I could, I don't think I've ever had a Margarita." Replied Chris.

"Trust me, they're soooooo good here, you'll love it." Pushed Jennifer.

"Andy, make that two of your amazing Margaritas" Stated Chris, then turned to Jennifer. *"Shall we take a seat?"*

"Well, I suppose we should now, as we've got some drinks coming." Jennifer replied with a bit of a grin on her face.

George had already sat down, and was just staring straight, at Jennifer. Although Jennifer couldn't see George, Chris could, and it was quite off, watching George Michael swooning at Jennifer. Chris wanted to give him a nudge but knew that would be a little bit suspicious.

"So how do you know George?" Asked Jen, somewhat embarrassed.

"Oh, we've known each other for a while, we're very close now, he's an amazing chap." Replied Chris

Jennifer let out a little giggle. *"That's very English."*

Chris giggled, "which part?"

Jen giggled again and said, *"chap."*

"Oh yes, that is a bit English, isn't it?" Giggled Chris. *"So, what would the LA version of that be?"*

"Oh, um, I'm not sure, man, guy, or I guess boy?"

"I'll try and remember those." Replied Chris.

"No no no, I like the whole English thing, don't stop being that chap." Giggled Jennifer.

Right at that moment, Andy returned with their margaritas. *"One margarita for you Ms Aniston, and one margarita for you, sir."*

"Oh god I've been looking forward to this." Came Jennifer grasping the glass, taking a long, but slow sip. *"Andy, bring me another when you can, these are sooo good."*

Chris took a sip from his and Jen was right, it was really good. *"Make that two Andy."*

"No problem, guys, enjoy."

"At least he didn't say chaps." Giggled Chris.

Jennifer nearly spat her drink out, at Chris's comment and then from behind Chris, came something he wasn't expecting.

"OHHHHHHHH!!   Haaaaaahaaaaaahaaaaa!   It's Aniston! Darling look, it's Jen Jen."

Chris sensed someone approaching, recognizing the voice without turning. The approaching footsteps created a symphony, and George's face confirmed Chris's intuition about the familiar friend's arrival. In that shared moment of silent recognition, unspoken camaraderie filled the air.

"Aniston, how you doing, George nice to meet you…………. You're not George? Jen you've been ripped off, this isn't the real George Michael! Jen, I hate to break the news to you but George has brown eyes, this isn't George!"

The actual George was in hysterics, while Chris was looking slightly embarrassed.

"Adam, I know it's not George." Yes Adam, Adam and Jackie Sandler. *"George had an accident at his hotel and triggered a back injury. He will only see his Osteopath, who's in Austria, so that's where George is heading."* Explained Jennifer.

"Ha ha ha ha ha! That's the best excuse I've ever heard! Hey Jackie, next time I don't fancy going out for dinner, don't be surprised if I jump on plane to Austria." Laughed Adam.

"Don't you dare, you're sooooo bad darling." Replied Jackie.

"So, who's this chap then?" Enquired Adam.

Jennifer, Chris and George, all burst out in laughter, both Chris and Jennifer spitting their margaritas back into their glasses.

"*Whaaaaaaaat? What's so funny.*" Asked, a now confused Adam.

"*Oh, don't worry, private joke.*" Replied Jennifer.

"*You guys have private jokes already?*" Enquired Adam.

Jennifer looked across at Chris and gave him a wink.

Adam reached out his fist for a fist thump from Chris. "*Don't leave me hanging!*" He laughed.

"*Oh right, sorry.*" Replied Chris, clenching a fist and bumping with Adams. "*Do we explode fists now?*" Asked Chris.

"*Noooooooo!*" Laughed Adam. "*It's a fist bump, there's no exploding.*"

Jennifer and Jackie rolled their eyes as the boys bonded, then Jen interjected. "*This is Chris, he's a friend of George and it was George who asked Chris to meet me today so I don't have a day wasted*".

"*Ohhhh okay, that's different, that must be an English thing.*" Replied Adam.

"*Adam, that's really sweet, makes George seem human.*" Asserted Jackie.

"*George is a mega star, he's not human.*" Insisted Adam.

"*I am human actually.*" Replied the invisible and silent George.

Once again Jennifer and Jackie rolled their eyes at each other.

"*So, Chris, you better look after my Jen Jen, I'll be watching you buddy!*" Laughed Adam.

"Don't worry she's in very safe hands, George wouldn't have asked me to come if he thought I was going to be an idiot." Replied Chris.

"Ahhhhhh that's cool." Chuckled Adam.

"Come on darling, leave Jen and Chris to their lunch, you can interrogate Jen later." Suggested Jackie.

"I'm sure Chris will be a complete gentleman Adam, I'm in safe hands." Replied Jennifer.

"Okay okay." Replied Adam.

Jackie grabbed Adam's hand and turned to walk away.

"Hey why don't you kids come over to ours tomorrow, we can have a BBQ, is that okay Jacks, can we have them over tomorrow?" Enquired Adam.

"Ummmm yes, we can do that!" Replied Jackie with a smile.

"Ohhhhh okay, ummm yes, I suppose we could, I don't have anything planned." Replied a slightly shocked Jennifer. *"Do you have anything planned tomorrow, Chris?"*

"Ummmm nope, I guess I could go to Adam Sandlers for a BBQ." Laughed Chris.

"Well, then it looks like we'll be coming to yours tomorrow." Said Jennifer.

"Yeaaaahhhhhh." Laughed Adam

"Yeahhhhh!" Laughed George.

"Yeahhhhhhh". Sighed Jennifer.

"Hey Chris man, Jen will bring you over, won't you Jen Jen?" Insisted Adam.

"Ummmm yes, that's fine, I suppose." Replied Jen.

"Cool, see you both tomorrow." Laughed Adam. *"Come on Jackie, I'm hungry as shit."*

"Ohhhh Adam." Sighed Jennifer.

Chris glanced at George, who sat there, utterly gobsmacked by what had just transpired. This peculiar man, thrust upon him, not only shared lunch with Jennifer Aniston, his other love, for which George was entirely grateful. Now, an invitation to the Sandlers' BBQ awaited him, a testament to the unexpected joys George had brought into his life.

The rest of lunch flowed smoothly, an unexpected reprieve after the intrusion by Adam and Jackie. Chris, never one for chat-up lines, simply enjoyed engaging in conversation. Jennifer proved to be incredibly easy to talk to, and surprisingly was eager to learn about him as he was about her.

As time passed, Chris forgot the grandeur surrounding their meal. He no longer noticed the other diners, their attention solely focused on Jennifer Aniston sitting across from a totally unknown man who vaguely resembled George Michael. They had no idea that the real George Michael had recently asked her out on national television. Yet, wonderfully surprising to Chris, Jennifer genuinely enjoyed his company. There were no ulterior motives, no hidden agendas. He was simply himself, albeit with a tinge of effort to mimic George Michael's appearance.

George observed in silence, relishing in the blossoming friendship between Chris and Jennifer. It reminded him of how quickly he had become a part of Chris's world, a mysterious gate crasher who turned into a trusted friend. George mused at how unexpected it all was. Surely, Chris had never imagined that his life would take such a turn when he went to bed on Christmas Eve just a few months prior. Now, he found himself best friends with George Michael, sharing lunch with Jennifer Aniston, and even securing an invitation to a BBQ hosted by Adam and Jackie Sandlers. Chris's formerly reclusive existence had been completely upended. Remarkably, he navigated this new world with ease, seamlessly fitting in with his newfound famous friends.

Lunch reluctantly came to an end, Jen had enjoyed herself, Chris had definitely enjoyed himself, and George was shocked to the core that the two of them had hit it off so quickly.

Chris caught Andy, the waiter's attention. "*Hi Andy can I get the bill please?*"

"*Of course, was everything okay for you guys?*" He replied.

"*Yes, fantastic.*" Replied Chris.

"*Lovely, thank you.*" Added Jennifer.

Chris paid the bill like the gentleman that he is, but quietly thinking to himself, that there weren't many men in the world who could say they had taken Jennifer Aniston out for lunch. Let alone by the fact that George Michael was sat next to him during that lunch and Adam and Jackie Sandler had invited them all of them to a BBQ the next day, not that they knew they had invited George to join them, but he wasn't going to miss that for the world.

As Chris, Jennifer and George headed for the door Adam piped up. "*See you both tomorrow!*"

"*See you tomorrow.*" Replied Jennifer. "*What time?*"

"*I'll get my assistant to let you know.*" Replied Adam.

"*What time, Jackie?*" Sighed Jennifer.

"*I'll give you a buzz darling but whenever you're ready.*" Giggled Jackie.

Adam laughed his head off and Jennifer and Chris gave a polite wave as they left the restaurant.

"Thank you, Chris, thank you for a lovely lunch I really enjoyed myself, even with Adam's impromptu arrival, I'm sorry about him."

"It was all my pleasure Jennifer, I really enjoyed myself too, and Adam was fine, it was great to meet him, and we got invited for a BBQ too, we are still going, aren't we?" Replied Chris.

"Oh yes definitely, that's if you still want to go?" Replied Jennifer.

"I can't wait." Replied Chris trying to hide his excitement.

"Excellent, I'm really looking forward to it." Retorted Jennifer. *"Hey, how are you getting back to your hotel?"*

"Oh, I was going to get a cab." Replied Chris.

"Don't be daft, I've got a car waiting, I'll take you back." Offered Jennifer.

"Wow that would be amazing." Replied a shocked Chris, just as George poked him in the ribs as if to say go buddy.

The hotel wasn't far from the restaurant and they chatted all the way there.

"Thank you for the ride, that was great." Said Chris as they arrived.

"No problem, I know where to come tomorrow now. I'll pick you up about 1.00 O'clock if that's okay?" Asked Jennifer.

"That will be brilliant, I can't believe Jennifer Aniston will be coming to pick me up to go to a BBQ at Adam Sandlers." Laughed Chris.

"*I know right.*" Teased Jennifer. "*Bring a change of clothes, they have a pool so we'll probably end up in there at some point.*" Giggled Jennifer.

"*Brilliant, thanks for the heads up. Should I take something? What do they like to drink?*" Questioned Chris.

"*Don't worry I'll pick something up.*" Replied Jennifer.

"*Only if you're sure?*" Replied Chris.

"*It's fine.*" Said Jennifer.

With that, Chris opened the door and went to get out of the car.

"*Thank you for putting up with me for lunch.*" Uttered Chris shyly.

"*I really enjoyed myself, thank you, I'm really looking forward to tomorrow.*" Responded Jennifer.

"*Me too.*" Replied Chris. "*See you tomorrow, Jen.*"

"*See you tomorrow, 1,00 o'clock.*" Retaliated Jennifer. Then to Chris's total surprise, Jennifer leaned across and gave him a kiss on his cheek. George's mouth dropped to the floor in surprise. His new friend's plan seems to have worked.

Chapter Twenty-Three

The following day, Chris and George made sure they were outside the hotel's reception in good time, so that Jennifer wasn't left waiting for them. Being on time was one of Chris's things, when he was in sales, he always took great pride in turning up at appointments bang on time, in fact he often challenged himself to plan his journey down to the minute.

Chris, a stickler for punctuality, stumbled into his ideal sales job when a chance meeting with Andrew, the Sales Director, turned an unplanned interview into an instant job offer. This unexpected twist left the rival company, also eyeing Chris, in disbelief.

The two companies argued over who was going to get Chris and then after Andrew's suggestion, they ask Chris who he would prefer to work and Chris chose the refrigeration company. It was a fantastic company and after a difficult first year and after a heart to heart with Andrew, just before Christmas break, when Chris actually thought he was going to be given his marching orders, Andrew reasserted his belief in Chris and that was the beginning of an excellent journey where Chris went from strength to strength becoming their top salesman and earning the privileged accolade of employee of the year.

Chris was on his way to work one very memorable morning when he got a call from one of his workmates,

Henry, with some unbelievable news. Chris lived in High Wycombe and his office was in Kent, so he had to negotiate the formidable and notorious M25 motorway. As usual Chris was in the car singing along, to a bit George Michael to wake him up and make the journey more enjoyable when the phone rang.

"Henry. What's up?" As Chris answered the phone.

"Morning, where are you?" Asked Henry.

"M25, just coming up to Gatwick junction, why?" Asked Chris.

"Are you heading to the office today?" Replied Henry.

"That was the plan, why?" Returned Chris.

"Have you heard the news today?" Asked Henry.

"No, I've got a CD on, why?" Replied Chris.

"Let me guess, George Michael?" Laughed Henry.

"Yeah, why?" Asked Chris.

"It's coming up to 7.30, listen to the news and phone me back." Insisted Henry.

"Okay." Replied Chris and without answering, Henry hung up.

In a sudden twist, Chris switched from CD to the radio, catching breaking news that George Michael had been arrested in Beverly Hills. The shocking details revealed a lewd act in a public toilet with an undercover cop, leaving Chris bewildered. Wondering why George, who he believed wasn't gay, would engage in such an incident, Chris couldn't fathom the motivation. Then it dawned on him— the attention he received while emulating George's style wasn't merely admiration. With a French crop hairstyle and a hint of George's essence in his work suit, Chris found himself unwittingly attracting the same attention George faced, a realization that added a complex layer to his own journey of self-expression.

The phone rang, it was Henry, again. "*Well?*" Came the first question.

"*I can't believe it, George isn't gay!*" Answered Chris.

"*I think he is, mate.*" Replied Henry. "*Have you still got that picture above your fireplace?*"

Chris had taken a picture from his programme from the Faith tour, and had it framed and it held pride of place in the centre of his wall, above his fireplace.

"*Turn around, I'll meet you at the house, I'm not far behind you.*" Insisted Henry.

Henry lived in Kent and was coming from the opposite direction, so it wouldn't have taken long for him to catch up with Chris and quite literally after Chris arriving back at the house, Henry pulled in behind him, another few miles of motorway and Henry would probably have caught up.

"*Right, let's get that picture down.*" Insisted Henry.

"*What?*" Questioned Chris.

"*You can't have a picture of a gay man on your wall mate.*" Pushed Henry.

"*What, what do you mean?*" Enquired Chris.

"*George has to come down mate.*" Insisted Henry.

"*Oh, right.*" Replied Chris.

It had taken about an hour from turning the car around and pointing it in the right direction to getting back to the house, and the radio had been full of the news about George. Chris had listened intently to what was going on and was trying to wrap his head around it. He didn't feel any less for George, how could he? They were so tightly entwined, it would have taken something much worse than this to split them up. Afterall, George had been trapped by a cop so it probably wasn't true anyway.

"Take it out of the frame, let's take it into the garden and burn it." Urged Henry.

"I'm not sure I want to do that H." Replied Chris.

"Sorry mate, but it's got to be done." Insisted Henry.

The two of them went into the back garden, lit up a cigarette and Henry attempted to set alight to the picture. He tried and tried, but for some reason it wouldn't burn. Maybe it was something to do with the ink, or maybe the paper had been coated in something, but it most definitely, and to Chris's relief, wasn't going to catch fire.

"Well, we tried." Said a somewhat disappointed Henry. *"I can't believe I've driven all this way and it won't bloody burn!"*

"Oh well." Replied a relived Chris. *"What now?"*

"I suppose we'll have to head over to the office." Replied Henry.

"I was nearly there when you insisted, I turned around and went back home." Retorted Chris

"Hmmmmm. Hey you know what we could do?" Came Henry.

"What's that?" Asked Chris.

"Let's go to Thorpe Park, I'm not in the mood to go to the office now." Stated Henry.

"Are you having a laugh?" Replied Chris.

"Come on, you won't be to concentrate now. Knowing George is gay, let's go and have some fun?" Retorted Henry.

"I suppose so. I don't think I would get much done today." Replied Chris

The boys, donned in business suits, jumped into their separate cars and headed to Thorpe Park for rollercoaster fun. Despite their attire, they looked entirely in place. However, for Chris, his thoughts were solely on George. Upon entering his car, he swiftly switched from radio to CD, immersing himself in George Michael's tunes. Along the journey, Henry called, finding it amusing that Chris was still tuned into George. Little did anyone, including Henry, fathom the profound bond Chris harboured for George.

Chapter Twenty-Four

Back at the hotel, George and Chris stood patiently waiting for Jennifer to arrive and just a few minutes after 1.00 o'clock, a silver Porsche pulled into the driveway of the hotel, and pulled up next to Chris.

"I'm not late, am I?" Shouted Jennifer, through the open window.

"Hi, no, not at all, bang on time." Laughed Chris.

"Oh good, I tried to get here on time." Replied Jennifer.

"I'm actually surprised you turned up at all." Replied Chris.

"Why? It's going to be fun. Adam and Jackie do an excellent BBQ; you're going to love it. Come on, jump in." Giggled Jennifer. *"Fasten your seat belt."*

"Oh my god is this going to be scary?" Asked Chris.

"Noooooo, I'm a brilliant driver." Laughed Jennifer.

"I used to be a driving instructor; you know." Laughed Chris.

"No way, seriously?" Screamed Jennifer.

"Seriously!" Laughed Chris.

"Hold on tight, Loverboy. I'll show you some real driving." With a huge grin on her face, Jennifer let loose down the hotel driveway, taking the briefest glance before

merging onto the highway with a squeal of the tyres as she lit up the rubber. *"Feeling safe?"* She laughed.

"I'll let you know in a minute." Replied a slightly shocked Chris.

"I love this car!" Squealed Jennifer as she roared down the road.

"It's a beautiful car." Replied Chris, holding on tight to the door handle.

After a few hundred yards, Jennifer lift off the gas pedal, and started to drive normally now, much to Chris's relief. It's not that he's a bad passenger, and he certainly wasn't going to offer driving advice to Jennifer Aniston on their second meeting. Let's face it, Chris wasn't meant to be her date, she was supposed to be out with George Michael, who unbeknown to Jennifer, had squeezed himself into the back seat, not in Chris's body, wasn't looking too worried, as he had no feelings so if Jennifer totalled the car, he wouldn't have felt a thing.

"I have to say, I'm liking your shorts, I would be surprised if you still have them on the way home, Adam is going to see them and want them, and he can be very persuasive." Giggled Jennifer.

"These are my Billabong specials, I love these, Adam will have to be a magician to get these off me." Replied Chris.

"Ohhhhh don't underestimate the Sandman, if he wants something, he won't give up, make sure they're done up well, in the pool." Teased Jennifer.

"Oh well, that wouldn't be embarrassing at all, would it? In a swimming pool with Jennifer Aniston and no boardies on." Laughed Chris.

"Ahhhhhhhhhhhh hhahhahahhhaaaa!" Shrieked Jennifer.

"You did ask to bring some swim shorts, just in case we ended up in the pool." Replied Chris.

"I'm pretty sure we'll end up in the pool, it's going to be hot today, it will be lovely to cool down, I hope you like my bikini, I wasn't sure which one to wear." Replied Jennifer.

"I'm sure you'll look amazing Jennifer, let's face it, you were gifted to have an everlasting bikini body." Giggled Chris, who was completely taken aback that Jennifer Aniston was he hoping he would approve her bikini. Of course, he was going to like her bikini, Jennifer Aniston in a bikini, what man in his right mind is going to disapprove of that? Even George was looking forward to seeing Jennifer in her bikini and was sat in the back, fanning himself with his hand.

"Christopher, please call me Jen, after all we're friends now, aren't we?" Returned Jennifer.

"I didn't want to assume anything; nobody likes cocky blokes." Replied Chris while George was behind him, sticking his finger down his throat having witnessed Chris's first and quite pathetic attempt to flatter Jennifer.

"Ohhhhh you're good, I'll have to keep an eye on you, it must be the English charm." Giggled Jennifer.

George couldn't believe Chris had got away with that one, clearly the English accent was appealing to Jennifer, Chris might actually pull this off, his chances were certainly looking up.

"Adam likes his beer, doesn't he?" Asked Chris.

"Yeah, he's partial to a beer or two, why?" Replied Jennifer.

"My flip flops have got bottle openers built into them." Announced Chris.

"No way, that's crazy, Adam will want those off you too. I hope you have another set of clothes in your backpack, or you'll be coming home naked." Laughed Jennifer.

George smacked his forehead, feigning a swoon. How could this quirky fellow, seemingly a George Michael imitator, pull off such absurdity? Was he oblivious to Jennifer Aniston, not just a millionaire but a hundred-millionaire? Meanwhile, Chris, substituting for George, lacked suave pickup lines but effortlessly engaged in genuine conversation. While he refrained from outshining George, in any genuine competition, Chris stood no chance against the charismatic George.

After spending a bit more time in the car, discussing about Adam and Jackie's meal and drink choices, their conversation resembled that of a seasoned couple, not two individuals who had coincidentally met the day before – a fact unbeknownst to Jennifer but clear to Chris, who knew the true story behind their encounter. As they approached a driveway, Jennifer stopped at a keypad, buzzing in with the press of a large silver button.

"That better be you Aniston, I'm hungry as shit." Came the response.

"Yes, it's us, can we come in?" Replied Jennifer.

"Come on up, is George with you?" Laughed Adam.

"No but Chris is, as well you know." Giggled Jennifer.

"Cmon up guys, I'll get some drinks going." And with that, the big black gates started to swing over and Jennifer made her way up the drive. As they got to the house, Jackie was waiting for them on the drive, waving like a mad woman.

"Hi guys, come on in, Adam is freaking out, wanting to get the food on," she sighed.

"Ohh God!" Replied Jen.

"I can't wait." Added Chris.

"Don't let him bully you Chris, he's very protective." Replied Jackie, putting her arm around Chris.

"It's George he needs to be questioning, I'm just keeping Jen company in his absence." Giggled Chris.

"Oh, don't be daft Christopher, I've enjoyed spending time with you, you're part of the gang now." Laughed Jennifer, as she took position on the other side of Chris, putting her arm around him.

As they walked through the magnificent Sandler household to the garden, Adam caught sight of the new boy wedged between the girls.

"OHHHHHHHH MY GOD! Look at you soaking it up!" Laughing his head off.

"Aren't I a lucky boy?" Giggled Chris.

"Don't get any ideas, Jackie is mine, do what you like with Aniston." Adam giggled.

"Thank you." Replied Jennifer sarcastically.

"Hope you're not one of those vegan nutters Chris, I've got a stack of good old American meat ready." Returned Adam.

"Definitely not, I love my meat." Laughed Chris.

"So does George, doesn't he?" Giggled Adam, giving Jen a friendly nudge and a wink.

"Ohh shut up, he's into me now, you're so rude." Replied Jennifer with a frown.

"Yeah yeah!" Giggled Adam. *"Maybe you should stick with Chris, at least he turns up."*

"If only he knew the truth." Whispered George in Chris's ear, slightly chuckling.

"Adam, don't embarrass him, or me for that matter." Retorted Jennifer defensively.

"I'm only kidding Jen Jen." Laughed Adam.

"I did warn you." Added Jackie.

"Oh Jackie, he's a nightmare." Laughed Jennifer.

"I know." Replied Jackie.

Adam laughed his head off and turned around to head over to his incredible outside kitchen. *"Chris what you drinking? And don't say spritzer. Jen Jen are you having a margarita?"*

"Ohhhh yes please, make it a cold one." Demanded Jennifer very excitedly.

"I'll take a beer, if you've got one." Replied Chris.

"Good man, straight out of the bottle?" Asked Adam.

"Perfect." Replied Chris, hoping to show off his flip flops with bottle openers.

"Don't you dare use your flip flops to open that bottle!" Urged George.

"I've got a bottle opener Adam." Giggled Chris.

"You didn't actually say that, did you?" Sighed George. *"I give up on you."*

Adam passed Chris a bottle of Budweiser, and Chris whipped one of his flips flops off and removed the cap.

"Oh man that's ridiculous, you've got bottle openers on your flip flops, I love it!" Gasped Adam

"I don't believe it." Sighed George *"You jammy sod!"* He added.

"I told you he would love them, I bet you don't leave with them." Giggled Jennifer.

"I suppose you'll want some of those now?" Asked Jackie.

"I have to get some of those, Jacs." Laughed Adam.

"Unbelievable!!!" Sighed George.

"I'll order you some Adam, what size are you?" Replied Chris.

"STOPPPPPPPPPP!!! " Sighed George.

"That would be awesome, let me see if yours fit." Asked Adam.

"Don't let him have them Chris, you'll never get them back!" Insisted Jennifer.

Too late, Chris had removed his flip flops and passed them over to Adam who slipped them on and started to walk around the patio.

"Ohhhhh my god these are so comfortable, they're like wearing trainers, Jacs, I have to have a pair of these, they're amazing!" Swooned Adam.

"They're bloody flip flops." Sighed George.

"Ooooo let me try them on!" Insisted Jackie. *"Oh god they're so bouncy, they're mental, do they do a girls' version?"*

"They do, but the girls' version has a secret compartment for a credit card." Laughed Chris.

"Jen you have to try these on!" Insisted Jackie.

"Ohhhh my, they are comfy, aren't they?" Indulged Jennifer.

"I can't believe you have-got away with your bloody flip flop fetish." Retorted an exasperated George.

This was Chris at his best, although everyone in the circle of friends were millionaires, Chris and George were actually the poor members of the party with only just over £100 million each, and yet he had impressed his new friends with a pair of £50 flip flops.

"I get a new pair every year, it's a must." Declared Chris.

"I don't blame you, wait till I show Spade, he'll love them". Insisted Adam. Spade being David Spade, good friend of Adam and fellow actor.

"I can't believe you've single-handedly created a new fashion trend in Hollywood with your friggin flip flops." Shrugged George. *"All we'll see on the red carpet from now on, is flip flops with bottle openers and credit card compartments."*

Chris was enjoying watching George get more and more bemused by something as basic as a pair of flip flops, especially as it was only Chris who could see and hear him get more frustrated by his idiotic friend.

The four of them soon moved on from the flip flops and started chatting more generally with Adam and Jackie quizzing Chris, with Jennifer standing by, and occasionally jumping in to defend him. Somehow, Chris was being targeted as Jennifer's date and Jennifer found herself defending him as he was her date and found herself feeling herself slightly drawn towards him. Chris was doing his best to stand his ground and not give away the grand plan that George and Chris had concocted. Although it was George who kept reminding Chris that Jennifer was expecting to be on a date with him and that Chris was only meant to be keeping her company.

Jennifer found herself constantly checking on him, ensuring he had a drink and Adam was behaving. She genuinely enjoyed Chris's company and, on this warm day, the four of them frequented the pool. During pool games, Jennifer always teamed up with Chris, and in their playful banter, they teased and tried to surprise each other, often ending up underwater. The close contact with Chris didn't seem to bother Jennifer; in fact, she relished it, and their joyous laughter echoed louder with each passing moment.

George, unable to join in with the antics, got as close to the action as possible, sat with his feet in the pool watching the goings on. This was one of the first times that he started miss having the physical ability to join in with the games. He was enjoying watching Jennifer and Chris starting to bond, after all, this was the plan that they had come up with. He was ever so happy for Chris, who he had also become very fond of, and was delighted that Jennifer seemed to enjoy his company. But he found himself wishing it was him, Jennifer was definitely great fun to be around. But there was a conflict, George had become very used to Chris's company, and a part of him was becoming worried that their friendship as short as it was, could actually be at risk.

"Could you excuse me, can I use your loo, Adam?" Asked Chris.

"You know where it is, help yourself." Replied Jackie.

"Thank you." Returned Chris climbing out of the pool. And surprisingly being followed by George.

"Looks like it's going well with you and Jen." Guessed George.

"I know, I'm so surprised how easy Jen is to get on with." Replied Chris.

"She is amazing." Replied George.

"You're not going to follow me into the loo, are you?" Asked Chris.

George Laughed. *"Don't worry I'll wait outside."*

"Are you okay George?" Asked Chris who just had picked up that George was feeling a bit left out.

"Yeah, I'm fine, I'm just glad that you and Jen are hitting it off." Replied George.

Chris and George had spent so much time in each other's company over the past few months, they had become incredibly synchronized to each other's feelings and Chris could tell George was not his usual sarcastic self. Chris started to think about how he could include George without letting the others know what he was up to. Chris wanted to show George how incredibly important he was, how vital, George was to Chris. He wanted to tell George that even if things went well with Jennifer, George would always be a massive part of his life, Chris had to prove to George that after over 30 years he wasn't suddenly going to fall out of love with George.

As George and Chris rejoined the others in the garden, they had all left the pool and were sat on the patio, on some very comfortable furniture, the sort of furniture that you wouldn't dare to leave outside in the UK. Chris looked at where everyone was sitting, and thankfully noticed that Jen had chosen to sit on one of the sofas, leaving plenty of room for Chris to join her, and there was still room for George to sit next him, although George opted to curl up in one of the huge chairs.

"Here he is!" Announced Adam. *"We thought you had flushed yourself down the toilet."*

"*Sorry, was I a long time?*" Giggled Chris. "*I was talking to myself.*"

"*That's the first sign of madness.*" Laughed Adam and George at exactly the same time.

"*So, I hear.*" Replied Chris.

"*The second is hairs on the palm of your hands.*" They both quipped then looking around to the reaction of the others. Jen and Jackie tried to discreetly take a look at their hands without making it too obvious. Chris knew where the joke was going so kept his hands firmly by his side.

"*The third sign is looking for them.*" They followed up with in perfect harmony, although apart from Chris the others thought it was just Adam.

"*Oh god*" gasped Jen knowing she had been caught out.

"*I hate you!*" Teased Jackie, then pretending to check her nails, knowing full well she had also been caught out.

"*I love that one, it works every time.*" Shrieked Adam.

Chris looked at George who was sat there very smug. "*I knew that.*" He announced grinning.

"*Chris, are you okay for a drink? I can see Jen is, she always has a drink.*" Giggled Adam.

"*Oh Adam.*" Retorted Jennifer.

"*I'll have a beer if that's okay?*" Replied Chris

"*You know where they are, help yourself buddy.*" Replied Adam who had clearly decided that he didn't want to get up.

"*Cool.*" Returned Chris "*Are you sure you're okay Jen?*"

"*I'm fine, thank you darling. Actually, top me up, why not.*" Giggled Jennifer.

"*There she goes!*" Shrieked Adam.

"*Oh god.*" Gasped Jennifer, nearly jumping out of her skin.

"How about you Jackie? Can I get you something while I'm up there?" Chris asked.

"*I'll have a glass of wine lovely.*" Jackie replied, handing Chris her glass.

"*How about you Adam?*" Asked Chris.

"*I'll have a beer and a flip flop buddy, please.*" Adam replied.

"*You know where they are, help yourself.*" Laughed Chris.

"*Ohhhhhhhhhh! Check him out.*" Laughed Adam.

Chris went off to the garden kitchen and put the drinks for his new friends together. Of course, the first person to be attended to, was Jennifer, followed by Jackie and then bringing over a bottle of beer for himself and Adam.

"*So, Chris what was the worst time you ever got drunk? Are you a secret drinker?*" Asked Adam.

"*Oh, I'm not sure, oh I did have one occasion where I misjudged it a little bit.*" Replied a thoughtful Chris.

"*Do tell?*" Asked Jennifer.

"*Oh god, it was years ago, I was still a teenager I think.*" Replied Chris.

"*Ahhhhh a novice drinker, they're always the best.*" Chipped in Adam. "*Spill the beans!*"

"*Ummmm, it was Christmas because I had been given a camera and was taking pictures of everything. We're all old enough to remember a time when mobile phones didn't exist, let alone, phones with cameras.*" Started Chris.

"*God yeah, I'm embarrassed to admit I remember those days.*" Added Jennifer.

"That seems such a long time ago." Added Jackie.

Adam just nodded, choosing not to comment on this occasion.

"I had gone to my mate's house, Jim, my other mates, Woody, Aggy and Andy B, were there too. We had been just sitting around talking and Jim had tempted the boys with some of his dad's Ouzo. You probably know Ouzo, don't you Jen, with your Greek blood?"

"Oh yes, I know all about Ouzo." Laughed Jennifer.

"What's Ouzo?" Asked Jackie.

"It's a Greek spirit, it's very strong, it can be lethal." Replied Jen.

"It certainly is." Replied Chris. *"So, I said I would have one and Jim poured me a small glass. It was when I asked him to top it up, the boys bet me that I couldn't drink a tall glass of Ouzo neat."* Carried on Chris.

"Oh god." Whispered Jennifer putting her hand across her mouth.

"So, I said I would do it, but only if they made it worth my while financially. They each chipped in a full £1 each giving me a full £4 to down a glass of Ouzo."

"Oh my!" Whispered Jen as she probably knew what was coming.

"So, I downed the Ouzo and took the money, no problem, piece of cake. Then Aggy chipped in, and said I couldn't do it twice." Continued Chris.

"Here we go." Whispered Jen.

"Jim poured me another glass of Ouzo, the boys got their pound coins out and I drank the Ouzo straight down in one go."

"Oh god!" Came from Jennifer again.

"It was fine, I had drunk two glasses and was a whopping £8 better off and felt absolutely fine. As far as I was concerned, I thought that I had spent the night at Jim's house, in the same chair, having a chilled evening with the boys." Explained Chris.

"Here we go." Came another mutter from Jennifer.

"Jen, you're expecting something bad to happen?" Asked Adam

"Trust me, this isn't going to turn out well, is it Chris?" Jennifer enquired.

"Well apparently, I didn't spend all night at Jim's, what actually happened is very different. Apparently, we left Jim's house and headed down to Andy B's house, which normally is about two or three minutes away but on this occasion, it took about fifteen minutes, because one member of the group wasn't able to put one foot in front of the other, let alone walk in a straight line. At one point, apparently, I veered off into the road, right in front of an oncoming car."

"Oh god." Gasped Jennifer again.

"It's okay Jen, it missed me." Laughed Chris. *"So, eventually we got to Andy's house, where his mum, dad, brothers and grandparents were all having an evening together."*

"Oh" came another gasp from Jen, who had clearly guessed things were going to go downhill quickly.

"I took it upon myself to keep the mood light, and as someone generally polite, especially with older folks, I was told I got a bit cheeky. After unintentionally offending everyone in the living room, I shifted to the kitchen where Andy's mom and grandma were deep in conversation. With enthusiasm, I declared my Christmas camera as top-notch, adding a playful twist by revealing a surprise beneath my jeans to the two ladies."

"Oh my." Giggled Jennifer.

"You legend!" Shrieked Adam.

"Oh no!" Giggled Jackie

"You fucking idiot." Announced George who as a Greek man, is very aware of the power of Ouzo.

"After that, I was asked to leave, as I had clearly crossed a line, even though I was totally oblivious to what was going on, as far as I was concerned, I was still in my chair in Jim's house, I had no idea that we had moved down the road to Andy's, it was only when I went outside it all got serious. I collapsed in a flowerbed and emptied the contents of my stomach all over Andy's mum's roses. After that, I passed out and was completely unconscious."

"Oh god, you poor thing." Exclaimed Jennifer with one hand over her mouth and the other hand on Chris's knee.

"Poor thing? My arse!" Muttered George. *"You're a moron."*

Chris discreetly looked towards George, with a mixture of a frown and a cheeky smile, to which George just shook his head back at Chris, whilst signalling that Jen had her hand on Chris's leg.

"Ambulance job I'm guessing?" Interrupted Adam.

"Ohhhh god." Added Jennifer again.

"Ohhhhhh no, they phoned my dad, that's much worse. He eventually found Andy's house and pulled his car onto the driveway, took one look at his unconscious son lying in a flowerbed covered in his own vomit, then turned to the boys and asked, what the hell has he been drinking? "Ouzo". They replied. "How much?" Asked my dad. "Two glasses." Replied the boys. "Is that all?" Asked my dad. "Two big glasses," added Jim. "Where?" Asked my dad. "My house." Answered Jim. "So, it's your fault, my son is almost dead in a flowerbed!" "Yeah sorry." Replied Jim. My dad made Jim and Woody get in the back of the car, then lay me across them with a carrier bag each, to catch any potential vomit. He then drove home damn quick and got the boys to carry me into the kitchen. My dad then put a chair in front of the kitchen sink and sat me on it, with my head tilted back under the tap."

"He didn't," urged Jennifer.

"He could have killed you!" Added Jackie.

"He should have killed you?" Laughed George.

"He didn't do what I think he did, did he?" Enquired Adam.

"Yep, apparently, he turned on the cold tap and tried to flush the Ouzo out of my system and I didn't have a clue that any of this was going on, you have to remember that I thought I had spent the entire evening in the same chair at Jim's House, I don't remember a single thing after downing the second glass of Ouzo."

"Aye, *you poor thing*". Said Jennifer sympathetically.

"No, he's an idiot." Piped up George, even though nobody else could hear him.

"I bet you suffered in the morning?" continued Jennifer.

"That's the thing," giggled Chris. *"My dad had his breakfast, and then waited in the kitchen for me to come downstairs with a plan of making me suffer even more. However, I came downstairs, took up my normal place at table, poured some cereal and had my breakfast as i normally do. It wasn't until my dad started to question*

me, on how I was feeling that any of the previous evening's events were bought to my attention. My dad's furious that I didn't have a hangover, I didn't even have a hint of a headache, I felt absolutely fine, my dad couldn't believe that I wasn't suffering in the slightest. All I remember, is thinking that all the talk about drink and Ouzo and the first thing that sprung into my mind was Club Tropicana by Wham! So I finished my breakfast and left my dad sat there fuming, while I disappeared out of the Kitchen singing. He was actually fuming." Giggled Chris.

Chris of course, headed back upstairs and put Club Tropicana on, and started singing along. Meanwhile, his dad was still sat the kitchen listening to the music coming out of his son's room and wondering how on earth he didn't have a hangover, not even a hint of a headache, and yet he was utterly clueless about the state he was in a few hours earlier. Even though Chris's dad should have been angry at the state his son was in, he also recognised it was serious, Chris was in a bad way.

"Clearly a big George Michael fan." Asked Jackie.

"Lucky me!" Announced George.

"Big fan and a great friend of George." Added Jennifer.

"Hmmmmmmm." Sighed George.

The new gang continued to tell stories of their experience with the booze, but Chris was definitely proudest that he had nearly died from Ouzo. He probably hadn't nearly died, but he wasn't sure if it was the quality of the Ouzo and the high levels of pure alcohol or his dad's attempt to nearly drown him. Either way he lived to tell the tale.

"I'm ready for bed." Announced Jackie. *"You're not driving home, you two have to stay here tonight."*

"Ohh, thank you Jackie." Replied Jennifer. *"I've lost count how many drinks I've had."*

Chris stayed silent, he was suddenly going to be given a dilemma, where was he going to sleep? And with whom?

"Yeah, I'll sort this stuff out in the morning." Announced Adam. *"I've had fun, thanks for coming."*

"Thank you for inviting me, it's been awesome." Replied Chris.

"Yes, thank you Adam, I've had a great day, thank you." Added Jennifer.

All Chris could think about was that he was there as George's friend, not as Jennifer's date. Chris and Jennifer obviously had fun and got to know each other very well, and there was definitely some flirting going on between them. As the day had gone, Jennifer had felt happy to be more tactile with Chris in George's absence, or though he wasn't absent at all, he had been there the whole time. The two of them had grabbed any opportunity to have a chat, either on the patio, while Jackie and Adam were busy with the BBQ, or in the pool cooling off. They had spent quite a bit of time, sat on the steps at the shallow end, chatting away and Jen didn't mind at all, punching Chris playfully when he wound her up, then rubbing his arm better afterwards.

Jackie took them upstairs. *"Here you go Jen, you can have this room, there's everything you need in the bathroom."*

"Thank you Jacs, oh I'm looking forward to bed." Replied Jennifer.

"You're most welcome, sleep well, see you in the morning, and no rush to get up!" Returned Jackie. *"Here you go Chris, this one is yours, make yourself at home, see you in the morning."* Jackie opened the door to the room for Chris

and then gave him a goodnight kiss and disappeared down the hallway.

As Chris entered the bedroom, he was pushed from behind. *"Let me see your room, it better not be bigger than mine?"* Enquired Jennifer as she grabbed him around his waist barged past into the room.

"Don't mind me!" Laughed Chris as Jennifer pushed him aside.

After a quick look around at the bedroom and checking the bathroom, assuring herself, the room was almost identical, she turned around and headed for the door, then stopped and turned back to look at Chris.

"Thank you for today, I've had a great time." Whispered Jennifer.

"Me too, thank you for bringing me, I've had a brilliant day." Replied Chris.

"It was a pleasure." Replied Jennifer, as she placed her hands on either side of Chris's face and pulled him towards her, placing her lips on his, giving him a soft but long kiss. *"Goodnight, sleep well, see you in the morning."*

"Night Jen, sleep well." Returned Chris and as Jen went to leave the room, he grabbed her hand and pulled her back towards him. Placing his arms around her lower back, just above her bum, he pulled Jen into his body and gave her another kiss. To his joy, Jennifer didn't pull away from him, she actually pushed her body tighter against his and was happy to hold the kiss for a while. Eventually, they parted their lips.

Jennifer looked up at Chris. *"Oh my, I wasn't expecting that!"*

"Did I cross a line?" Asked Chris.

"No, not at all, I liked it." Replied Jen, who was a little bit flustered. *"I really liked it."* She giggled.

Jen then planted another long kiss on Chris's lips, giggled and left the room. *"I had better go, or I'll be here all night kissing you."*

"I wouldn't mind that." Replied Chris.

"No, nor would I." Returned Jennifer. *"I have to go, oh my, that was lovely, goodnight."* As she was off giggling all the way to her room.

"Goodnight" Chris whispered as he watched Jen disappear through the door, his eyes drifting down to her perfect bikini clad bottom.

Chris closed the door then turned around to go back into the room, to see George sat on the bed shaking his head from side to side.

"How the hell did you manage that?" George asked.

"I haven't got the foggiest idea!" Replied Chris.

"You an absolute nobody, has got mega star beauty, Jennifer Aniston to like him?" Continued George.

"I know, how the hell did that happen?" Asked Chris.

"Why are you so down on yourself? Why do you have such little faith in yourself? Why do you rely on me to get on in life?" Asked George.

"Well, if it wasn't for you, I wouldn't be here now, George." Returned Chris.

"Well, yes, yes, on this occasion, but I've been watching you today, and when you drop the George Michael facade and just be Chris, you manage to impress Jen, but you can't tell when you're being me and when you're being you." Pushed George.

"Because in my head the two are the same." Insisted Chris.

"Are you trying to tell me that you can't tell the difference anymore?" Asked George.

"I guess not!" Responded Chris quietly.

George stopped pushing Chris to be himself, he had obviously touched a nerve, but more so, George had discovered that Chris had spent so much time trying to be somebody else, he really had lost track of who he was. Chris was completely lost in his own head.

George actually felt sorry for his crazy friend and decided it would be wrong, even for him, to try and take Chris out of his fantasy world. George may have gate crashed Chris's world, but Chris was already completely lost in it, and decided it would probably be best to facilitate his fantasy rather than try and change him.

"Well, I can tell you for free, I am not sleeping on the floor!" Announced George.

"Well, I can't, what if Jen walked in and saw me sleeping on the floor, she would think I'm some sort of nutcase." Replied Chris.

"Ohhhhh and you certainly, are not a nutcase, are you?" Replied George.

"That was a cheap shot." Giggled Chris.

"I talk the truth my friend, and that is the truth." Laughed George.

Up until now, the boys had either been in one of their houses with their own rooms or if they were staying in a hotel, they had a suite with separate beds, this was the first time they had been put in the dilemma of only one bed.

"Right, well you're not sleeping naked, George." Insisted Chris.

"Fine by me." Replied George.

"And no spooning!" Added Chris.

"I'll try not to." Replied George sarcastically. *"But I can't promise, you're so irresistible."*

"Very funny? Jen finds me irresistible." Giggled Chris.

"But Jen isn't in bed with you, is she? But I am." Teased George.

"Hmmmmm, you had better behave." Laughed Chris.

"Like I said, I'll try my best, lover boy." Replied George who had rediscovered his sarcastic side.

Chris turned his back and nervously stripped out of his board shorts into a pair of boxer shorts and without turning around, asked George. *"What side of the bed do you want?"*

"All of it. Nice bum by the way!" Giggled George.

"You can't have all of it." Replied Chris. *"And leave my bum alone."*

"I'll take this side; I prefer to be on the right side of my partner." Answered George. *"It's quite pert, isn't it"?* He giggled.

"Okay." Replied Chris slipping under the duvet. *"Leave my pert arse alone."*

"Do me a favour Chris, relax and go to sleep, I really won't try and shag you." Laughed George.

"No chance of a cuddle then?" Giggled Chris.

"You would crap yourself if I started to give you a cuddle buddy." Laughed George, *"You couldn't handle me."*

"That's okay then, night." Smiled Chris.

"Love you." Chuckled George.

"Love you more." Returned Chris.

"Ohh but you do, Chris." Laughed George.

"Go to sleep, George." Giggled Chris.

Chris made himself comfortable, closed his eyes and started to think about his day with Jennifer and how amazing it had been, he couldn't believe how well it had gone, and how she had made a special effort to come and give him a kiss goodnight. Just as Chris was starting drift off, Chris felt a hand on his bum starting to caress his butt cheek.

"George, stop it, right now!" Chris said sternly.

"So easy?" Giggled George.

"I knew you wouldn't be able to keep your hands off me." Giggled Chris.

"Don't I get a kiss goodnight?" Teased George.

"Nope." Replied Chris.

"Jen did." Giggled George.

"Ohhhh come on then!" Replied Chris rolling over to face George.

"Seriously?" Shrieked George.

"No, go to sleep." Replied Chris.

Unimpressed, George punched Chris on the arm. *"Tosser."* He whispered.

"Yep" replied Chris.

In the morning light, Chris awoke, greeted by the realization that he was sharing a bed with George. Rolling over, he studied George's peaceful form, wrapped in the warmth of the duvet. Despite occasional annoyance at George's sarcasm, Chris cherished every moment of their tangible connection. George, a man of faith shaken by loss, made Chris ponder the what-ifs. Would George's fate have differed if Anselmo were still here? Did George ever question why he ended up with someone as complex as Chris? Chris, feeling chosen and intrigued, wondered if he was destined to be George's companion. The unanswered questions lingered, weaving a tapestry of connection and cosmic mysteries between the two friends.

George started to stir and then rolled over, ended up looking straight into Chris's eyes.

"What are looking at weirdo?" He asked still half asleep. *"I was sleeping."*

"Nothing, just making sure you were okay." Replied Chris.

"I'm fine thanks, stalker." Replied George.

"If I was a stalker, I would hope you would be a bit more shocked that I was in bed with you." Returned Chris.

"Maybe my luck would be in?" Laughed George

"Sorry, not this morning." Laughed Chris.

"What, not even a kiss?" Asked George.

"Not even a kiss." Chuckled Chris.

"You're so selfish!" Giggled George. *"After all I've done for you?"*

"Aren't I just?" Replied Chris, who actually did feel a bit guilty, because George really had done a lot for him, and on the spur of the moment, very quickly leaned forward and gave George an awkward kiss on his forehead.

"Oh thanks, is that all I get?" Asked George.

Fortunately, Chris was saved by a knock on the door.

"Morning, I'm putting some coffee on, we'll be in the kitchen." Called in Jackie.

"Awesome, I'll be straight down." Said Chris.

"Huh, saved by the bell?" Laughed George.

"Yeah." Replied Chris.

There was another knock, but this time Jackie was knocking on Jen's door.

"Coffee in the kitchen, when you're ready Jen Jen."

Chris got out of bed and made his way to the bathroom for a shower, he didn't want Jen to see him with bed head and he wanted to clean his teeth, just in case she wanted to give him a morning kiss.

"Tarting yourself up for Jennifer then?" Came the first sarcastic comment of the day from George.

"Just having a freshen up." Replied Chris.

"Tart?" Retorted George.

By the time they got downstairs, Adam, Jackie and Jen were all sat at the breakfast bar.

"Heyyyyyyyyy, here he is!" Announced Adam. *"How are you this morning, sleep well?"*

"Morning guys, yes very well, that is a very comfortable bed." Replied Chris.

As Chris walked past Jennifer, she gently let her hand brush his. *"Hi"* Jennifer said, in a quiet flirtatious sort of way.

Adam had noticed the brushing of their hands and also picked up the flirtatious way that Jen had greeted Chris with, and asked, *"okay?"*

"What?" Shrieked Jen.

"*Nothing, no no nothing!*" Replied, a curious Adam as he looked across at Jackie, who gave him a knowing wink.

Chris looked at Jen and gave her a cheeky little grin, and Jen actually started to blush, this was clearly a good sign and an excellent start to the day. George on the other hand, rolled his eyes and shook his head in disbelief.

Jackie made a fresh batch of coffee and made some proper American pancakes which were amazing, there was also a choice of sauces, but Chris played it safe and went with Maple syrup. After breakfast, Jen and Chris said their goodbyes, thanked Adam and Jackie for an awesome time and hit the road back to Chris's hotel.

On the way back, the two of them had a good giggle about the events of the night before, and some of the conversations they had indulged in. Chris was keen to let Jen know how surprised he was at how easy she was to talk to and how he never thought they would have got on so well. Jen assured Chris that she found him very easy to be around and how comfortable she felt in his company and how difficult it is to meet people when you're as famous as she is. They were clearly in agreement that they worked well together and that there was something brewing between them. As they pulled into the hotel driveway, Jen looked for somewhere to pull in rather than stopping right outside reception.

"*There you go, home safe and sound.*" Announced Jen as she pulled into a space.

"*Thank you for driving me back and not making me get a cab.*" Giggled Chris.

"*I couldn't make you take a cab, could I?*" Replied Jen with a wink.

"*I have to head back to UK tomorrow.*" Announced Chris.

"*That's a shame.*" Replied Jen.

"*I know, I wish I had longer here.*" Returned Chris.

"*That would be nice, I would quite like to spend some more time with you.*" Returned Jen with a cheeky grin.

"*I didn't think this would happen when I booked the hotel.*" Replied Chris.

"*Well, if nothing else, I owe you lunch?*" Giggled Jen.

"*Are you suggesting we go out again, Jennifer?*" Asked Chris.

"*It sounds like that, doesn't it Christopher?*" Smiled Jen.

"*Well, that would mean that I would need to get my arse over here, quick sharp?*" Suggested Chris.

"*Yes, I think you should. I think as soon as you get home you should book a flight back over?*" Insisted Jen.

"*Really? You want me to come back over?*" Asked Chris.

"*Well, it sounds that way, doesn't it?*" Questioned Jen.

"*It certainly does.*" Replied Chris.

"*Let me know which flight you're on and I'll meet you at the airport.*" Pushed Jen.

"*You'll pick me up from the airport?*" Asked Chris.

"*I'm already looking forward to it.*" Said Jen.

"*Right. Well, I will get straight on it as soon as I get home.*" Giggled Chris.

In the car, Chris and George talked about Chris's return, and George saw his unlikely plan starting to happen. George felt happy that he was helping Chris make his dream come true.

"*I had better go.*" Said Chris eventually.

"*I guess so.*" Replied Jen.

"*I'll let you know when I'm home.*" Replied Chris.

"*More importantly, I want to know when your plane is going to land?*" Stated Jen.

"*Don't worry, as soon as it's booked, you'll be the first to know.*" Replied Chris.

"Well, I had better be, Christopher." Giggled Jen.

They stopped talking and looked deeply into each other's eyes and then slowly came together for a goodbye kiss. It seemed to last forever, especially for George who had to sit and watch them, but for Chris, it was over way to soon. As Chris and George stepped out of the car, Jennifer dropped the window.

"*Don't you dare forget to phone me when you land, Christopher.*" Shouted Jen through the window.

"*Oh, I most definitely won't forget, Jennifer.*" Giggled Chris.

"*You had better not.*" Smirked Jen.

"*Ohhhhhhhh give it a rest!*" Shouted George.

Jennifer pulled the car out of the space and disappeared down the driveway, beeping her horn and waving out of the window, while Chris stood waving.

"*Come on Loverboy, we've got a flight to catch.*" Urged George.

Chapter Twenty-Five

It was a quiet flight to home, unsurprisingly as it would have looked like George was talking to himself, which no doubt would have led to a media frenzy. Once they got out of the airport and into the safety of the car, they were able to get back to normal.

"Well, that was a trip and half, wasn't it?" Ventured George

"Ohhh my god, wasn't it crazy?" Replied Chris.

"I'm still not sure how you managed to pull that off." Returned George.

"We pulled it off, George, it would never have happened without you." Insisted Chris.

"Yeah, we are a good team, aren't we?" Replied George proudly.

"Thank you, George. I mean it, thank you for everything." Replied Chris.

"I've enjoyed it." Laughed George. *"I know I might not have shown it, but I have enjoyed it."* Insisted George.

"It must have been difficult to watch and not be able to be involved." Asked Chris.

"That was the hardest part, indeed." Admitted George. *"But I am so happy that you and Jen hit it off, that in itself is a bit of a miracle."*

"A bit of a miracle, George?" Laughed Chris *"We have just achieved mission impossible."*

"Bloody right, we have!" Guffawed George.

In the last few months, life had embraced George and Chris with an enchanting rhythm. George's tour, bathed in sold-out venues and raving reviews, mirrored the success of a new album conquering charts. Straight to number one, it held its reign, unyielding for weeks. Singles, too, soared to the pinnacle, with George achieving the rare feat of securing both top spots. Yet, in this musical symphony, George's greatest triumph was overcoming adversity. After a harrowing battle with illness, his scarred throat not only survived but flourished, delivering a voice that echoed strength and resilience. Every note, crystal clear, resonated effortlessly, a testament to newfound joy and unparalleled versatility.

George was in so much demand, every radio station, news and entertainment show wanted his presence on their show, they all wanted a piece of George and George had the fitness and motivation to take on every single one of them. He was in perfect form, proving everybody what a charming, charismatic professional George Michael is. New listeners were getting to know George Michael, and they were all falling in love with him. Parents were telling their kids that they've been listening to George for years and it wasn't until they realised how long George had been around.

While George and Chris were rushing around doing the interviews, it was Chris who was feeling the pressure and George who was providing the energy, George was becoming stronger and stronger by the day. George Michael fever was again spreading across the globe, which meant George and Chris were flying literally around the world on a crazy promotional tour. That tour of course, included the USA which meant that Chris was able to spend time with Jennifer and they were going from strength to strength. Jennifer was in the middle of filming a new movie, so she was quite happy that Chris was going to and from the states. This way, she could concentrate on her work, without being distracted by Chris hanging around.

Chris was no longer staying at a hotel, Jen insisted him to stay with her, so that they could spend quality time together. Chris couldn't believe how normal Jennifer was away from the spotlight of Hollywood, not like she had ever seemed to come across like some of the pretentious actors you see on the telly. They hung with each other, went for lunch, dinner, shopping or just hung out in the park, or in Jen's beautiful garden. Jen loved the beach, and they could be often seen messing around in the waves. A few of the papers had picked up on their relationship, but so far, Jennifer Aniston's new partner was known, only as, George Michael's, friend. Nobody knew who Chris was, nor would they be likely to find out. George had been asked during interviews what happened to his romance with Jennifer, and he bluffed his way through it, but never gave up any information about Chris.

In an enchanting twist of fate, Jennifer found herself engaged in a heart-to-heart with George, a moment both charming and unusual, as Chris silently observed. Amidst laughter and confessions, they attributed missed encounters to their bustling professional lives. George, aware of the unfolding plan, couldn't help but feel a twinge of envy for the incredible Jennifer, a woman he deemed perfect if only he were straight. Unbeknownst to Jennifer, a whimsical scheme brewed between George and Chris. Despite her initial contentment with singlehood, Chris changed Jennifer's perspective, weaving joy back into her life. As they shared a warm hug, a unique trio was born, with George's invisible hand shaping a bond that became an unexpected masterpiece—a testament to the beauty found when hearts intertwine.

While the boys were in the UK, they split their time between the different houses and as summer arrived, they spent quite a bit of time at Chris's house in Cornwall. In the daytime, they would be found lounging around the pool, getting drinks from the pool bar, Club Tropicana, and listening to music. George was very happy to listen to his own music and the two of them would sing along with the tracks while floating around the pool on their inflatable chairs. George loved swimming and was constantly doing lengths. Chris couldn't help but notice that George was getting stronger and stronger. When George first gate-crashed Chris's world, there was very much a spiritual presence about him. However, as time went on, he took on a more physical presence, Chris had even noticed that George was starting to tan. This would be expected from a man with Greek blood, and normally George would tan very easily, but as something extraordinary had taken place, up until recently, there wouldn't be a hope in hell that George would have tanned. Something new was happening, it seemed that George was changing.

Chris could hear George giggling to himself from the other side of the pool and reluctantly Chris looked across to see what he was up to.

"*Really?*" Asked Chris as he caught sight of George.

"*Hell yeah! I look bloody brilliant.*" Laughed George.

"*You should have waited till it was dark to get the full effect.*" Suggested Chris.

"Ohhhhh yeah, bugger!" Said George, who was sitting by the side of the pool in a pair of white speedos, trying to pull off his iconic Club Tropicana pose. *"I still look bloody good though."*

"Yep, I gotta say, you've pulled it off." Laughed Chris. *"Have you noticed that you're looking better, George? Are you feeling better?"*

"I really am feeling good Chris, something is happening to my body, it's a little bit weird." Replied George.

"Yeah?" Said Chris, who was pleased that George was looking and feeling so good, but part of him worried that they didn't know why.

"There must be something in the water or the Cornish air?" Teased George. *"I'm getting a drink, do you want one?"*

"What you having?" Asked Chris.

"Only a coke." Replied George. *"Want one?"*

"Yeah, I'll have one too." Replied Chris.

"Please." Returned George.

Something they had in common was that they both love diet coke and could drink it till the cows come home. Chris struggled to drink it slowly and downed it in a few gulps, so George always bought him two, one to gulp down and the other to sip slowly.

"You really love that stuff, don't you? I thought I liked it, but you reaaaally like it." Laughed George.

"Ohhh god, it's just so good, especially in the sun, it just goes down sooooooo well." Returned Chris.

"Most people like a beer or a glass of wine?" Giggled George. *"You have to be different, don't you?"*

"I just love the taste and the way it feels as it goes down." Replied Chris.

"It's only a can of coke?" Stressed George.

"I know, but damn it tastes good." Urged Chris.

"You're a freeeek!" Laughed George. *"I still don't get you?"*

"What do you mean?" Asked Chris.

"The whole me thing, that you have let rule your life." Continued George.

"I thought we had moved on from that?" Returned Chris.

"It still confuses me why have you dedicated so much of your life trying to be a completely fictional character?" Pressed George.

"I've explained why, George." Pushed Chris.

"Yeah yeah, I know you have tried to explain, but I just don't get it. I get George Michael out of a box to do a show, or personal appearance on the telly, or radio, but the rest of the time, I'm just normal me, living a relatively normal life. I get up late, I slob around in scruffs all day, I don't shave, sometimes I don't even bother to clean my teeth. I put my feet up in front of the telly, or take Abby for a walk, but pretty much I'm just a normal bloke.

Sometimes it's months or years between public appearances and in between, I can assure you, George Michael is nowhere to be seen." Explained George

"I don't try and be you 24/7." Returned Chris, defensively.

"You probably try and be George Michael far more of the time than I do." Argued George *"When you go to Morrisons, you go hoping to be confused for me. When I go shopping, I go hoping not to be recognised as me."* Returned George.

"I've never been asked for an autograph?" Giggled Chris.

"I wonder why? Maybe it's because most people wouldn't expect George Michael to be doing his weekly shop in Morrisons in Newquay?" Suggested George.

"Maybe you're down here on holiday?" Argued Chris.

"Every week?" Returned George. *"Tell me you don't take in your own bags?"*

"I might!" Replied Chris.

"Do you really think that I can't afford a few plastic bags?" Laughed George.

"Maybe you think the environment is worth protecting." Retorted Chris.

"I should, but I don't." Chuckled George.

"When you designed this amazing house, did you design because it's what you wanted or how you thought I might have designed it?" Asked George.

"How I wanted it." Returned Chris.

"There you go, you designed it how Chris wanted it, so this is a part of Chris and not a part of what you thought might be George Michael." Explained George.

"Don't you like my house?" Questioned Chris, spontaneously.

"I love your house, and if I had designed a house from scratch, it may have looked like this because you have very similar taste to me, if I was building it in Greece." Replied George. *"But as you know, my homes are more traditional."* Explained George.

"It's my permanent piece of Greese." Returned Chris.

"It's a great house Chris, and it came from your heart, not mine." Tried George.

"Thank you." Replied Chris.

"You crack me up Chris, or should I say Yog 2?" Laughed George.

"I'll take that!" Laughed Chris.

"You bloody will not! You've hijacked George Michael; you're not having Yog too." Insisted George.

"Nope, I like Yog 2, I might hold onto that." Teased Chris.

"Put Yog 2 down, you're not having him, and you would never get anyone to take it on anyway." Laughed George.

"You don't know that?" Questioned Chris.

"I do." Laughed George.

"How?" Asked Chris.

"It's simple, you're a recluse, you haven't got any bloody friends." Laughed George.

"I've got Jen, Adam and Jackie and, you?" Returned Chris.

"They're not going to start calling you Yog 2 and I'm certainly not going to, you freeek." Laughed George.

"Hmmmmm." Shrugged Chris.

"Oh, come here idiot, give Yog 1 a hug?" Laughed George reaching out his arms for hug, knowing full well Chris wouldn't respond.

"Nob off!" Laughed Chris.

"Ohhhh come on, give uncle George a hug!" Tried George again.

"No." Sulked Chris.

"Spoiled sport!" Laughed George.

Chris looked at George with a stern stare, beaten by his more realistic friend, who had actually just described Chris perfectly.

In the tranquil moments by the pool and the secret rehearsals for Glastonbury, George's remarkable resurgence led him to close the festival. A casual conversation with Chris birthed a colossal collaboration, spiralling into a frenzy of grand ideas beyond their music. Enthusiasm soared as plans unfolded, weaving dreams of an unprecedented Glastonbury set. Amidst meetings and discussions, they delved into special effects and light shows, investing a fortune for an unparalleled experience. Every penny spent, a promise for a Glastonbury finale that transcends imagination, bound to leave an indelible mark.

Chapter Twenty-Six

The pyramid stage fell into silence, darkness had fallen across Glastonbury, the crowd had spent the last few days waiting for the grand finale and the atmosphere was electric, and then from nowhere the ground started to vibrate. The tremors running through the floor were strong enough to take you off your feet. The audience were holding onto each other, so they didn't fall over as they gained their balance. On the big screens on either side of the stage, it appeared as someone had inserted the wrong disc in and instead it looked like the beginning of a 70s porn film starting. Then the sirens started as if the whole venue was being raided by the police. It sounded like the whole of Glastonbury was being buzzed by helicopters and then from above the sky was lit up by search lights from a fleet of helicopters swooping in and scoping out the crowd.

"LET'S GO OUTSIDE GO OUTSIDE GO OUTSIDE!"

"OUTSIDE.......... OUTSIDE......... OUTSIDE!"

The intro had begun, the event of the weekend was starting, this was going to be epic.

The ground was literally thumping, it was difficult to stand up, the big units placed around the main field in front of the pyramid stage, erupted into life. The helicopters above, flew around, scanning the audience with their search lights.

"Back to nature, outside, human nature nature nature!!" Backing singers.

"Back to nature, outside, human nature nature nature!!" Backing singers.

"Back to nature, outside, human nature nature nature!!" Backing singers.

"Back to nature, outside, human nature nature nature"!! Backing singers.

"Back to nature, outside, human nature nature nature!!" Backing singers.

"I THINK I'M DONE WITH THE SOFA!"

"I THINK I'M DONE WITH THE HALL!"

"I THINK I'M DONE WITH THE KITCHEN TABLE BABY!!" Boomed the deep low vocals of George.

"GOOD EVENING GLATONBURY, HAPPY SUNDAY, ENJOY THE SHOW!!!!!!" Announced George Michael

"LET'S GO OUTSIDE!"

"LET'S GO OUTSIDE" Backing singers.

"IN THE SUNSHINE, I KNOW YOU WANT TO, BUT YOU CAN'T SAY YEAH"

"LET'S GO OUTSIDE"

LET'S GO OUTSIDE" Backing singers.

"IN THE MOONSHINE, TAKE ME TO THE PLACES THAT I LOVE BEST"

"Ladies and gentlemen, good evening, have you had a good weekend?" Shouted George as he paced around the stage, trying to see as many of the audience as he could.

The audience erupted into applause and the ground shook even more, this was the first time anybody had experienced anything like this, the effects could almost be described as violent.

"Ladies and gentleman, please can I introduce you to some very good friends of mine, a group of guys that I like to call COLDPLAY!!!!!!!!!!!!!!"

Well, that was it, the crowd went absolutely mental, this must have been one of the best kept secrets of the century. George had been advertised as with special guests, but nobody had linked him to Coldplay. Chris Martin ran out onto stage in his usual enthusiastic manner, and straight into George's arms, followed by Guy, Will and Jonny. One by one they all came over and greeted George, then took their places on the stage, all the while the beats of Outside and the backing singers had been keeping the atmosphere electric.

"Hello everyone, are you having a good time?" Shouted Chris Martin, waiting for the obvious response.

"Well, you ain't seen nothing yet, George! Let's rock!" Cheered Chris.

The two of them took it in turns, to run up and down the stage, taking it in turns to lead the hysterical audience through the song, eventually bringing the song to its conclusion. The stage fell silent and the floor stopped thumping but the crowd were still on cloud nine, and they had only heard one track. And then once again the floor started to vibrate, gradually, getting more and more violent.

"COZ YOU'RE A SKY, COZ YOU'RE A SKY FULL STARS"

"I'M GONNA GIVE YOU MY HEART"

"COZ YOU'RE A SKY, COZ YOU'RE A SKY FULL OF STARS."

"COZ YOU LIGHT UP THE PATH"

"AND I DON'T CARE, DON'T WANNA TARE ME APART"

"I DON'T CARE IF YOU DO, OO OO."

"COZ IN A SKY IN A SKY FULL OF STARS, I THINK I SAW YOU OO OO OO, I THINK I SAW YOU OO OO OO."

The stage lit up, the backing musicians came alive, George joined Chris centre stage, and the ground started to vibrate even more if that was possible.

George took over the vocals.

"BECAUSE IN A SKY A SKY FULL OF STARS I WANNA DIE IN YOUR ARMS"

"AND YOU GET LIGHTER THE MORE IT GETS DARK"

"I'M GONNA GIVE YOU MY HEART, OHHHHHH"

"AND I THINK I SEE YOU OO OO OO"

The stage burst into dazzling light as strobes flashed behind the band. George and Chris owned center stage, their energy and laughter bouncing off each other. Running and rolling, they immersed themselves in the performance. The meticulously designed boxes lining the field were a joint creation, holding immense power to synchronize with the music and elevate the audience experience.

The duo's secretive million-pound investment in the boxes became evident within just two songs. These powerful structures, strategically placed with lights, added an extra layer to the immersive experience. The spectacle showcased meticulous planning, creativity, and a significant investment, leaving the audience in awe.

The boys eventually came to the end of A Sky Full of Stars, and the stage fell silent again, Chris and George made their way back to the main stage and grabbed a drink of water to prepare themselves for the next track. The audience were loving it, it was the best collaboration they had ever seen and they were only two songs in. Why had George never done Glastonbury before? This was going to go down in Glastonbury's history as one of the best sets ever, and anyone else would have to come up with something out of this world to match it, let alone better it. George and Coldplay had set the bar so high, it would be almost impossible to beat.

The spectacle resumed, and the ground seemed to pulsate, creating the sensation of an incoming stampede. The audience, surrounded by strategically positioned lights, felt trapped in a dazzling cage. As the lights burst brightly, it evoked the illusion of a massive herd closing in. The air filled with screams of monkeys, adding an unexpected and thrilling element. Some younger children clung to their parents, adding to the suspense.

Then, the lights began to move, giving the impression of the cage rocking the audience. The pounding floor threw everyone off balance. In this electrifying moment, Chris seized George, pointing at the audience, both laughing at the out-of-body experience they were creating. The immersive show reached a crescendo, blending suspense, excitement, and an unforgettable journey for everyone present.

"BETTER WATCH OUT, BABY WHO'S THAT, DON'T LOOK NOW THERE'S A MONKEY ON YOUR BACK" Shouted George.

"BETTER WATCH OUT, BABY WHO'S THAT, DON'T LOOK NOW THERE'S A MONKEY ON YOUR BACK" Came Chris.

"BETTER WATCH OUT, BABY WHO'S THAT, DON'T LOOK NOW THERE'S A MONKEY ON YOUR BACK" Chris and George synced.

"WHY CAN'T YOU DO IT?" Again sang George.

"WHY CAN'T YOU SET YOUR MONKEY FREE?" Added Chris.

The strobe lights lit up the stage and scanned the sky line, sending everything into slow motion. The floor was rocking and the way they had programmed the bass boxes, each one the size of a car, the floor actually moved like a wave, making it very difficult to stay on your feet. The audience were all looking at each other and laughing as they got thrown around in a field, this was like nothing else they had ever experienced, not even in Disney or Universal Studios had they had such huge senses overload.

As the song came to an end, the heavy bass was slowly filtered into a heartbeat. The floor went from a thunderous thumping to a gentle dum dum, dum dum, and gave the audience time to regain their balance, matching their own heartbeat with that coming through the floor. Everything seemed to calm down and take on a level of normality.

Then the screens on the sides of the stage came to life, and the famous dancing gorillas appeared, Chris Martin took centre stage and started to copy the dance the Gorillas were doing on the screens and unbelievably George was right behind him also taking on the dance.

Adventure of a lifetime kicked in and Chris took the lead with George, backing him up and joining Chris for the harmonies, both of them clearly enjoying every second. They seized every opportunity to engage with the audience, actively seeking maximum participation. The huge boxes around the arena were in full heartbeat mode, then interspersing the screams of the Gorillas, giving the impression that beyond the main field, Glastonbury was surrounded by screaming Gorillas. The ground was thumping and the audience seemed to sync with the beat and were in complete harmony with every beat.

After a few up-beat fast tracks, it was time to slow things down, the stage went dark and the base line was faded right down. Slowly, the mega boxes scattered around the field, began to stir to life. A peculiar wave-like motion rippled through the ground, creating the illusion that the earth itself was gently rolling in a harmonious dance. The stage was lit up in blue, and the guitar started to ring out from the stage and everybody in the audience, screamed with delight as they all knew one of the most famous introductions of all time. However, instead of George stepping forward and taking the lead, Chris Martin took the lead for A Different Corner. The audience watched mesmerised and swayed from side to side, as George made his way forward to join Chris centre stage. If you would like to know how this might have sounded you can look up Chris Martin singing A Different Corner on YouTube, but have some tissues to hand.

Next came Coldplay's Yellow, and they turned the tables again. George took the lead with Chris acting as support. The stage went from blue to yellow and the boys stood back, letting the audience take the lead for an extended introduction. Once again, the floor began to bounce to the rhythm. As the Coldplay band, with Chris unleashing his prowess on the instruments, George stepped forward, taking the lead vocals until Chris joined him in the sections where the crowd was also involved. You could see on the faces in the crowd, that they were almost overwhelmed by the set that George and Coldplay had put together. It was immaculate and they had obviously spent a lot of time secretly rehearsing, as well as keeping the collaboration top secret.

This was undoubtedly one of the best closing sets Glastonbury had ever witnessed, if not the best. The audience were in a euphoric state, with the mixture of George Michael and Coldplay tracks, meshing seamlessly while George and Chris sharing and mixing the vocals to perfection. But now it was time to really turn up the heat and give the audience an experience they most definitely wouldn't be expecting. Some of the true George Michael fans may have known about some of George's remixes and how he's more than capable of turning up the vibe but this was going to go the extra mile.

The floor started to thump, the stage lit up with white search lights and the lights situated around the main stage, came to life also acting as search lights. The base boxes were making the ground vibrate below the crowd's feet and George took control while Chris bounced around the stage like a mad man. This was clearly a very different version of 'Amazing' and the crowd was loving it. Nearly eight minutes into this extravaganza, and it took on a whole different life, imagine George Michael and Faithless and you have it. (Check out George Michael's Amazing Red Light Edit the 10-minute version on YouTube) The stage was lit up in a mass of colour and strobe lights, the ground was thumping harder than it had at any point during the set and crowd were jumping around, clapping their hands. This was a lesson on how to do the final set at Glastonbury, and one that would be talked about for years to come, with the saying "You had to be there" on the lips of everybody who attended. It was unlikely anyone would have ever experienced anything quite like this before, nor would they ever again.

With everybody buzzing, their bodies taken to a totally new place, that they would not have been expecting, it was time to settle things down a little bit. You could normally expect to come out of a concert with your ears ringing, but to have your whole body vibrating was another level.

George and Chris took centre stage, and watched as the crowd regained their balance and started to relax after their 10-minute explosion. If any of them had any energy left, they weren't letting on, they looked ready for a load more of what they had just had dished up to them.

"*Thank you everyone, we hope you had a good time!*" Shouted George.

The audience screamed and started to chant "*More....... more .... more!*"

Chris stepped forward with a huge smile on his face surrounded by his band mates. "*Thank you everybody we had an excellent time; we hope you enjoyed it as much as we did!*"

The crowd was still chanting "MORE MORE MORE MORE MORE!!!"

Along with George, they took centre stage and took several bows over the constant chant of "More"

One more bow then, they turned around and ran off stage waving.

The crowd wasn't having any of it, they wanted more, no they demanded more.

With the stage still in full darkness,

"Hey George, do you think we have time for a couple more?" Came the voice of Chris Martin.

"*I'm not sure Chris, maybe we should ask the audience.*" Replied George.

"*What do you think guys? Do we have time for a couple more?*" Chris asked the audience.

The audience went absolutely wild.

"*Well George, I reckon that's an overwhelming yes.*" Laughed Chris.

"*I think you could be right Chris, let's do it!*" Said George with a huge smile on his face.

The audience went wild and the guys took their place on the stage, and just as the bodies of the audience had started to settle down, Chris sat down at his piano and starts to play with the keys, keeping the audience in curiosity of what's coming next. George was centre stage swaying as Chris played, then the lasers, one by one started to light up the sky, and on top of the stage a whole wall of white light lit up the sky, so bright it could possibly be seen from space.

Slowly, but surely the intro became obvious as to what was coming and the audience started to sing along. George stepped forward.

"I wanna hear all of you sing, I wanna hear all of your voices!"

With that the whole of the audience started to sing Hymme for the weekend, and the stage became a kaleidoscope of colour. Chris joined George, and the pair of them let rip driving the audience into a frenzy. The boys let rip on stage and the audience who were all lit up in a mass of colour from the light show, they made it last as long as possible.

As the song gracefully concluded, there was no breath between it and the next, seamlessly transitioning into the next track. George, Chris Martin, and the Coldplay ensemble, accompanied by George's band and backing singers, had no intentions of granting the audience respite. Their mission was clear: to deliver a show of a lifetime, and they executed it flawlessly. The floor pulsated once again, and the unmistakable riff of "Killer" resonated with an incredible bass line. George and Chris prowled the stage, alternating lead roles, showcasing a finely tuned performance that stretched to provide the audience maximum value for their money. Effortlessly flowing into

"Papa Was a Rolling Stone," a mashup beloved by long time fans, the energy continued to escalate. In nearly fifteen minutes of musical mayhem, each band member had their solo moment.

As the night's final song commenced, every George Michael enthusiast in the crowd anticipated what was coming, and they were not about to be disappointed.

"Hey George, what is the one thing you want most of all? " Asked Chris.

"It would have to be a little bit of FREEDOM!!!!!" Replied George.

That was it, everything went ballistic, the stage lit up so bright that it could probably have been seen from space. There were lights on stage, around the stage, on top of the stage, around the field, they were absolutely, everywhere. The bass boxes came to life again and everyone tried to regain their balance as George and Chris took to centre stage and let rip. The audience couldn't believe what was going on, this was mind blowing, it was so loud it could have been heard in Bristol. George and Chris loved every second of it and at times lost their way a little bit, but it didn't matter and nobody in the audience cared, they were loving it. The vastly extended version of Freedom came to an end at that point the audience must have thought that was it the show must be over after that extravaganza, but as the stage fell into darkness the delightful tones of a saxophone filled the air and once again one of the most well, known, introductions filled the stage, yes Careless Whisper was going to give the audience the time they needed to come back down to earth.

Chris sat this one out and let George close the set on his own, because only George could do Careless Whisper and it was a perfect way for the audience to just enjoy the soulful perfection of George's new vocal range. He hit every note with perfection and when invited the audience joined in with the classic.

"*Thank you, Glastonbury! I hope you had as much fun as me!*" Announced George.

The audience went wild clapping and cheering.

Chris joined George on stage, "*Thank you, George, for letting me be a part of this, I had a great time, did you enjoy yourself?*" He shouted out to the crowd.

Johnny, Guy and Will joined them on stage to take full advantage of the appreciation from the audience.

"*That was mental!*" Announced Johnny.

"*That was so good.*" Added Guy.

"*That was so much better than I imagined it could possibly have been, we absolutely nailed it.*" Joined in Will.

"*I can't believe how well that went.*" Added Chris

"*Ohhh my god, that was ridiculous.*" Added George.

The boys continued to soak up the applause from the audience for several minutes, before the lights went down and the boys left the stage for the last time, but the audience continued to applaud for some minutes, even though the stage was empty. Glastonbury was over for another year and George Michael and Coldplay had rocked the festival to its core, good luck anybody else trying to top that. There was nobody who could have done that better, certainly none of the poor selection trying to compete with George Michael in the form of his career, he was on fire, his energy levels were off the scale, his voice was perfect, he and Coldplay were going to go down in Glastonbury folk law.

⋯◄◆►⋯

Chapter Twenty-Seven

George woke up, it was early, and Glastonbury seemed a long time ago, even though it was going to be a night that George would never forget. Everybody was raving about the final set of the festival and the performance of a lifetime, people were talking about it for weeks and those who were lucky enough to have been there, could only tell those who weren't there one thing, "You had to be there, man" That performance without a doubt, will be talked about for years to come and every year that Glastonbury comes around people will say. "Do you remember George Michael and Coldplay? You had to be there, man."

George pulled the duvet off and rolled out of bed, stood up, and had an overwhelming desire to stretch. George couldn't remember the last time he needed or wanted to stretch, let alone remember how good it felt. George stood there stark naked, in the middle of the room and had the best stretch he could have imagined. He couldn't remember the last time his body didn't ache, or his internal organs weren't crying out in pain. He looked in the mirror and saw a trim, tanned, slim reflection, with even a hint of some abdominals showing. He couldn't remember the last time he looked in the mirror and actually liked what or who was looking back at him.

He pulled on some speedos and a bathrobe, and headed downstairs to the indoor pool where he wandered around for a couple of minutes before hopping on the training bike and started to pedal. He wasn't going mad, just a gentle pace, but what he did notice was his head was crystal clear, his every thought was clear as day, he was thinking about his future. George stayed on the bike for about fifteen minutes, and found himself thinking about a new song, and not surprisingly it was about a certain person who had entered his life. George wiped his brow and kept peddling, then stopped. George had just wiped his brow; he hadn't needed to do that for a long time. It didn't register immediately what had just happened, he just thought that he had done a good warm up and now it was time for a swim. He jumped off the bike, threw his bathrobe on a sun lounger, and dived into the pool.

As George leisurely glided through the pool, the melody of his favorite tunes filled the room, painting his aquatic journey with a rhythm of joy. Each stroke, whether front crawl or breaststroke, harmonized with the music, carrying him effortlessly through the water. Pausing at one end, he realized the music had ceased, only to be replaced by a familiar tune emanating from another part of the house. Wrapping himself in a towel, he ventured towards the source, his curiosity piqued. Upon entering the living room, he was greeted by the sight of Chris at the grand piano, serenading the air with George's beloved song, "A Different Corner." Overwhelmed by the unexpected gesture, George couldn't help but smile, appreciating the heartfelt moment shared between friends.

This was the first time George had heard Chris sing properly, with some real feeling, they had messed around in the car and by the pool, but this was first time George had heard Chris really sing. George crept through the hall to the living room door, and held back to listen to his friend sing. He wasn't bad, he certainly put the feeling into it, in fact, George could really feel Chris singing from his heart. Chris was singing as if he was in pain, not actual pain, not like a strangled cat, but like someone who had found love. George knew he wasn't singing about Jennifer, because they were so loved up it was embarrassing, those two were totally meant for each other, no, Chris was singing about someone else?

"*Do mind if I join you?*" Asked George as he gently entered the room.

"*Oh, I didn't know you were there? That wasn't embarrassing at all.*" Answered Chris without stopping playing the piano.

"*Well?*" Asked George, sitting next to Chris on the piano stool.

"*Umm okay.*" Replied Chris.

There was something in his voice, something different, that George couldn't put his finger on.

"*Where we up to?*" Asked George.

"*Just join in when you're ready.*" Replied Chris and then pretty much started from the beginning.

"I'd say love was a magical flame." Chris on his own.

"I'd say love would keep us from pain." Chris on his own.

"Had I been there, had I been there." Chris on his own

"I would promise you all of my life." Chris and George.

"But to lose you would cut like a knife." Both of them.

"So, I don't dare, no I don't dare." Both of them.

They sat at the piano, and sang the same song another three times, unless it was just one very long extended remix, and then George stopped.

"Is everything okay, Chris?" He asked. *"I've never seen you like this before."*

"I'm fine, but thank you George." Chris replied.

"Are you sure? That sounded like it was really coming from your heart." Quizzed George.

"Was it okay?" Asked Chris.

"I was really impressed, but it sounded like someone in pain." Replied George.

"Oh thanks." Returned Chris.

"Not that sort of pain, stupid, like someone in love." Explained George.

"Hmmmmm, I can't explain it." Replied Chris.

"You and Jen are okay, aren't you?" Asked George.

"Yeah, Jen's amazing, we're totally fine." Explained Chris.

"So, what's up then?" Laughed George. *"From where I'm sat, it looks like you've got things pretty good."*

"I know, you're absolutely right George, I'm so lucky, it's not true." Said Chris.

"So?" Enquired George.

"Like I said, I can't explain." Retorted Chris.

"Can't or won't?" Asked George again.

"Can't, definitely can't." Replied Chris.

"Anything I can do?" Offered George.

"No.........Just make sure you're around. Please George?" Asked Chris.

"Of course, I'm not going anywhere." Replied George, putting his arm around Chris.

As George held Chris, he received the first bit of affection from his weird little friend since they had been thrown together. Chris had opened up to George about how he had wanted to be him, how he dressed like him, and how he hardly listened to anybody else's music, apart from Coldplay of course, but Chris had never afforded George any real affection. As George held Chris, he felt Chris rest his head on George's shoulder, not just briefly, but resting and leaving it there. They had stopped playing the piano and just sat there in silence for several minutes.

Chris suddenly lifted his head off of George's shoulder.

"You been for a swim then?" He asked.

"Yeah, it was really nice, you should've joined me." Answered George, sensing the moment was over.

"Yeah, I should have come in." Answered Chris, who still seemed distracted, but George could not work out why. *"I'm going over to Jen on the weekend, you coming with me?"* Asked Chris.

"Yeah, I might come, or maybe I'll stay here with Abbey, she's loving the beach." Replied George.

"Oh, okay!" Replied Chris.

The boys had been living in each other's pockets for months now, it would be strange if they weren't together. Nobody else knew that they had been inseparable, because for the outside world, only one of them could be seen at any one time. If George needed to be seen, then he used Chris's physical body, but Chris was still there obviously. If George didn't need to be noticed, he'd vanish, but usually lurked nearby, teasing Chris. When alone, especially at Chris's house, they didn't have to play their usual game of George entering Chris's thing. They could just be themselves, and it had been a while since they merged into one.

"Are you sure?" Asked Chris. *"It will be strange if you're not there, making sarcastic comments in my ear."*

"You and Jen need to have some time on yourselves, you don't want me loitering around." Replied George.

"I like you being there." Explained Chris.

"You spend some time with Jen, and I'll stay here with Abbey." Replied George. *"And don't forget to take your own passport, you'll be flying as you, not me, remember."*

Despite having Jennifer Aniston as his girlfriend, Chris returned home after just a week, leaving George puzzled. George spent his time swimming and working out, driven by an unexplained urge to exercise. Abbey observed his workouts, seemingly understanding him on a deeper level, even while she remained silent.

George was in the living room watching telly with Abbey, when her ears pricked up and she sat up bolt upright, looking towards the door. A few seconds later, George could hear the key in the door and giggling, as Chris and Jennifer barged in, clearly excited about something. Abbey went and sat by the living room door, but didn't actually venture into the hallway.

"Hello cutie, who are you?" Asked Jen spotting Abbey sat in the doorway. *"Are you going to come a say hello?"*

Abbey stood up and started to wag her tail.

"Oh, that's Abbey, George's dog." Replied Chris.

"Well, hello beautiful, aren't you gorgeous, where's your daddy?" Asked Jennifer and she headed for the living room.

George didn't bother getting up from the sofa, there didn't seem much point, Jen couldn't see him, so she would just think he was somewhere else in the house or gone out.

"Hello gorgeous." Said Jen giving Abbey a big cuddle. *"Aren't you beautiful? Oh, hi George, don't get up!"*

"Ummmmm hi Jen, sorry, how lazy of me." Replied a stunned George, Jen had seen him!!!!

"Don't I get a kiss; I have forgiven you for standing me up." Giggled Jen.

"Yes of course, how rude of me!" Replied George.

Chris was stood in the doorway gobsmacked, how the hell could Jen see George, it wasn't possible?

"Alright George, has everything been okay?" Asked Chris, trying to act as normal as he possibly could while trying to figure out what was going on.

"Do you know? Thinking about it. For two guys who are such close friends, this is the first time I've seen you both in the same place at the same time." Suggested Jen.

"No, surely not?" Replied George and Chris at exactly the same time.

"Yep, I think I would have remembered, and this is definitely a first." Replied Jen. *"So, George, have you been house sitting? I thought mega stars like you had better things to do with your time?"*

"Ummmmm no, Chris said you were coming over, so I wanted to see you." Replied a very confused George.

"Ahhhhhhh, how lovely, it must be a British thing?" Giggled Jen. *"Well, come and give your Jen a kiss then, it's so lovely to see a mega star being so normal."*

Jennifer was oblivious to the sheer panic going on, in the heads of George and Chris as they tried to work out what was going on. For months now, Chris had been the only person able to see George and now Jennifer could. They were looking at each other in bemusement, whilst trying to avoid any suspicion from Jen.

"Can I get you a drink darling?" Chris asked Jen.

"Yes please." Replied Jen and George at the same time.

"Ohh that's so funny George? You thought he was calling you darling, that's so sweet. Ohh ohhh ohhh! Is there something I should know about boys?" Giggled Jen.

"I wasn't really listening to him; I just fancied a drink." Said George, desperately trying to defuse his response.

"I'm only joking George, not even you could take this young man off me, I dare you to try." Laughed Jen.

"I wouldn't do that Jen, you're welcome to hang out with a weirdo." Returned George, looking straight into Chris's eyes.

"What do you fancy, Jen?" Asked Chris.

"I think it's margarita time, don't you?" Laughed Jen. *"Margarita, George?"*

"I make an awesome margarita Jen, keep Abby company, I'll show Chris how to make a good one." Replied George, grabbing Chris in an armlock around the neck and dragging him out of the room. *"Cmon Loverboy."*

"Aaarrghhh!" Shrieked Chris as George dragged him towards the kitchen.

As they got to the kitchen, George shut the door behind them and reached out to Chris, resting his hands on Chris's shoulders firmly.

"Jen can see me." Whispered George.

"Ohh ohhh I did notice that too." Replied Chris sarcastically.

"Sarcasm, now, really?" Sighed George. *"Jen can fucking see me, and what's going on? What have we done?"* Questioned George, shaking Chris.

"I don't know Yog, I'm actually quite scared by what's going on. You did say you've been feeling better recently. No?" Suggested Chris.

"That'll mean I'll have to do things on my own again. I've got used to having you around." Replied George very seriously.

"I'm not going anywhere George, I'm not losing you, I don't want to go back to just having your music." Replied Chris.

"Thank you." Replied George taking his hands off Chris's shoulders and wrapping them around Chris, giving him a massive hug.

Chris embraced George tightly, unwilling to part, as they shared a lingering hug. Eventually, George gently released his hold and pressed a loving kiss to Chris's cheek, which was met with acceptance and reciprocity. Their connection transcended words, expressing a depth of affection beyond measure.

"Abby! Abby! Where are you going!" Jennifer shrieked as Abby decided that she wanted to be with the boys.

The boys ended their hug, just as Abby and Jennifer came bursting into the kitchen, Abby barking and Jen giggling her head off as she almost fell through the door while she tried to grab hold of Abby.

"She got away from me, I couldn't keep up!" Giggled Jen.

"Hello babe." Said George, bending down to greet Abby.

"Where's my margarita? Does a girl have to make her own drink? What have you two been up to?" She asked curiously.

"Oh, just having a catch up." Replied Chris. *"C'mon George, show me how to make a perfect margarita!"*

"Don't worry I'm here now, we can make it together." Interrupted Jen.

Amidst the rhythmic clinking of glasses and the sweet tang of margaritas, Jen and George settled into the comfort of old friendship, exchanging tales of their extravagant adventures as global icons. Chris, reclining in his chair, savoured the sight of their animated faces, his heart swelling with gratitude for their enduring bond. Lost in the nostalgic haze, he couldn't shake the memory of his intimate moment with George, pondering the depth of their connection. As laughter danced in the air, each sip of the cocktail seemed to deepen the camaraderie that enveloped them, a testament to the beauty of their shared history.

It was a few days later when George woke up feeling very fresh and well rested, he also feeling inquisitive about Chris and had the desire to quiz his friend some more about the whole being George Michael, as although Chris had constantly answered George's questions, George still wasn't convinced that he understood Chris. He got out of bed and went to find the nutcase so that he could interrogate him some more. George hadn't made his mind up if he was going to be good cop or bad cop yet, it would depend on what mood Chris was in. What George had discovered was that if Chris was on his time of the month, he didn't open up much. Yep, George had decided that Chris had a time of the month, probably most men do, they're just not as obvious as Chris. It was probably all part of being a recluse and hiding away from the public, well not just the public, but anybody. Although the very same moody recluse was also going out with one of the most famous people on the planet, and still presented himself as George, even though

George was his closest confidant these days, which George found highly amusing.

"*Morning lovely?*" George asked once he found Chris, testing the mood level.

"*Morning.*" Replied Chris, not giving much away.

"*How are you today?*" Tried George.

"*Not bad. You?*" Returned Chris, still not making it easy for George to judge the mood level.

"*Well, I am feeling dandy.*" Laughed George. "*Are you feeling dandy dear?*"

"*Dear?*" Laughed Chris.

"*I'm sorry, don't you like me calling you dear?*" Asked George, feeling at last he was getting something back from Chris.

"*I don't mind, whatever you call me fruit bat.*" Laughed Chris.

"*Do you love me?*" Tried George, thinking this must surely get a response.

"*You know I do.*" Replied Chris.

"*You have a funny way of showing it.*" Giggled George.

"*Come here, give your Chris a hug.*" Replied Chris, who was now beginning to show, he was in a good place and feeling playful.

"*I thought you would never ask?*" Laughed George, happy that he had cracked Chris and could now start the questioning, after getting a hug first.

They were both in a good place these days and could share moments of affection knowing that they were just moments and Chris was obviously crazy about Jennifer, but relaxed enough to give George some affection, knowing

George wouldn't push his luck. They were both in a place of mutual affection, not quite the friend zone, a lot more than the friend zone, but not quite the full hit the sack and shag like rabbits. George didn't, actually feel that way about Chris, he would probably have preferred to hit the sack with Jennifer.

"So, how's your George today?" Asked George.

"How's my George?" Laughed Chris.

"Yeah, are you still being George?" Asked George.

"Maybe!" Replied Chris sheepishly.

"That's fine." Replied George. *"I'll let you have a bit of George."*

"You'll let me have a bit of George?" Giggled Chris.

"Yeah, but not that bit." Laughed George grabbing his crotch.

"Oh, thank you, I appreciate you not letting me have your shlom." Laughed Chris.

"Shlom?" Laughed George. *"What's a shlom, when it's at home?"*

"Your shlom. Your dick." Laughed Chris.

"You're a dick." Laughed George.

"That's mature?" Returned Chris.

"I just wondered if you still needed to rely on me, now you're with Jen?" Asked George.

"Ahhhh, are you feeling unwanted!" Returned Chris.

"No just wondering!" Replied George.

"Don't worry George, you're still required." Replied Chris in a very sincere tone.

George had got Chris, just where he wanted him, he had primed him perfectly to be questioned.

"That's good, I wouldn't want to be dumped now that you have Jen." Returned George.

"You still don't get it, do you George?" Replied Chris, but a little more sternly.

"Possibly not?" Replied George, feeling that he might not have to ask too many questions as Chris might just spill the beans without being pressed.

"I thought you understood now?" Returned Chris

"I thought I did too, maybe I was wrong, maybe I didn't quite understand?" Replied George, now worried he had hit a nerve.

"When you are with someone, even if you love them to bits, Kenny or Anselmo, did you tell them everything? Could you tell them everything? Especially the stuff that scared you?"

It was Chris's turn to question George now.

"Not everything, but who does? " Replied George.

"And that's my point, George. No matter what the problem was, no matter how scared I was, when I lost my dad and my two best friends, when a relationship wasn't going to plan. When a job didn't work out, when money wasn't stretching far enough, when there seemed to be no escape from some very deep depression, it didn't matter, because you listened, you made things better, you gave me the strength to keep going. I am alive because of you George, you gave me the strength, you let me talk to you and you listened without judging me, without prejudice. If it wasn't for you George, I doubt I would be here, which would possibly mean that you wouldn't be here now." Explained Chris.

"Fuck, now that I wasn't expecting!" George replied a little shocked at what Chris had just spilled.

"As I have told you before, it's very difficult, in fact I would go as far as to say impossible to explain. Can you imagine having someone in your life that you can tell absolutely anything that is going on in your life?" Asked Chris.

"No, I can't say that I can!" Replied George, who was now racking his brains for who he might have been able to tell absolutely anything, and he couldn't think of anybody.

"There you go, that's why you're so important to me, because you have been that person and I know for a fact, you always will be." Assured Chris *"It's knowing I can talk to you while you sing to me, it's like an allergy, different things trigger different allergies."*

"Oh, so I set off your allergy now?" Teased George.

"No, of course not. But like an allergy, there is something about your voice that puts me in a calm place where I can think clearly. Whatever's worrying me, I can go to a calm place and put order into my life." Replied Chris.

"I don't know what to say to that." Said George sympathetically.

"You don't have to say anything Yog, just know how grateful I am that you've been there the last 30 years." Insisted Chris.

"You're welcome." Returned George, who was so shocked by Chris's confession.

"Don't try to understand it, I don't think there is an answer to it? I do occasionally try to understand it, but give up, because it's beyond my understanding." Explained Chris.

"I would like to understand." Replied George.

"That is absolutely fine, but will it make any difference?" Enquired Chris.

"No, it probably wouldn't make any difference." Confided George, who strangely enough, now that he didn't need to understand, actually started to.

"Can we have some fun now?" Laughed Chris. *"Or have I blown your fuses?"*

"Damn Right!" Giggled George, although it would take a while to snap out of his deep thought. The plan was to interrogate Chris and here he was feeling like he had been interrogated. That was one of the most intense moments he had shared with Chris, and one he should never forget.

Chris seemed to shrug off the deep conversation the two of them had just shared, and George couldn't help but think, either it was Chris's way of protecting himself, or, he was just so used to his feelings, they felt completely normal. The two of them headed down to the pool and did a bit of swimming then just lazed around on the inflatable chairs. It was Chris who tried to inject some humour into the time, George was definitely struck by the admission by Chris, especially the remark about not being here, if it wasn't for George. Could he have been that influential in Chris's life? Could he have intervened to thwart a foolish decision in a moment of desperation? If that was the case, it certainly made sense about how connected Chris was to him. In fact, it made the whole relationship make sense, and completely explained why they had become so close. George started to think about how wonderful it was to be connected in such a unique, unexplainable way, actually he was starting to think like Chris, and it felt amazing.

Chapter Twenty-Eight

<<<<<<<<<<<<<<<< PLAY >>>>>>>>>>>>>>>

December 19th 2017

As George slowly opened his eyes, he looked around the room. Light flooded in as the sun shone outside. The first thing that entered his mind was a level of confusion and then how good he felt. He didn't have a headache, none of his limbs hurt, none of his internal organs were crying out in pain, he felt fabulous. George threw the duvet off, rolled out of bed, grabbed his bathrobe and headed for the door. As he adorned his bathrobe whilst walking, the aroma of fresh coffee entered the room. George made his way downstairs to the kitchen.

"Morning my lovely." Announced George as he entered the kitchen.

"Morning my George." Replied Noom. *"How are you feeling today?"*

"Absolutely fabulous!" Exclaimed George.

"I must say you look pretty good, for someone who's just rolled out of bed." Teased Noom.

"Pretty good?" Laughed George.

"Someone's in a good mood!" Chuckled Noom.

"It's nearly Christmas Noom, the best time of year, apart from the crap telly." Laughed George.

"Can I get you some breakfast darling?" Asked Noom.

"Oooo yes please, my lovely." Replied George.

What George didn't do was head over to the back door and light up a cigarette, instead, he sat down at the kitchen table and poured a coffee.

"Do want a coffee, Noom?" Asked George

"Ummm yes please." Replied Noom.

As they sipped their coffee, a warm anticipation filled the air, tinged with excitement for the upcoming festivities. George's eyes sparkled with enthusiasm as he envisioned the familiar warmth of his favorite pub, bustling with holiday cheer. The thought of lending a hand behind the bar brought a sense of belonging and joy to his heart. Amidst the preparations, there was an underlying sense of camaraderie, a shared anticipation for the candlelight parade. George's spirit danced with mischief, eager to join in the playful antics of the procession. The prospect of connecting with his fellow villagers, exchanging stories and laughter, infused him with a sense of community and belonging. As they spoke of their plans, the air buzzed with the anticipation of cherished traditions and shared moments. George's anticipation swelled with each passing moment, a delightful mix of excitement and nostalgia for the holiday season ahead.

Chris slowly opened his eyes and looked over to see who was lying next to him as he did every morning, he couldn't believe he was waking up next to Jennifer. Jen was already awake and as Chris looked across at her, she met his eyes with one of her beautiful smiles.

"Morning honey." She sighed with a huge grin.

"Morning Gorgeous." Replied Chris.

"Are you going to get your lazy arse out of bed and make me a coffee?" Giggled Jen.

"For you, my darling. Anything!" Giggled Chris

"Excellent", sighed Jen, in a way, only she could make sound so sexy.

Chris made his way downstairs to the kitchen with a huge smile on his face, remembering how a chance encounter with Jennifer whilst in Hollywood, led to coffee, then lunch, then dinner and then to dating. Chris thought he was the luckiest guy in the world to be able to change Jennifer's mind about living the single life. She could have any man in the world and for some reason she decided she would give Chris a chance, the odds of that happening were probably higher than winning the lottery, but Chris had done that too.

He wandered into the kitchen, switched on the telly and selected YouTube, then selected his playlist and as per usual, George Michael filled the room. The playlist picked up on what Chris had been listening to most recently, so it was a mixture of George's more upbeat tracks. While the kettle boiled, Chris strutted around the kitchen practising his favourite George Michael moves. Chris had spent the last few decades performing these moves and excelling at them. Freedom 90 was playing, and Chris was doing one of George's trademark moves, where he steps back, then forward, then back with the other foot, then sways side to side while dipping down. Chris loved this move, especially as it took him ages to get right, it wasn't a simple move at all. Chris then strutted around the breakfast bar as if he was on stage performing to an adoring audience, because of course, in Chris's eyes he was George Michael, even if he was in a pair of pyjama bottoms, he could still shake his arse, because they notice fast.

"What, are you doing?" Laughed Jennifer as she stood in the doorway watching Chris strut his funky stuff around the kitchen.

Chris burst into laughter. *"How long have you been there?"*

"Long enough George." Returned Jennifer in hysterics. *"Nice moves though!"*

"Come, join me?" Asked Chris reaching out to Jennifer.

Jennifer was only wearing one of Chris's T-shirts and a pair of Chris's boxer shorts.

"Are they my boxer shorts?" Asked Chris.

"Yep, they looked really comfy." Giggled Jennifer

"They look better on you than they do on me." Smiled Chris.

"Well of course they do, they're on my butt." Replied Jennifer in a very deep and purposely over the top sexy voice.

"I'm never going to wash them, ever again!" Laughed Chris.

"Oh, I hope you do." Returned Jennifer.

Jennifer made her way across the kitchen and joined Chris in a frenzy of arms movements, rocking out, throwing her hair around, and gyrating her hips in a circular motion. In the cozy kitchen, Jennifer's vivacious energy radiated as she belted out tunes alongside Chris, her laughter filling the air like sweet music. Chris watched in awe, utterly enchanted by the sight of the iconic actress letting loose with such abandon. It was a moment of pure delight, a snapshot of joy that Chris knew he'd treasure forever. As Jennifer's laughter echoed off the walls, Chris couldn't help but feel grateful for this unexpected, magical morning.

"Come here Loverboy, dance with me!" Shrieked Jennifer, grabbing Chris's hands and sweeping them from side to side, then out of the blue, leapt up, wrapping her legs around him, clinging onto him like a monkey and giving him a huge kiss on the lips.

"I love mornings with you Christopher!" Squealed Jennifer above the music.

"They certainly are different!" Laughed Chris, with his arms wrapped around Jennifer, holding her close to him with his hands strategically placed on her bottom. Then Fast Love, The Buddha Café Del Mar version came on, a very slow and sensual version of Fast Love. You couldn't even get a cigarette paper between Jennifer and Chris as they swayed around the kitchen, their bodies entwined and grinded against each other, as they took in every beat and pulse, looking into each other's eyes, love oozing from them. Jennifer looked incredible with her hair over her face as she leaned back and swayed as Chris held the base of her back, how could anybody look that amazing after falling out of bed, she was unbelievable.

Then as if you could make it up, "Wicked Game" by Chris Isaak came on, and Chris remembered the video featuring Chris Isaak and Helena Christensen on the beach and imagined himself and Jennifer being alone on a beach all loved up.

"Oh, I love this song." Sighed Jennifer as she pulled Chris tight against her.

"It's a good one, isn't it?" Replied Chris, not believing how lucky he was.

After a couple more minutes of the pair enjoying a dance around the kitchen, they both took a moment to catch their breath, whilst laughing uncontrollably and holding onto the breakfast bar counter top.

"*Ohhh my.*" Laughed an out of breath Jennifer.

"*I'm knackered.*" Chuckled Chris.

"*Me too.*" Giggled Jennifer. "*Where's my coffee, ohhh my?*"

George had made himself busy getting ready for the day, he had been upstairs and spent ages in the shower soaping and re-soaping himself. He then sorted out what he was going to wear and again spent ages doing his hair, blow drying it, waxing it, more blow drying, then copious amounts of hairspray to keep it make it look perfect. Once he was convinced that he couldn't look any better, he finally made his way downstairs.

"*Noom!*" He shouted as he came down the stairs. "*Where are you?!*"

Noom jumped out of her skin at George's shouting, wondering what she had done wrong and why George was seeking her immediate attention.

"*Noom, where are you?*" George shouted again.

"*I'm here, what's wrong?*" Called Noom from the kitchen.

"*Where?*" Called George.

"*The kitchen!*" Returned Noom.

"*What are you doing?*" Demanded George.

"*Washing up the breakfast stuff.*" Replied Noom.

"*Leave that, get your coat, we're going Christmas tree shopping!*" Called George.

"*Ohhhh lovely, wait for me.*" Giggled Noom.

"*C'mon, or they'll all be sold out!*" Shouted George.

"I doubt they will." Mumbled Noom.

"I heard that!" Shouted George.

"How does he do that!" Asked Noom silently to herself.

"I heard this one too!" Returned George with a giggle.

"Idiot." Replied Noom.

"C'mon, come on!" Insisted George.

"I'm coming." Returned Noom.

"Where we going to get one?" Asked George.

"Ummmmm let's go to the garden centre, they'll have some." Suggested Noom.

"Nice plan, I want a big one, a big bushy one!" Replied a very excited George.

"How exciting!" Gasped Noom.

The two of them jumped into George's Land Rover and headed straight to the garden centre, where George had no intention of wasting time, he had a plan to grab a member of staff to take him straight to the best trees.

"Have you got your tree up yet?" George asked Noom.

"I have. I put it up the other night." Retorted Noom.

"Where did you get your tree from?" Enquired George.

"The loft." Replied Noom.

"Where's that?" Asked George.

"At the top of my landing." Giggled Noom.

"Ohhhh, you have a fake one?" Asked George.

"It's a very nice fake one." Stated Noom.

"Do you want me to get you a real one?" George offered.

"Thank George, but no, my fake one is very nice." Smiled Noom.

Once George had commandeered a member of staff, they searched through the selection of trees. George got the poor lad hold up numerous trees for inspection, putting them in a 'maybe' or a 'no way' pile, eventually a decision was made and the tree was purchased. George being the generous guy that he is, made it worth the lad's time and stuck a £20 note in his pocket to say thank you for his time.

With excitement buzzing in the air, George and Noom eagerly dove into the array of decorations, determined to create a tree unlike any other. George's vision for a fresh start infused their efforts with renewed purpose, sparking a creative frenzy. As they returned home, the day unfolded in a whirlwind of festive cheer, accompanied by the merry melodies of Christmas songs. George's leadership as the "Tree Decorator Manager" brought a sense of order to the chaos, guiding Noom with infectious enthusiasm. Amidst the laughter and shared moments, Noom cherished every second spent alongside her eccentric yet endearing boss, George Michael.

"*Well, that's it, we've done it!*" Announced George eventually.

"*It looks beautiful, George.*" Replied Noom.

"*It feels like Christmas has already started.*" Laughed George.

"*It's going to be a great Christmas!*" Announced Noom.

"*It certainly is, my lovely.*" Replied George, wrapping his arms around Noom, giving her a huge kiss on her cheek.

"*Ohhhhhhh George?*" Giggled Noom, slightly embarrassed by the affection from her boss.

The Final

In the midst of his seemingly perfect life with the love of his life, Chris felt a nostalgic pull to visit Goring-On-Thames. Suggesting a spontaneous drive to Jennifer, they embarked on a journey to discover new lunch spots. As they strolled through the village, enveloped in a festive atmosphere, warmth radiated from the locals, oblivious to Jennifer's celebrity status. Amidst the holiday charm, Chris found solace in the simple pleasures of exploration with his beloved.

The people of Goring-On-Thames were used to celebrities, they had one of the biggest celebrities on the planet, living in their village, so they knew how to let Jennifer feel relaxed, but they were obviously excited about her being there. It was a cold day and Jennifer's hands were freezing.

"OOOOOh jeez, my hands are freezing, why did I let you convince me to come to the England in December?" Shivered Jennifer.

"I'm sorry, don't let me do that again!" Giggled Chris.

"Can I have the car key; I'll go and get my gloves." Returned Jennifer.

"Shall I come with you?" Asked Chris.

"No don't worry, it's only round the corner, stay here, I'll be back in a minute." Replied Jennifer.

Chris knew where he was, so was happy to stay put, or stay roughly where he was. *"I'll be here."* He said. Jennifer turned and headed for the car and Chris looked down the alley and started to wonder further down the path.

"Abby! Abby! Wait for me!" Came a voice down the path.

From around the bend in the path, came a big blonde Labrador, waddling along, tail wagging, tongue hanging out. The Labrador came up to Chris, had a quick sniff then kept walking straight on past.

"Hey Abby! Don't go too far!" Came the voice.

Then to Chris's surprise, George Michael walked around corner.

"Hiya, you haven't seen my dog, have you?" Asked George.

"Urrrrrrrrr yeah she's just up there by your front door." Replied Chris

"Thanks, mate, she's gagging to get back to the fire." Laughed George.

"I don't blame her, it's freezing." Replied Chris

"Tell me about it?" Said George as he kept walking.

Then out of the blue, George stopped in his tracks and turned round to look at Chris.

"Do I know you?" He asked.

"Ummm no, no I don't think so"? Replied Chris

"Huh. You look familiar." Said George.

"Nope, I don't think so." Replied Chris, desperate to tell George the truth.

"You must have one of those faces, or I've eaten too much cheese? I heard someone say that once." Laughed George.

"We must have met in another life somewhere." Replied Chris.

"Yeah, that must be it." Replied George as he turned to walk away. *"Take care, Happy Christmas."*

"Yeah, Happy Christmas, George". Returned Chris as George walked away.

Then as Chris turned to continue down the path. *"HEY! HEY! WAIT FOR ME!"*

Chris turned around and with a huge smile on his face, raised his arms to receive his pursuer, who as they met, landed their lips on his and gave him a beautiful lingering kiss, that Chris hoped would never end, it was beautiful.

"C'mon Loverboy, I think you should take me for lunch, I'm starving and very cold."

"Lunch sounds like a perfect idea." Retorted Chris.

As they turned around and walked back up the path and past a front door, Chris turned to Jen and spoke. "Apparently George Michael lives there."

"No way!" Replied Jennifer.

"Apparently." Returned Chris.

"Shall we see if he's in?" Giggled Jennifer.

"He's probably busy." Replied Chris nervously, imagining Jennifer knocking on George Michael's front door and inviting herself in.

"Yeah, probably, anyway, I'm hungry. Let's get some lunch, we'll try George later." Laughed Jennifer.

Dear Reader!

Thank you for making it this far, I hope you enjoyed my story and the journey that you have been on. George of course, continues to be my guardian angel and is always there whenever I need him. He never argues and never makes excuses, he is just there, and I will always be grateful and continue to love him.

Love to George.

One last request, to understand where my heart is please play, A Different Corner, my favourite song of all time, thank you.